**Rozlan Mohd Noor** served as a police officer in the Royal Malaysia Police for 11 years as a crime investigator and court prosecutor before joining the private sector. He has published several crime/thriller novels. Five of them feature Inspector Mislan as the main protagonist, with *Philanthropists* being the latest. The Inspector Mislan novels are now published internationally by Arcade Crimewise, New York, starting with *21 Immortals* in 2020 and *DUKE* in 2021.

FIXI NOVO MANIFESTO

1. We believe that omputih/gwailoh-speak
is a Malaysian language.

2. We use American spelling. This is because
we are more influenced by Hollywood than
the House of Windsor.

3. We publish stories about the urban reality of
Malaysia. If you want to share your grandmother's
World War 2 stories, send 'em elsewhere and you
might even win the Booker Prize.

4. We specialize in pulp fiction, because crime,
horror, sci-fi and so on turn us on.

5. We will not use italics for non-American/
non-English terms. This is because those words are
not foreign to a Malaysian audience. So we will not
have "They had *nasi lemak* and went back to *kongkek*"
but rather "They had nasi lemak and went back to
kongkek". Nasi lemak and kongkek are some of the
pleasures of Malaysian life that should be celebrated
without apology; italics are a form of apology.

6. We publish novels and short-story anthologies.
We don't publish poetry; we like making money.

7. The existing Malaysian books that come closest
to what we wanna do: *Devil's Place* by Brian Gomez;
and the Inspector Mislan crime novels by
Rozlan Mohd Noor. Look for them!

8. We publish books with the same print run
and the same price as those of our parent company,
Buku Fixi. So a book of about 300 pages will sell
at RM20. This is because we wanna reach out to the
young, the sengkek and the kiam siap.

CALL FOR ENTRIES.

Interested? For novels,
send your synopsis and first 2 chapters.
For anthologies, send a short story of between
2,000-5,000 words on the theme "KL Noir."
Send to info@fixi.com.my anytime.

# OJ Is Dead

Rozlan Mohd Noor

*Published by*
**Fixi Novo** *which is an imprint of:*
**Buku Fixi Sdn Bhd** (1174441-X)
B-8-2A Opal Damansara, Jalan PJU 3/27
47810 Petaling Jaya, Malaysia
info@fixi.com.my
http://fixi.com.my



**OJ Is Dead**
© Rozlan Mohd Noor

First Print: October 2021

Cover illustration: Mugunthan Loganathan
Layout: Teck Hee
Consultant: Alyssa Mohamad & Ted Mahsun

ISBN 978-967-2328-69-8
Catalogue-in-Publication Data available from the
National Library of Malaysia.

*Printed by:*
Vinlin Press Sdn Bhd
2 Jalan Meranti Permai 1, Meranti Permai Industrial Park
Batu 15, Jalan Puchong, 47100 Puchong, Malaysia

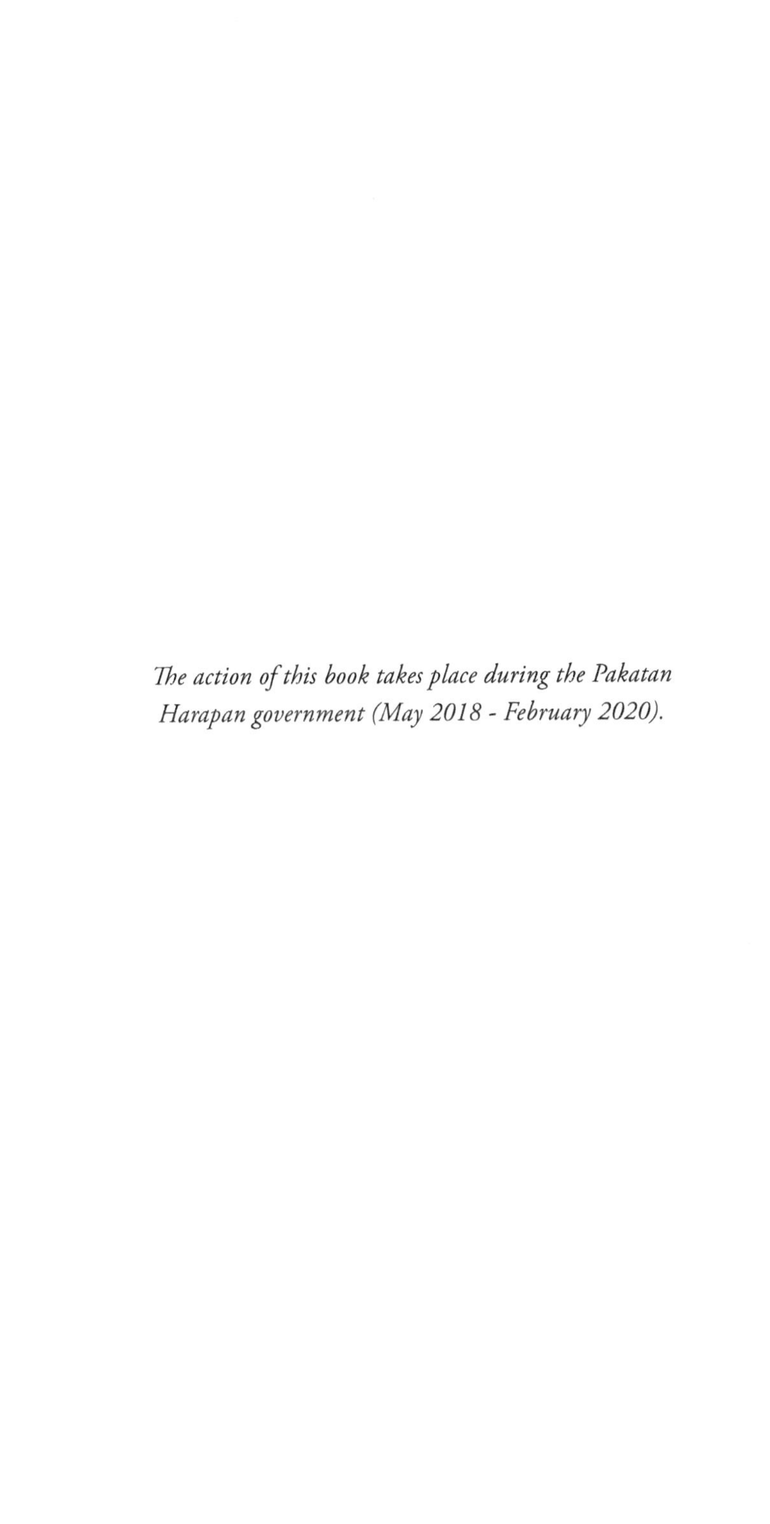

*The action of this book takes place during the Pakatan Harapan government (May 2018 - February 2020).*

# 1

Folding two RM1 notes into his palm, Jeffri stepped out of his car. A Bangladeshi petrol kiosk attendant hastily approached, shouting something from the far end of the station while frantically waving at him. Although his shout was drowned out by the traffic noise, Jeffri knew what was implied by the vehement waving. Grabbing a thin brown folder file and a wrinkled black jacket from the back seat of the car, he locked his beat-up Proton Wira. Nonchalantly he turned and flashed a warm, friendly smile at the approaching attendant.

"Bos, sini tarak boleh taruk kereta," the Bangladeshi intently said.

Ignoring what was said by the petrol kiosk attendant, Jeffri proffered his hand for a handshake. Caught by surprise, the attendant took the hand as any civilized individual would. The folded two ringgit changed palms.

"Sekejap saja, saya mau pergi bayar bil cukai pintu, okay."

The attendant's hand slid into his pocket, and he smilingly replied, "Okay, Bos."

*These foreign workers learnt local donation culture fast,* Jeffri said to himself. With the jacket draped around his arm, he hurried across the ever-busy Jalan Pandan Perdana into Menara MPAJ-Ampang Jaya City Council Tower. He was not about to stick around for the attendant to discover he had just risked his job for a miserable two ringgit bribe.

Ampang is one of the districts in the state of Selangor bordering the city of Kuala Lumpur. As the capital city was fast becoming too expensive for average-income workers to live in, Ampang became a choice alternative due to its proximity. You can still breathe the smog of the capital city but at a lower cost. Over the years, Ampang bustled with rapid developments of new affordable housing estates. The spin-offs raised crime rates and undocumented immigrants, which were claimed to contribute to the former.

It was only 8:40 in the morning but the heat was unbearable, and the humidity was making him sweat like a fat cigar-smoking man in a sauna. Living in a city with bumper-to-bumper traffic like Kuala Lumpur, the first skill you learn is crossing roads without being mowed down by pea-brained motorists. Malaysians are generally courteous and patient, but being seated behind a steering wheel or motorbike handle can turn them into assholes.

The crowded but cool council building lobby was a welcome relief from the heat and humidity. Standing in a corner to catch a breather, Jeffri slipped on his jacket, nodding to other Black Jacketers hurrying past or loitering about. Anxiously, he scanned the sea of faces for his yet-unknowing financial saviors. Unfortunately, they were nowhere to be seen. Grudgingly he headed down the passageway toward Court 13. Standing by the door, he gave the packed gallery a hopeful slow left-to-right pan. No saviors. *Adoooi*, he whimpered. Driving here this morning, he'd worked his brain on how to squeeze a few extra hundred ringgit from his only paying client to stay afloat, at least for this month.

He was now almost two months behind on the office rent and car instalments. Not to mention the salary, or whatever the Employment Act cared to term the meager amount he paid his one and only staff in the law firm of Jeffri & Associates.

Crestfallen, he slowly made his way to the already overcrowded defense table. As he expected before the start of morning proceedings, there was not a single empty chair available. He nonetheless squeezed into a tiny gap between two court attendees in the front pew of the gallery. His action caused irate attendees to shift their butts tighter to each other. *I'm a Black Jacketer. That gives me the right to move your butts, and I'm not in a charming mood today*, he mentally responded to their muttering.

The wall clock read 9:20 am, but the magistrate bench was still empty. The court staff were leisurely chatting and sorting out papers or charge sheets. The Black Jacketers at the defense table were engrossed with their smartphones. *If there is one thing social media has overachieved, it is making waiting bearable and toilet visits longer, especially when doing the big thing,* Jeffri reflected. Straightening his clip-on necktie, he checked his handphone— not that he expected any message or missed call, but more out of having nothing to do and wanting to look like he belonged, a twenty-first century kind of guy.

The gallery's humming dropped a few decibels as heads turned to look to the entrance. An all-women prosecution team made their entrance, chatting gaily and walking to the prosecutor's table. Two of the team members were Black Jacketers, and one was in police uniform. They were each carrying a bundle of files. Jeffri noted a few new files but most were worn-out files from over-handling due to the obscene number of postponements. Files the police termed as 'Investigation Paper', or 'IP'. Jeffri knew there was no way in hell all the cases carried by the prosecutors would be heard. Most, if not all, would be postponed. If the accused person or complainant was lucky, it would only be for a few months, but otherwise it would be years.

A normal day in court began with the mentioning of new cases or fresh charges. This usually took a couple of hours at the very least. After the mentioning of fresh cases, the court moved on to the sentencing of previous PG-ed cases — cases where the accused persons pleaded guilty upon the charge being read or on the previous appearance. The handing down of the sentence was dependent on the availability of the Chemist Report, Juvenile Report, Medical Report or whatever other reports needed and the Fact of Case. Another couple of hours slipped by, and by then the court would adjourn for lunch. More often than not, it would be a long extended lunch before the sitting resumed to a draggy, heavy-stomach session. If a case was lucky enough to be called for hearing, chances were only one or two witnesses would take the stand before the case was postponed as part heard. The postponement, of course, would be accompanied by the magistrate's empty promise that it would be given top priority on the next hearing date.

At long last at 9:51 am, the booming voice of the court policeman called out—BANGUUUUUUN. *Funny how they always manage to find a policeman with a deep baritone voice to make the call,* Jeffri thought. He, the Black Jacketers, prosecutors, and attendees stood up as instructed. He didn't know about the rest of them, but he was always amused by this time-honored charade.

A door behind the magistrate's bench cracked open, and a woman's head emerged. Standing beside the chair, she gave the slightest bow and sat down. The rest followed. Those seated at the prosecution and defense tables could only see her head and the top of her shoulders. *Why do magistrates and judges have to sit so high up? Why can't we all sit on level ground? Why the bow and not a wave, smile and hello? Better still, why not follow like the rest of the government offices – an Assalammualaikum followed by a prayer,* Jeffri grunted to himself. Clearly, he was in a foul mood this morning, grumpiness perpetuated by the failure to spot his saviors.

Eventually, the proceeding got on its way with the mention of new cases. One after another, the accused person or persons were paraded in by the police from the holding cell, and those on bail emerged from the gallery. Charges were read, pleas recorded, bails set, and hearing dates fixed for those who claimed trial. Dates that both the prosecutors and Black Jacketers knew the probability of being heard on was next to zilch. You have a better chance at striking the lottery than getting your case heard on the first fixed hearing date. For a handful of cases where the accused persons were unrepresented and pleaded guilty, they were asked to stand down for the fact of the case to be prepared by the prosecutor. All in all, it was an age-long circus of a legal merry-go-round.

The defense table started thinning out of the Black Jacketers, whose cases were called and postponed. Spotting an opening, Jeffri moved from the gallery's pew to the defense table. Another twenty minutes passed, and then his client with another individual were escorted and ushered into the accused dock. His client immediately turned to search the gallery, Jeffri following his line of vision. *A child can smell his/her parents,* flashed through Jeffri's mind. *Voila—* there at the far corner stood his saviors: his client's parents. Jeffri held his sight until they made eye contact; he nodded with a smile of acknowledgement. The smile was more to himself, to his rekindled hope of gain.

A bored-looking court staff stepped away from his table, holding a charge sheet. Stopping halfway between the accused dock and the bench, he read out the name of the two accused persons.

"Mohd. Ridwan Bin Jajis?"

The first accused person nodded.

"Abdul Latif bin Abdul Khasan?"

The second accused person, Jeffri's client, nodded and then turned to look anxiously at his parents.

"Kamu ada peguam?"

The first accused person shook his head, but the second eagerly nodded, pointing to the Black Jacketer's table. Jeffri stood and introduced himself to the court and got placed on record as the counsel for the second accused person before retaking his seat.

Without any precursor, the bored court staff read out the charge against the two accused persons and asked, "Do you understand the charge read to you?"

Mohd. Ridwan, the first accused, nodded. Abdul Latif turned to gawk at Jeffri. The bored court staff took Jeffri's nod as a 'yes' for his client. Walking back to his desk, he disinterestedly announced for the magistrate's benefit: both the accused understood the charge. Then from where he stood, he demanded rather than inquired, "How do you plead?"

"Salah," Mohd. Ridwan admitted, looking just as disinterested as the court staff.

"What?" the bored court staff snapped, "Speak up, the court can't hear you."

"Guilty, guilty," Mohd. Ridwan barked back.

"The first accused pleaded guilty, Puan." It was said as if the magistrate was hard of hearing and it was his solemn duty to inform her.

Turning to Abdul Latif, he jerked his head, lifting his eyebrows questioningly.

The guilty plea by the first accused person was like a sign from above to Jeffri — YOU HAVE MY BLESSING TO SQUEEZE MORE MONEY FROM YOUR SAVIORS. Springing to a stand, he addressed the court.

"Puan, my client pleads not guilty to the charge and claims trail." As an afterthought, to apply pressure on the prosecutor he added, "For the record, we're ready to proceed with the hearing."

He snuck a glance at the prosecutor's table. None of them paid any heed to his comments. They were thoroughbred public servants, totally immune to any form of pressure from the public.

"15 August next year is the earliest available date, Puan," another bored court staff wearing a gaudily sequined hijab announced from her seat.

"Hearing is fixed for the fifteenth of August next year, bail is set at five thousand with one surety," the magistrate announced without looking up. "Prosecutor, are you ready with the fact of the case?"

The prosecutor in the police uniform half-stood and said she was.

Hearing the bail amount, which Jeffri anticipated would be an obstacle in squeezing money from his saviors, he immediately stood up.

"Puan, I pray the court to reconsider the bail amount. My client is an accounting student in UiTM and is preparing for his finals. The flight risk is virtually non-existent, and setting such a high bail will only cause my client to be incarcerated and miss out on his final. His father is a respectable retired public servant with no means to come up with such a big amount. I pray—"

"Mitigation noted, bail is set at one thousand with one surety," the magistrate said and banged her gavel of authority, cutting Jeffri's rambling short. He hated it when the bench cut him off like that. *Don't they know we're merchants of words? Clients love to watch us give them as many words as possible for their money,* Jeffri cursed under his breath.

Instead, Jeffri said, "Very much appreciated, Puan," then turned to his saviors and winked.

As Abdul Latif was escorted out of the dock, Jeffri stood, gave a slight bow to the bench, walked to the back of the gallery and beckoned for his saviors to follow. Outside the court room, he told them to go to the general office to arrange for their son's bail and wait for him. When they left, he returned to the defense table.

The prosecuting officer, Woman Assistant Superintendent of Police (ASP) Mala Manivil handed the bored court staff a written fact of the case. The bored and by now most likely bored and hungry staff, insipidly read it to the accused person who seemed to be already thinking about his lunch too.

"Do you admit to the fact of the case?" he asked, walking back to the bench and handing the sheet to the magistrate.

The accused nodded.

"The accused admitted to the facts, Puan."

"Mitigation?"

"Ada apa-apa nak rayu?"

Mohd. Ridwan shook his head. His expression said it all: *Let's get this over with. I'm fucking hungry and tired.*

"Nothing to mitigate, Puan."

"Prosecution?" asked the magistrate.

"The accused has two previous convictions, Puan," ASP Mala announced, handing a copy of the criminal record to the court staff. "In 2013, he was fined 1,500 ringgit in default of three months imprisonment for possession of stolen property. The accused failed to pay the fine. In 2015, he was sentenced to one-year imprisonment for a similar offence. The accused is a habitual criminal, and Prosecution prays for a deterrent sentence."

"Three years imprisonment effective from the day of arrest."

The gavel banged with finality. Mohd. Ridwan was escorted out. Jeffri stood, bowed, hiding a grin, and took his leave.

## 2

Out in the court's general office, Jeffri located his client's anxious mother and irked father seated at the waiting area. Before approaching them, he reminded himself, *If you're to wheedle something out of this one, the only client you have for the entire month, you have to work the mother.* Experience had taught him, *When it comes to their children's wellbeing, the mother is the sure hand into the father's pocket.*

"Puan Kalsom," Jeffri greeted, psychologically placing her as the alpha parent instead of the husband.

Jeffri was right. Kalsom sprang to her feet as he approached. The father remained seated, looking disengaged.

"Mana Latif?" Kalsom asked anxiously. "We've paid the one thousand as required, but where's Latif?"

Jeffri told her to wait as he went to the counter to inquire. Coming back, he informed them Latif's bail was being processed, and he would be brought out soon. He spotted ASP Mala, one of the prosecutors, walking back to her office. He again excused himself and firmly reminded them to wait until he came back.

Poking his head in the doorway of the prosecutor's office, Jeffri signaled to ASP Mala his intent to have a chat with her. She beckoned him in with a nod to the visitor's chair.

"Puan Mala, I'm Jeffri from Jeffri & ..."

"I know. What can I do for you, Encik Jeffri?" Mala asked as she continued sorting out the bundle of investigation papers.

"I'm wondering, sorry, I'd like to seek your advice," Jeffri immediately corrected himself. He knew just too well; if there was any chance of getting what you wanted when dealing with bureaucrats, you have to patronize them. To put it mildly: kiss ass, thus the correction from 'wondering' to 'seeking' her advice.

Mala looked at him skeptically.

"The first accused PG-ed and admitted to the facts, which stated he was riding the stolen motorcycle. My client was a pillion rider and most likely did not even know the motorcycle was stolen. I mean, who would ask the driver if the bike was stolen when getting a lift?" Jeffri said with a smile. "Perhaps, you could advise me if I should seek for the charge against my client to be dropped."

"You know I don't have such authority. I suggest you write to the DPP."

"Yes, yes, good suggestion. However, I'm sure the DPP values your views on it. I'm ever, and my client's parents will be ever grateful if you could put in some favorable words to support my request. My client is the only child, and the parents really depend on him to be able to take care of them in their old age," Jeffri added a lie for melodramatic effect.

"Funny how they all seem to have only one child and are desperately hoping for that child to care for them," Mala, who had heard it all, mocked.

Jeffri ignored her sarcastic remark.

"Thank you, Puan, for your advice. I'll do that and revert as soon as I've the DPP's consent. And thank you for your support," Jeffri said, smiling politely.

Stepping out of the office, he was already working his brain on how to play it with his saviors, to squeeze a few extra ringgit, to unlock their bank account with something untrue but plausible.

His client Abdul Latif was already seated next to his mother, who was doting all over him when Jeffri walked back to the court's general office. The father remained as irked as when he left them. Putting on a grave face, Jeffri approached. On seeing his expression, the mother stood up, looking desperately concerned.

"Is something wrong Encik Jeffri?" she queried.

"I just came from the prosecutor's office, and I'm afraid it doesn't look too good for Latif." Jeffri paused for effect. He liked the expressions on the mother's and son's faces, especially the mother.

"Ya Allah," Kalsom uttered in anguish.

Jeffri knew he had her unwavering attention and went in for the kill. "The other accused, the one that PG-ed — sorry, pleaded guilty, what's his name…" Jeffri started.

"Ridwan," Latif blurted out, all ready to burst into tears.

"Yes Ridwan, was sentenced to three years imprisonment. The DPP has offered him a deal: should he be willing to testify against Latif, the Deputy Public Prosecutor will seek a reduced sentence," Jeffri explained.

"Is he?" Latif asked, agape.

"Is he going to?" echoed Kalsom, her mouth gaping even wider than her son's.

"The prosecutor said Ridwan has not reverted on the offer. But more importantly, we need to stop the offer by the DPP." Jeffri used the word 'we', making sure to include the parents as if they had a big role to play. "We need to file an urgent motion to the court to stop the offer from being made."

It was a blatant lie, but a lie he needed to tell to survive.

Kalsom and Latif nodded earnestly in sync. The father, however, gazed at the lawyer distrustfully. His expression said it all: Lawyers have a reputation for making bad things worse or more difficult than they really are, for obvious reasons. As an ex-public servant, he despised the word 'urgent' for it usually translated into extra work and, in a lawyer's world, more money.

Ignoring the father's irritated expression, Jeffri continued. "I'll need to bring in a temporary paralegal to assist in the precedence research and another for the filing." His spin-doctor's brain was working on overdrive. "I could do it myself, but in our case … time, or the lack of it, is critical. The motion must be filed immediately to have any chance of stopping the DPP's offer."

"Yes, we must act immediately," Kalsom agreed. "Along's future must be protected at all costs," she added and instinctively wrapped her flabby arm over her son's shoulders.

"Yes, Along's future must be protected," Jeffri regurgitated her sentiment. "Now, this is what I need to do immediately. I'll need additional funds to engage the two paralegals. As this is rushed work, I'm sure they'll charge us a little more than the normal fee. However, to be fair, I'll offset that by not asking for additional fees for my firm. I'll need five thousand immediately to secure the two paralegals' assistance."

"Thank you, that's very kind of you," Kalsom commended. "May Allah bless you for your kind heart."

"But you said the fee is five thousand on engagement and five upon conclusion," the father protested. "I understand it to be inclusive of everything, I mean everything."

"Abahhh!" Kalsom admonished, "Encik Jeffri already said he is not adding an extra fee for his firm. This five thousand is for the extra two persons, not him."

"But…" the father opened his mouth to table his argument.

"But what! You know I have a weak heart. You want Along to go to prison and for me to die?"

Jeffri watched in silence, feeling a touch of guilt as the mother reduced the father to chicken-shit. He saw no necessity for him to say anything. His battle was being fought and won by the mother. He consoled himself by remembering a quote from PAS leaders: *It's OKAY to lie for the party's salvation.* In his case, it's OKAY to lie for Jeffri & Associates' salvation.

"Go across to Maybank and draw out the money, or I'll never forgive you if Along goes to prison, never!"

With those commanding words, Jeffri's financial status significantly improved. He would still have an office, his car and most likely his helper for another month.

3

✕

With a bulging pocket, Jeffri walked out of MPAJ Tower a rejuvenated man. Crossing the ever-congested Jalan Pandan Perdana to his car, the heat and humidity did not bother him as much. After taking off his jacket and clip-on tie, he threw them onto the backseat of his car. As he opened the driver's door, he heard his name being called. Turning around, he was surprised to see his university mate, Kim On Juan, standing in front of the station's sundry shop.

"OJ," Jeffri managed, stupefied. OJ was what Kim On Juan used to be called during their university days.

"How're you, Jeff?" OJ greeted, beaming.

"Fine, fine," Jeffri said, closing the car door. "What brings the corporate suits down to this part of town?" he asked, stepping away from the car and extending his hand. "Wait, wait … don't tell me. Business is so bad the corporate suits are muscling in on our kangkong actions."

OJ grinned at Jeffri's joke, not responding in like.

"Jeff, let's have a drink," OJ said, gesturing toward the mamak restaurant across the road next to the petrol station.

Jeffri gazed at his university mate, trying to read something into the invitation. They had not met since they graduated and started chambering. There was the occasional phone call to touch base, but that was about it. Both were busy making a living. At least he was. OJ, on the other hand, was probably learning the tango in the corporate hassle and tussle, working in his father's law firm Kim & Kim. An old and well-established firm specializing in corporate law. Somehow Jeffri doubted this meeting was by chance, and his curiosity was piqued.

"Sure. So, what actually brings you here?"

"I was at the land office and remembered your office is located close by. I called your office and was told you were in court. When I came down from the land office, I saw you walking out of the lobby and followed you."

Jeffri knew that was a lie and an insane one at that. *OJ came out from the station's sundry shop when he spotted me walking to my car. That meant he must've been waiting for me.* OJ had always been a lousy liar. During their university days, he couldn't even bluff his way out of a boring lecture. Jeffri let the fib slide. He needed to know what his university mate had in mind.

"Lucky you saw me, otherwise I would've left and missed the chance to catch up," Jeffri said, playing along. "How's business?"

OJ did not reply. Instead, he pointed to a table along the sidewalk, away from the early lunch crowd. They ordered their drinks, but both declined lunch. The ensuing silence and sporadic minuscule smiles were rather awkward for two grown men sitting at the same table. Other customers might take them as a couple. OJ seemed rather lost in his thoughts. Jeffri waited. Their drinks arrived, and finally, OJ started talking.

"How's practice?" OJ asked, kicking off the conversation.

"So-so. Pickings are slim as usual, but we try to manage."

An uncomfortable silence ensued with OJ staring into the iced lemon tea glass as he toyed aimlessly with the straw.

"OJ, what's up? You seem distracted. Is there something you want to get off your chest?" Jeffri asked, offering him an opening.

"Actually, there's something I'd like to ask of you."

Jeffri waited as OJ again lapsed into his 'deep thought staring into glass' routine.

"I know you have your hands full with litigation, but I'd like to…" He hesitated, searching for the right words. "The firm would like to offer you some of its cases."

"Oh, that's nice of your firm, but you know I don't do corporate paper-pushing stuff."

"Yes, no, I mean, it's not corporate work. It's criminal litigation, your area of expertise."

"I thought your firm didn't take on criminal cases," Jeffri remarked, surprised.

"We don't, but sometimes it's unavoidable. It involves some of our major clients, and the firm took them on as favors, or rather to retain their business. It's sort of keeping them happy. You know how they lump us; lawyers are lawyers," OJ said with a forced half-smile.

"All this while, how were they handled? I mean, who were the defense counsels?"

Again, the awkward silence followed. OJ suddenly raised his head to look at Jeffri straight in the face.

"My father is leaving the firm," OJ blurted out off-topic.

OJ's statement caught Jeffri by surprise, but he said nothing. He was certain there was more to follow and waited. It took a little longer than he anticipated, but it came.

"He has told me of his desire to retire on numerous occasions, but last week, last Monday to be precise..." OJ stopped mid-sentence. "He's retiring immediately. He did not go into detail but said his decision is firm. I'll be made a partner in his place."

"Congratulations are in order then," Jeffri offered, extending his hand.

OJ took the hand, flashing a half-smile of acknowledgement, then pulled it away rather too quickly. He sipped his iced lemon tea.

"All this while, criminal litigation was farmed out to firms, friends of my father."

A long silence followed, and Jeffri waited patiently for the 'but' punchline.

"Don't get me wrong, they're good lawyers and loyal to my father, but that's as far as it goes. In their eyes, I'm Kim Junior, and I'll always be that to them, never their equal. I cannot and never will gain their respect and loyalty, nor can I be absolutely certain they're doing their best or are being aboveboard with me. I need someone I can trust, someone who sees and treats me as equal. I need to be absolutely sure the firm's clients are given the best possible representation."

"And you came to me?" Jeffri asked wide-eyed. "I'm honored, but why me? There're hundreds of reputable firms that'll jump at the opportunity to work with your firm. Kim & Kim is no rookie player in the industry."

"I've known you for, what, more than five years now. Granted, you're not a reputable litigator yet, but I know you, and that's what I need. Someone I know. Someone I trust and that'll be upfront with me."

It was Jeffri's turn to be silent and deep in thought.

"If you're agreeable, I've two cases awaiting immediate farm-out. They're yours at whatever rate you're charging. By the way, what's your going rate?" OJ asked, baiting the offer.

"Eh?"

"Your retainer?"

"Oh, it depends," Jeffri said, buying time to answer a simple question, but a question his law firm was unaccustomed to. Most of his clients were members of a street-pack that he used to run with or those referred to him by them. Almost all of them were not able to pay much in hard cash. Still, they compensated the shortfall with markers or deeds-in-kind, something Jeffri envisaged he might need a lot of, one of these days.

"On?"

"The case, its complexity…"

"Ballpark?" OJ asked, cutting him short.

"Twenty for retainer, two for each appearance, less miscellaneous of course."

"Of course. Let's say five or six appearances, give or take thirty thousand to tapau?" OJ said, grinning.

"That should cover it, less miscellaneous expenses," Jeffri repeated with a grin of his own.

"Yes, yes, of course. It's a deal then," OJ prompted. He stood up, offering his hand. "Let's shake on it, and I'll get my office to forward you the two cases."

Stunned by the speed of the windfall, Jeffri remained seated yet somehow managed to grab OJ's extended hand for the gentleman's agreement handshake to conclude it.

"It's really nice seeing you, and I'm looking forward to seeing you more regularly. Perhaps we could relive our uni days and pick up from where we left off," OJ said, smiling broadly. "If you ask me, those were the best days of my life."

"Yes, it's really great seeing you, and thanks. Thanks for the farm-out, really appreciate it."

Several minutes after OJ left, Jeffri was still seated at the table nursing his drink, dazed by what had just happened. He was afraid to stand and leave, afraid that should he walk away from the table, the offer just made across it would disappear, poof into the hot and humid Pandan Perdana air.

4

✕

Driving back to the office, Jeffri made a call to his one and only loosely termed staff, Juliana Osman, known to him and her close friends as Ju. She informed him there was a call for him from a man, but when told he was at court, the man said thanks and hung up. The information brought a sly smile to Jeffri. He was right: OJ was waiting for him and the so-called chance bumping into him was a lame cover story.

"Ju, had your lunch?"

"Not yet. You buying?" Juliana asked, chuckling.

"Why don't you come down? Let's have yong tau fu. I should be there shortly."

The law firm of Jeffri & Associates was housed on the second floor of a three-story shophouse, right above Ampang Yong Tau Fu restaurant — a place patronized by Malays craving for Chinese dishes. The office was devoid of any associate's cubicle, save for one room left behind by the previous tenant. That room was turned into Jeffri's office. Similarly, there were no associates, contrary to what was boldly expressed by the firm's signage. The 'associates' was something Jeffri, or for that matter, most lawyers, romanticized of having when starting their own firm, spurred by the illusion that setting up a law firm was a breeze and there were clients aplenty. However, after operating for two years, Jeffri & Associates was still a one-man show, with Juliana Osman as the only staff helping out with the day-to-day office work. She was a genuine McCoy full-package: receptionist, clerk, secretary, cleaner, security, dispatcher, and whatever else needed to be done for the office by a human being.

After driving three times around Ampang Point, Jeffri finally managed to find a parking spot in front of the Sports Toto betting outlet, about 500 meters away from his office. Walking in the hot and humid air, he entertained the thought of securing a reserved parking bay in front of his office. He wondered how much that would cost him.

Juliana was waiting in front of the yong tau fu restaurant as he arrived all sweaty yet only mildly grumpy from the walk.

"Here, let me take those," Juliana offered to grab the jacket and file from him. "How did the case go?"

"Better than expected," he beamed, digging into his pocket to pull out a wad of money. "Here, use it to pay the rent and take some for your own needs."

"Woah, who did you rob?" Juliana asked, genuinely amazed.

Jeffri laughed and placed their order with an aged Chinese woman who, from his memory, seemed to have worked at the restaurant forever. He ordered four deep-fried dumplings, four rolls, two eggplants, two red chilies, a plate of spinach with oyster sauce, two plates of rice and two sugarcane drinks.

"You want anything else?"

"That's more than enough. Tell me, how did the case go?" Juliana insisted.

"It went five K more than agreed," Jeffri said, rather pleased with his achievement. "I need to write to the DPP to drop the charge against our client. The first accused has a career in thieving and retaining stolen goods. He PG-ed and was given three years. Spoke to the prosecutor, she advised me to write formally to the DPP. I think the DPP will drop the charge. They already got whom they wanted, already charted a win, and to go to trial will be a waste of taxpayers' money."

"You think they care? I mean, about wasting taxpayers' money? Didn't you read about the AG's appeal on the Yellow Balloon case?"

"Yes, that was the ex-AG, the previous government. Perhaps the new one got more sense. Anyway, I'll still remind them of the wastage," Jeffri said, laughing.

"The new AG and government are worse than the previous, if you ask me," Juliana said spitefully. "Just a bunch of liars and hypocrites."

"All politicians are," Jeffri stated, smiling.

Their food arrived, and the conversation died off temporarily while they focused on filling their stomachs with the supposedly healthy diet of fish, taufu and vegetables. Halfway through, Jeffri broke the news.

"Met up with an old uni buddy at the court. No, not in court, outside MPAJ at Petronas."

"Good for you," Juliana said as she dipped her fried dumpling into the sauce. "What did you guys talk about? Girls?"

"No. He offered me work," Jeffri said, stopping midsentence on seeing Juliana's reaction.

She dropped her chopsticks rather clumsily, causing the utensils to roll off the plate onto the table. She stopped chewing the fried dumpling and gawked at him.

"Did you take it?" Juliana asked with her mouth full.

Jeffri nodded, puzzled. "Why? It is work I need, I mean, we need."

"And what am I to do?! I'm not a lawyer!" she mumbled.

Jeffri saw tears welling in her eyes as she bowed slightly to hide her face from him.

"What do you mean 'what'll you do'? You work with me."

"But you'll be working with your buddy."

"I said he offered me work. I didn't say he offered me a job or employment. He offered me, or the firm, farm-out work, cases. They don't do criminal cases."

"Ooh," Juliana emitted, hiding her embarrassment at misconstruing her boss's statement. "So the firm's still there, and you'll still work from it?"

Ju can be pigeonholed into the 'accidental employee' slot. It all happened about a year and a half back when Jeffri was in court representing one of his street-pack members for disorderly conduct in a public place. Juliana's case was a fresh mention and was called ahead of his case. Waiting for a case to be called was like waiting to see a doctor in a government hospital, except there was no number or muted television high up on the wall, and you were not allowed to be entertained by your smartphone apps. To avoid boredom, Jeffri focused on Juliana as she was escorted by a policewoman from the holding cell into the courtroom.

Juliana was in her late twenties, but she looked in her forties. She was in soiled jeans and T-shirt, with unmade hair and devoid of any cosmetics or jewelry. She was tall and clearly undernourished and exhausted, Jeffri thought, probably from the lack of sleep while under police detention.

On entering the courtroom, she seemed disoriented and terrified. At first, Jeffri thought she was going through drug deprivation withdrawal syndrome and thought, *This should be entertaining.* Jeffri noted with fascination that she jerked her shoulder away, followed by a menacing get-your-filthy-hands-off-me-bitch glare every time the policewoman tried to steer her to the accused dock. When she was finally in the dock, she gripped the dock railing tightly with both hands until her knuckles were bloodless. She turned rigidly in the direction of the slightest sound or movement like a cornered raccoon. When she turned to stare at the gallery, Jeffri was captivated by her eyes. He noted the absence of the all-too-familiar blurry, watery, glazed red eyes associated with drug users. There was no discontent, hatred or anger in them either, just fear — extreme fear.

Startled by the approaching court staff, she spun around from staring at the gallery. She leaned forward against the railing, shaking her head from side to side like a chained matriarch elephant. Her low grunt sounded animal-like, causing the court staff to stop in her tracks. Taking a couple of steps back, the clerk hastily read out the charge and hurriedly retreated to the safety of her desk. The policewoman standing by the dock hissed something to Juliana, which she replied with a deadly laser glare. Annoyed by the situation, the magistrate sternly instructed the court staff to read the charge again. The clerk read it from behind her desk.

After the charge was hurriedly reread, Juliana was asked if she understood it. Juliana started to rock her body from side to side while shaking her head. The charge was for the theft of a box of baby milk powder and a pack of Pampers totaling RM42.50 from Giant Supermarket. When the court staff repeated her question, Juliana closed her eyes tightly, and Jeffri figured she probably thought everything would just go away, that the whole thing was just a bad dream. She opened her eyes when admonished by the clerk. In a tiny trembling voice, she pleaded, "It was for my baby. He had not eaten for two days." The court staff admonished her again, saying she could mitigate later, and then repeated the question, "Do you understand the charge just read to you?"

That was the crazy moment Jeffri jumped to his feet, introduced himself and got placed on record as her counsel. His impulsive action attracted an irritated gaze from the magistrate who was caught off-guard, which he ignored. He pleaded not guilty for his new client and asked for a hearing date.

He caught the court by surprise, silencing it momentarily. Juliana turned to look at him. He spotted fear and puzzlement in her eyes. Waiting for the clerk to give the hearing date, Jeffri came to a shocking realization of his gallant but foolish action. He grinned awkwardly at the gawking court staff and policewoman. A hearing date was fixed, and Juliana was offered bail, which Jeffri managed to get one of his street-pack members to arrange for her, and his firm picked up yet another non-paying client.

The next day, Jeffri sent one of his street-pack members to pay a visit to the supermarket manager. The amount of RM42.50 was paid, with a few words of friendly persuasion. As expected, the charge against Juliana was withdrawn.

A day after the charge was withdrawn, Jeffri found Juliana holding an adorable toddler, sitting at the stairwell leading to his office. From that day on, she became an integral member of Jeffri & Associates. She refused to talk about her past, and Jeffri never asked.

When the embarrassing moment passed, Jeffri said, "OJ said he'll be sending two files for us to handle."

"When?"

Jeffri shrugged. "Soon, I hope."

"What's the fee like? These are paying clients, right?" Juliana added, her eyes narrowed.

"Thirty big ones each."

"You're kidding!"

"Nope, I never kid about money. That's what was agreed."

Juliana let out a long low whistle. "Can I have a new table, computer, fridge and microwave?" she asked teasingly.

"While you're at it, why don't you get yourself a forty-two-inch flat-screen TV," Jeffri said laughingly.

5

The law office of Kim & Kim was on the sixteenth and seventeenth floors of Citibank Tower, along Jalan Ampang. A prestigious address in the heart of the city in close proximity to the headquarters of the MCA, a component party of Barisan National, the previous government for sixty years; and Petronas Twin Towers, the country's iconic landmark.

OJ, together with 22 other associates, was housed on the sixteenth floor, which had the moniker of the Salt Mine. Each associate had a tiny open-concept cubicle while Section Head offices lined the walls. OJ was the head of Mergers and Acquisitions, and therefore allocated an office, a secretary and four associates: salt miners.

The partners were located on the seventeenth floor. It used to be Kim, the grandfather and Kim Senior, the father. After the passing of Kim the grandfather, a non-Kim was taken in as a partner, but the name Kim & Kim remained. In the legal community, the firm was known as the grandfather and father law firm. No son was ever mentioned.

The interior design, decor, fixtures and furniture of level seventeen were a total contrast with the Salt Mine. The partners' floor was fashioned with the ambiance of an old English barrister office. Yet the Chinese roots were evident everywhere, especially the wall adornments. The floor opened into a large reception area with lush dark brown Duke leather armchairs, polished cherry-finished coffee tables, hospitality counter and neatly displayed international magazines. The conference room was furnished with an oblong, sleekly polished oak table lined with black leather chairs, a state-of-the-art conference system, drop-down plasma screen, electronic whiteboard and a secretary table at the far corner with a digital recording system: all the comforts and latest gadgets needed to do a legal battle in the modern world. Next to the conference room was the library lined with law books and journals. Unlike the Salt Mine, the entire seventeenth floor only housed the two partners and their secretaries.

OJ had just signed off the farm-out instructions for the two cases to Jeffri & Associates with a 50 percent retainer fee payment when his secretary buzzed him.

"Mr. Kim, Mr. Kim Senior requested for you."

"What's it about?" OJ inquired, rather disturbed. His mind instantly connected the summons to his farm-out instruction.

"Ms. Lim didn't say. She just said your presence is required."

"Okay, thanks."

He replaced the phone, took his notepad, and headed out for the emergency stairs to go up one floor. Climbing the stairs, he resolved to stand firm by his decision to engage his university buddy as the counsel for the two cases, should his father raise the subject. Stepping into the reception area, Ms. Lim, his father's secretary, motioned him to the conference room.

Tapping softly on the door, OJ poked his head in. As expected, Kim Senior was seated on his throne at the head of the table, and a woman was sitting to his right facing him. Kim Senior gestured for OJ to come in. Noticing Kim Senior's gesture, the woman turned around to face the door, flashing the sweetest smile OJ had ever received. It took a few seconds before OJ managed to command his legs to move.

"Juan, I'd like you to meet Ms. Sarah," Kim Senior said without formality as OJ approached them. Juan was what OJ was called by his parents. "Sarah was referred by an old friend of mine. She is seeking some legal assistance which I'm sure could be adequately handled by you."

Without standing, Sarah extended her hand. Her hand was most certainly the softest of hands OJ had ever touched. The smile that accompanied it was hypnotic and her eyes, with the lightest of blue, were the loveliest eyes he had ever seen. OJ stood motionless, totally enchanted.

"Pleased to meet you," Sarah said, lightly pulling her hand from OJ's grip.

"Eh, yes, pleased to meet you too," OJ stuttered.

"Juan, I'll leave you with Ms. Sarah to work out what is needed." Standing, he turned to Sarah. "It has been a pleasure meeting you, and I'm sure we can assist you with your needs. Do give my warmest regards to Darren, should you meet him."

"Likewise, thank you, and I certainly will," Sarah responded, shaking Kim Senior's hand.

No sooner had Kim Senior stepped out of the door, when Sarah asked if she could smoke. OJ informed her the office had a no-smoking policy, but if she did not mind discussing it in his office, the policy could be overlooked.

"What're we waiting for?" she asked, getting to her feet.

OJ, who was still standing, pulled the chair aside for Sarah to step out and followed her to the door.

"It's just a floor down. Perhaps we could take the stairs. It's faster," OJ suggested as they reached the elevator lobby.

"Lead the way."

OJ headed for the emergency staircase, holding the door open for her. As Sarah squeezed past him, her hand lightly brushed his side, sending a surge of electricity through his body. When he released the door leaf, a whiff of her tantalizing perfume enticed him. The walk down to his office was both agonizing and delightful for OJ. He had to work very hard to control himself from taking every half-opportunity presented to touch her hand or shoulder, which were inches from him. To a mixed feeling of frustration and relief, they finally reached the landing. Just as he took the lead toward his office, Sarah's handphone rang.

She pulled it out from her handbag, glanced at the screen and said, "Sorry, I need to take this."

OJ nodded as Sarah stepped away for some privacy.

Standing by the main entrance to his general office out of Sarah's peripheral view, OJ gave her microscopic scrutiny. Her blend of Mediterranean and Asian features and light tan told him she carried some Caucasian blood in her. He put her in her late twenties. Height about five foot five, lush shoulder-length black hair, very curved and edged. His verdict: Sarah was exotically beautiful. She was casually dressed in designer jeans, a white cotton three-quarter sleeve blouse, medium-height brown heels, and carried a matching light brown handbag. She looked so natural with no or very little makeup. To OJ, Sarah had to be the most gorgeous woman he had ever met in person and was now in a position to assist and impress. If love at first sight did really exist, then OJ was experiencing it.

Faking disinterest, OJ strained his ears, eavesdropping on Sarah's phone conversation. He heard her say, *"Nothing … just waiting for your call … of course … just let me get ready … in 20 minutes."* Sarah terminated the call, conscious of OJ looking at her, and flashed a sweet smile that was intended to tame a lion's heart. In OJ's case, it did just that and more.

"Mr. Kim I'm sorry, but I really need to go and meet someone."

"Oh," was all OJ managed.

"What time do you finish? Perhaps we can meet after. It'll give us more time to talk."

"5:30, but I can leave anytime you decide to meet."

"I'll call once I'm finished if that's okay with you," Sarah said, putting her hand on his arm, a deliberate act to soften his disappointment.

"Yes, yes, certainly."

Sarah gave his arm a lingering light squeeze before heading for the bank of elevators. OJ watched motionless, eyes unblinking until she disappeared into one of the elevators. Dismayed, OJ made his way back to his office with Sarah occupying a permanent residence in his mind.

Kim On Juan, or OJ, was what Jeffri classified as a Mummy-Daddy boy. Born as the only son in an overtly traditional family with wealth, he was raised with the strictest of discipline, as preserving the family name was everything. He was a millennial kid looking outside at the world through a glass panel but never able to be a part of it.

Law was never OJ's choice of profession, nor was it his forte. From an early age, he dreamed of being an architect, something he loved with a passion and believed he would excel at. Reading Law was forced upon him by his father. Although he suspected his mother was against his father's resolve, tradition prohibited her from voicing her protest. To protest was to be disrespectful of the wishes of the house's master and a severe breach of the Kim house rules. OJ empathized with his mother's lowly status and never held her silence against her. His father's favorite citation: *Your grandfather worked very hard in those old days to be a lawyer, he worked very hard to put me through Law school to be a lawyer, and as the man who'll carry the family name, you should be honored to continue the family legacy.* What choice did he have but to bury his dream and read Law?

OJ's life took a turn for the better or worse when he enrolled in university and met Jeffri Abdullah. He was instantly attracted to Jeffri for his maverick, adventurous and vibrant personality. Qualities he was prohibited from even dreaming of having. He was a blue-blooded Kim, and that was that. Jeffri, on the other hand, saw OJ as a person who could be useful to him. Someone with brains and money; a timid conformist who would keep him informed of lectures and assignment schedules.

Their friendship bloomed with each benefiting from the other. OJ was introduced by Jeffri to all the wonderful immoral, unhealthy, and illegal things the world had to offer. In return, Jeffri got to enjoy the same without any expense, while at the same time was assisted in his term papers and updated on all assignment deadlines, lecture scheduling, and rescheduling. OJ's escapade ended when they graduated, and he returned to the fold of the Kim's world.

Sitting in his office, OJ was unable to get any work done. His mind kept asking what Sarah's legal needs could be. Was she in some sort of criminal mess? If that was the case, he had his Jeffri to rely on. But why was she referred to the firm by his father's friend? He was sure his father's friend knew they didn't handle criminal matters. And why did his father call for him? He remembered his father saying, *"Juan'll be able to assist."* No, not criminal; it had to be some other legal issue, perhaps a divorce or child custody or property division. *Yes, that has to be it, a divorce and property division*, OJ reflected smiling.

His handphone rang, distracting him from his thoughts. Horror surged through his mind as he realized he did not give Sarah his number. *How the hell is she going to call you, dumbass?* His handphone rang on, the number unfamiliar.

"Juan," he answered grudgingly.

"OJ, Jeff, got the files and I'm wondering if you can arrange for me to meet with Kenny. His bail is due, and I'd like to work on his case first."

"Sure. This is your number? When do you want it?"

"Yes, sorry I didn't give it to you earlier. Any time you can arrange for it, the sooner the better. I'll make myself available."

"Let me get back to you."

"Yes, and hey, thanks for the handouts."

"Don't mention it, the balance will be at the conclusion of the case."

"Yes, plus miscellaneous should there be any," Jeffri reminded, chuckling.

"Yes, of course," OJ said, tickled by his university mate's unchanged qualities.

6

Earlier that morning, before Jeffri made the call to OJ to set up the meeting, Juliana received a parcel from Kim & Kim. The address on the parcel excited her as she ripped off the wrapping. There were two super-thin brown paper files, a payment voucher to be acknowledged and returned to the sender, and a check for RM30,000 made payable to Jeffri & Associates. According to the payment voucher, the amount was for 50 percent of the two cases' retainer fees and the balance of RM30,000, plus any other agreed miscellaneous expenses, shall be payable within fourteen days upon completion of the cases.

Juliana could not hold back her joy. She immediately called Jeffri on his handphone.

"It's here," she blurted out when Jeffri answered.

"What is? The landlord with an eviction order?" he asked, thinking about the two months' overdue rent.

"No, silly, I paid the rent yesterday as you told me."

"Then what is here?"

"The retainer's check for the two cases, thirty frigging thousand," she literally screamed. "Oh my god, I can't believe it, I'm holding it in my hand," she said, waving it as if Jeffri could see through the handphone.

Jeffri, who was making the turn onto Jalan Putra Sulaiman out of his residence at Fawina Court, pulled over by the roadside.

"Jeff, are you still there?" Juliana asked, still waving the check.

"No shit, that was fast!" he exclaimed, smiling broadly.

"Where are you? What do you want me to do with it? Can we buy all the things we discussed…"

"Ju, Ju, slow down and take a deep breath," he said, cutting her off. "First things first, make a copy of the check, and I want it enlarged and in color."

"Why?"

"To frame it, what else? It's not the amount that's significant. Well, it is but mostly what it signifies: the breakthrough I've been hoping and working my butt off for. It's our ticket into the big league, the reputation and money league."

"You know how much it costs to photostat in color?"

"Hey, we just got paid thirty big ones, let's splash a little," Jeffri laughed. "Okay, I'll be in shortly. See you soon."

Jeffri ended the call, eased the car onto Jalan Putra Sulaiman, and made a left on Jalan 4, then onto Jalan 3, passing along rows of luxury condominiums. Property that up to a minute ago, he'd never dreamed of having the means to own. Making the curvy right bend, he stopped at the traffic light intersection at Jalan Ampang. The light was red, and while waiting for it to change to green, he started daydreaming of where all these new developments would take Jeffri & Associates: him. Would he from now on be playing with the big boys, the heavyweights, or was this a one-off?

Heading toward Ampang Point, he spotted a vacant parking lot and swerved in, claiming it. Jeffri believed this had to be his day, first the RM30,000 and now an easily found parking lot. As he stepped out of the car, he heard Juliana calling him. Turning around, he saw her standing in front of Ampang Point shopping mall, waiting to cross the road. Jeffri waited for her by the car.

"Where did you go?" he asked as Juliana approached.

"You asked me to photostat the check, so that's where I went," she replied, showing him the blown-up color copy of the check.

"Now, isn't it a beauty," he remarked, holding it up. "The prettiest thing I've ever laid eyes on. Can you see it? It's our beginning. Where's the check?"

"Banked in."

"Laaa, you didn't give me the chance to kiss it," he said, faking disappointment.

"Don't worry, I did it for you and me like a hundred times," Juliana said, laughing.

At the office, Juliana handed him the two thin case files and asked if he'd had breakfast.

"No."

"I bought some donuts. You want some?"

"Thanks, and coffee please. Ju, any instructions came with the files?"

"Didn't see any, just the payment voucher and check."

"Okay."

Jeffri headed for his office. A 22 by 12 feet bare-walled office, furnished with a used Formica top chipboard table as the centerpiece, a used black PVC swivel chair, two overused visitor's chairs, a used faded steel cabinet, and a stained light brown fabric sofa. An ancient but still functioning desktop computer from his university days sat on the right corner of the table, completing the setting. *All these will soon change.*

He switched on the computer, which gave out swirling squeaks and jangles unfamiliar to the youngsters of today, with their laptops and tablets. *If the youngsters were to hear the swirling sound, they probably would think aliens invaded their computer.* Waiting for the computer to wake up, he flipped open the first of the two very thin case files.

It was a case of voluntarily causing hurt with a dangerous weapon or other means, under Section 324 of the Penal Code. An offense which carries a sentence of imprisonment of not more than ten years or fine or whipping or any two of such punishments. Kim & Kim's client, for whom he would act as First Chair, was Kenny Lim Yoke Lai, a 21-year old male living with his parents in Ara Damansara.

According to the arrest report, he assaulted Jonathan Kite at Beach Club with a beer bottle. The victim sustained an injury on his jaw, but there was no mention of the extent of the injury, and no medical report included. Kenny, the suspect, was currently on police bail, which would expire in eight days. The case investigator was listed as Sergeant Mohd Khalifah Budiman of Dang Wangi police district.

The second case was under Section 5 of the Betting Act 1953. Lau Wee Meng, a 37-year-old man living in Kepong Baru, was arrested for allegedly advancing or furnishing money for the purpose of establishing or conducting a common betting house. If convicted, the punishment was a fine of not less than RM10,000, but not more than RM100,000. He could also be imprisoned for a period of not more than five years. Interestingly, Jeffri noted the police bail was just extended for another month. The investigating officer was Inspector Kok Mok Min of the Anti-Gaming unit from the Kuala Lumpur Police Contingent Headquarters. In Jeffri's mind, the bail extension could only mean the police were unsure of their case. Otherwise, Lau would have already been charged in court.

The first case was garden-variety for Jeffri: the most popular charge for his non-paying street-pack clients. The second, however, was new to him, something he had to put in some reading to understand. He decided to take on Kenny's case first and seal off the retainer.

"Ju, can you dig up old court cases on Section 5 of the Betting Act? I've never come across them. Perhaps you can find some on the internet. See if you can use your charms and chat up Inspector Kok Mok Min of Anti-Gaming, find out what they've got on the case," Jeffri told Juliana from inside his office.

"If he's cute, can I seduce him?" Juliana called back, chuckling.

"If you do, then I'd like a copy of his investigation paper," Jeffri replied, laughing.

Juliana came into his office and parked herself in one of the overused visitor's chairs. "What's the case about?"

"It's about funding a betting house. I cannot recall having read any case of that nature," Jeffri said, passing her the file.

Juliana read the police report. It was made by Assistant Superintendent Police Paliani of the same department or unit, but nothing in the form of evidence was stated in the report. The words 'suspected of' repeatedly appeared before the allegation of Lau's involvement.

"It says here he was suspected of financing a betting house they raided in Kepong Jaya five months back," Juliana pointed out.

"That could be translated into: one, they have no direct evidence and their accusations were purely based on circumstantial or hearsay; and two, they're still fishing and if he's charged, they're hoping he would PG," Jeffri deduced.

"Or three, they did not get their monthly paychecks," Juliana said, laughing.

"Let's hope it's the third," Jeffri agreed.

"Okay, let's move on to more pressing issues. Remember our discussion yesterday?"

Jeffri gazed at her questioningly.

"The office needs, can I start hunting for them?"

"Yeah, go ahead. While you're at it, get yourself a new PC and scanner, you know the one that can also do photostating."

"I'll see if they have one that can make coffee too," she jested. "What about the microwave and fridge?"

"If you must, but I'd rather we get new tables and chairs, something more presentable."

"Okay, let me see what I can get. I'd like to change the office signage. Do something that looks more like a law firm."

"What's wrong with the one we have now?"

"Plastic. Kedai Urut Ah Chong in Chow Kit has better signage," Juliana said.

Jeffri cringed at the remark, but he relented. The present signage outside the office on the ground floor was a 24 by 18 inch black plastic plate with white stencil. It was not reflective of the firm's status as a barrister at law.

"Okay, but just the one outside. Leave the one downstairs as it is for now."

"I'll do the brass plate with the wooden back, you know, like those real law firms."

"That costs a bomb," Jeffri protested with narrowing eyes.

"Investment. Believe me, it'll be worth it. Anyway, we've got money," Juliana said, stood and swaggered out.

"Investment, right. Why stop there? Why not gold-embossed letterheads, envelopes and a private parking bay for me upfront?" Jeffri joked.

A meeting with Kenny Lim, the suspect, was arranged by OJ for 12:30 p.m. at Tony Roma's in Pavilion — a restaurant normally beyond Jeffri's financial means but he was optimistic all that would soon change.

Jeffri Abdullah never knew his father and had always wondered about the name 'Abdullah' listed as his father in his birth certificate. The name Abdullah, which means 'the servant of Allah' in Arabic, was normally listed as the father of Muslim converts or a Malay child whose father's identity was unknown — an illegitimate child in Islam. Jeffri was born a Malay and, therefore, automatically a Muslim in Malaysia. He had never seen his father or a photograph of him. Yes, there are Malays actually named Abdullah by choice, and in these cases, their personal particulars, like identity card numbers and addresses, are recorded in the birth certificates. However, in his birth certificate, all those were listed as 'unknown'.

In his younger years, Jeffri met a lot of 'Uncles' coming and going. However, none hung around long enough to fit as a father figure. He had on numerous occasions, when he was in primary school, asked his mother about his father, especially when he got some kiddy achievement award at school. While most kids had their parents there, he only had his mother. Whenever he asked her the question, she did not get upset or sad. In fact, she did not react at all. She just pretended it was never asked and talked about other things. Finally one day, he stopped asking. Since he never knew his father and his mother had refused to talk of him, Jeffri strongly believed 'Abdullah' fell in the 'unknown father' category.

His mother, whom Jeffri loved and adored, was a KTV hostess, or glamorously termed Guest Relation Officer (GRO) in her younger days. Back then, they lived in a rented single-room City Hall flat at Jalan Pekeliling. It has long since been demolished to make way for upper-middle-class apartments and make some individuals very wealthy. As a karaoke GRO, his mother worked from around 7 p.m. till the early hours of the morning. Jeffri somehow managed to adjust and settle in with her routine. She was there for him when he left for school in the morning and when he came home in the evening. She was all dolled up by the time he completed his schoolwork and had his dinner. Soon after, she would leave for work, and he was all by himself.

Without a father figure to keep him in line, Jeffri ran loose. The street became his school after school, his universe. He started running with the street boys, always making sure he was home before his mother.

Jeffri was gifted with a shrewd mind. He saw and figured things out long before any of his street-pack members could or did. He was witty and always ready to take on a sticky situation whenever required. He could talk his or his pack's way out of tough spots and yet make the other party felt they came out on top or, at worse, broke even. His courage and attitude made him a natural leader of the pack.

By the age of 15, he was already drinking beer and enjoying sex. He tried cigarettes but never got the hang of it. He didn't do drugs of any form and sternly warned his pack against it. Drugs were a big no-no if they wanted to remain in the pack.

As a teenager, Jeffri was fascinated with Law. How laws were used to curtail or legitimize illegal or unethical activities. More intriguingly, how legal technicalities were used to delay, defer or even escape unfavorable decisions and conviction. Unlike other boys his age, he was never hooked on *Ultraman, Transformers, Captain America, Ninja Turtles* or the like of them. He was hooked on *Suits, Boston Legal, The Good Fight* and *Law & Order*. Apart from the intricacies of laws itself, he was enthralled by the lawyers on television: the showmanship, the arguments, their lifestyles and the beautiful women that came with it. The desire to be a lawyer was seeded in him long before he completed his secondary education — not just a paper-pushing corporate lawyer, but a trial lawyer, one that sings and dances in front of the jury, bringing them to his corner. Till today, his favorite novel is *The Lincoln Lawyer* by Michael Connelly. Unfortunately, long before he graduated with a law degree, the country disposed of jury trials.

One night during dinner, just a few months before sitting for his SPM, he earnestly told his mother of his aspiration to read Law. What he saw in her eyes was sadness. She did not have to say it. He knew. She did not have the financial means to put him through university. To hear her son express his dream but be in no position to assist must have broken her heart. That night, Jeffri made a promise to himself that he would achieve the grades to qualify for a government scholarship.

Two weeks after getting his SPM results, his mother woke him from sleep. It was 5:40 in the morning, and Jeffri thought something must be very wrong for her to wake him at that hour. She gazed intently into his apprehensive, sleepy face. After what seemed like forever, she hugged him tightly and handed him an envelope, whispering, "Go chase your dream." He did, and scraped through with First Class Honors.

After graduating, he chambered with a medium-sized law firm, and upon passing his Certificate in Legal Practice, he was admitted to the Bar. He was offered a junior associate position by the firm, where he volunteered for litigation work. Jeffri was happy.

Then one day, one of his street-pack members came calling, seeking legal representation. When his request was forwarded to the firm's partners, it was brusquely turned down with the remark: *These are not the type of clients the firm wishes to associate itself with.* Dejected by the partners' decision and angered by the uncalled-for humiliating remark, Jeffri quit. The next day, Jeffri & Associates was born with its first client on record.

Life was difficult, very difficult. The competition was murderous; it was a lawyer-eat-lawyer world. For those with no track record or powerful contacts, chances of failure were high. Jeffri started engaging his street-pack members to solicit for clients, chasing ambulances and Black Marias. He knew it was unethical, but ethics didn't pay his rent or bills or put food on the table. *I'll be ethical when I have the money to be ethical.*

Jeffri was early. He liked being early. It put him at an advantage, gave him time to check the area out, to pick a seat that offered positional superiority. On top of that, it allowed him to put on an expression of being annoyed at the other party's lateness, for being disrespectful of him and his precious time. A waiter approached his table, and Jeffri declared he was waiting for his guests and would order when they arrived. While waiting, he reviewed the menu.

Tony Roma's house specialty was ribs, and the picture looked delicious with the caption, 'A taste legends are made of.' Screw the price, he was going to have the 'taste legends are made of'. He was certain OJ would pick up the tab and charge it to the client. Over the top of the menu, he spotted OJ walking in alone. Putting down the menu, he waved OJ over.

"Sorry, am I late?" OJ asked, glancing at his watch.

"No, not late, just later than me," Jeffri joked.

"Seen Kenny around?" OJ asked, giving the restaurant a quick glance as he slid into one of the vacant chairs.

Jeffri shook his head. *What a presumptive question. How the hell would I know what Kenny looks like?*

"He should be here any moment. Have you ordered?" OJ picked up the menu, giving it a cursory view. Putting it down, he beckoned to one of the waiters. "Let's order while waiting for Kenny."

"You're in a hurry?"

"No, but let's order anyway." Truth be told, he wanted to be in his office waiting for an important call from a woman who had been on his mind since their meeting.

Turning to the waiter, OJ ordered Caesar Salad and plain water. Already having decided what he wanted, Jeffri pretended to review the menu, then asked the waiter about the lamb ribs. The waiter gave him a rehearsed endorsement to which Jeffri reluctantly said he would give it a try. For the sauce, he told the waiter to surprise him. Just as the waiter turned to place their orders, Kenny appeared at the entrance. OJ told the waiter to wait and take Kenny's order together. Kenny asked for Shrimp Scampi Pasta without looking at the menu.

OJ made the introductions and nodded for Jeffri to take over. Jeffri started by asking Kenny about himself. Kenny Lim Yoke Lai was 21, he had just completed a degree in Civil Engineering, following in his father's footsteps. *Keeping the family wealth within the family*, Jeffri thought to himself. Kenny worked in his father's construction company as a Site Supervisor. In Jeffri's eyes, Kenny was very similar to OJ: a sheltered life from a well-to-do family, unused to the harsh reality of street-level dealings.

Their orders arrived. The conversation momentarily turned to food commentaries as they dug in. Then it moved to the topic of 1MDB and the ex-Prime Minister being charged in court, and to the new government's failures to fulfill its election promises, the third national car pushed by the Prime Minister and concluded with the ridiculous announcement by a minister that the country would introduce a flying car that looked like KDK table fans being fitted to a double chair. By then, they had cleaned their plates and were fully satisfied with their overpriced meals.

"Kenny," Jeffri began, "I'm sure Mr. Kim has told you I'll be taking your case as the first chair."

Kenny nodded, although Jeffri was certain he did not know what 'first chair' meant.

"Okay, here's the deal. For me to give you my best, I'll need you to be truthful. Totally honest about what happened. The truth in my book is the complete truth, not half, not three-quarters. If at any instance I find out that you lied or hid something from me, we're through. Do you understand what I just said?"

Again Kenny nodded, but this time he shot a worried glance at OJ.

"Good. Tell me what happened on the night of your arrest."

Kenny looked to OJ, who gave him a go-ahead nod.

"That night, I picked up my girlfriend, and we went to KLCC for dinner. After that, we decided to catch a movie. It was…"

"Okay, okay, hold it there. When I asked you to tell me everything, I don't mean what you did with your girlfriend. Just everything to do with your case," Jeffri interrupted.

Jeffri's animated gesticulation in stopping his client's detailed narration melted the tension. Kenny laughed and was joined by the two lawyers.

## 8

Setting up the meeting with Kenny Lim as requested by Jeffri was the only productive task performed by OJ for the day after being left by Sarah at the elevator lobby. The rest of the afternoon was spent on agonizing when or if the woman would call for a get-together. The woman who made his heartbeat skip with her smile and whiff of her scent that made him want to hold her for eternity. Sarah — he didn't even know her full name.

At 30, OJ had been around the relationship block a few times, and had his share of pleasures. A few serious ones, but none lasted. With Sarah, he felt something different, stirring emotions within him he could not explain. It was like the lyrics to the song '*The First Time Ever I Saw Your Face*' by Roberta Flack— a song he and Jeffri used to belt out under the influence of alcohol in their numerous karaoke outings during their university days.

Sarah Jasmine O'Neil was a child from a failed mixed marriage between Muhamad O'Neil Abdullah and Khatijah Mansor. Muhamad O'Neil, or James O'Neil at birth, an Irish-American, was a Communication Marketing Consultant assigned to Grand Hyatt Kuala Lumpur. There he met the Director of Sales, Khatijah Mansor. After a brief romance, he converted to Islam, and they tied the knot. Soon after Sarah Jasmine O'Neil came into the world, the excitement of romance withered away. Khatijah, or Katty to James and her friends, was a liberal-minded and easy-going person but then started covering-up, physically and mentally. The teachings and demands of Islam became the scapegoat for their estrangement.

Suddenly everything became too inhibiting to Muhamad O'Neil Abdullah. In no time, a crack emerged in the marriage and divorce was inexorable. Muhamad O'Neil reverted to James O'Neil and moved back to the Big Apple. There was no official record of his reconversion to his original faith, for there was no necessity for it over in the United States.

Sarah was then a toddler. It was agreed by both separating parents that there was no necessity to go into a custody battle and turn their failed marriage into a media circus. Anyway, James knew the Islamic religious court would surely side with the mother. Added to the fact, James did not think he was capable of caring for Sarah as a single parent with thoughts of women constantly on his mind. An amicable child support arrangement was agreed upon, which was more than generous to see Sarah get the best education and continue living in comfort.

After completing her 'A' levels, Sarah moved to the Big Apple, where she enrolled in one of the colleges, majoring in Public Relations. Although James had offered her one of the spare rooms in his apartment, Sarah decided to rent her own place with a friend close to campus. The father and daughter relationship picked up where it left off, and James was grateful to have her back in his life. He played the role of Sarah's big, strong, and friendly provider and protector.

In her second year, Sarah fell madly in love with an Italian heartthrob Alessandro, who worked at a diner where she and her college mates hung out. She took a sabbatical, and they scooted off to Florence, Italy, where they lived out their dreams. Late one night, about a month into their dream life, they were rudely awakened by loud banging on the door of their rented apartment. When Alessandro went to answer the door, he was confronted by two huge men in black leather jackets and two similarly huge men in Carabinieri uniform. That was the last she saw of her heartthrob lover. As she did not know anyone there and was not formally related to him, she never knew what happened to him.

After two days of being alone in the apartment confused, frightened, and dried out of tears, Sarah contacted James. Five hours later, she was on a flight back to the Big Apple. Through his old boys' network, James managed to readmit his daughter into college. Life picked up from where she left off. Little did she know, her heartthrob Alessandro had left a part of him in her. When she missed her period, Sarah attributed it to stress caused by the incident in Florence, but when she missed it the second month, she stopped by a local drugstore and bought a rapid test kit. In the privacy of her apartment's bathroom, it informed her she was pregnant.

A lengthy consultation and discussion with James ended with Imran O'Neil Abdullah being brought into her life.

After graduation, James again, through his old boys' network, managed to secure Sarah an apprenticeship with one of the state's well-known political lobbyists. Her exotic beauty and charm were assets that gave her the competitive edge over other apprentices. She was taken under the wing of the veteran himself. Life was working out well for her. She and Imran lived in a decent middle-class area, and during the day, Imran was placed in a reputable nursery.

One day after work, when she went to pick Imran up, the nursery custodian informed her that a man came in the afternoon asking questions about Imran: where he was from, who his parents were, where he lived, etc. In compliance with the nursery policy, nothing was revealed, and the man left without leaving any contact number.

Sarah panicked. Her thoughts immediately brought her to the night in Florence. Had Alessandro heard of their child? In Sarah's mind, all Italians were somehow linked to the Mafia. Having watched movies and hearing how dangerously obsessed the Italian Mafias are with bloodline, she consciously decided not to seek him out to inform him. There was no way her son was going to be associated with the Mafia.

On reaching her apartment, she packed a suitcase with basic necessities, gathered all their important documents, and boarded a plane to Bangkok. After three days of cooling off, she boarded a plane to Kuala Lumpur. Upon arrival, she contacted her best friend, Lina, a divorcee with a son about Imran's age. She begged Lina to take Imran under her care until she could work something out for herself. She made Lina promise not to say a word to any living soul about Imran. That arrangement had gone on for more than a year now.

The sharp ringing of his office phone jerked OJ out of his woolgathering. Answering it, he was informed by his secretary that a woman by the name of Sarah was on the line. However, she refused to state her business.

"It's okay, put her through please," OJ said excitedly, taking a deep breath. Bracing himself for rejection, he answered, "Hello, Ms. Sarah."

"Mr. Kim, sorry for the delay in calling, the meeting took longer than I anticipated. Are you still available for a drink?"

"Yes, yes, where shall we meet?" OJ asked excitedly. "Where're you? Perhaps I can meet you there."

"Wonderful, but there's no need to do that. Why don't we meet at InterContinental, Bentley's Pub at 6? Is that fine with you? I know the traffic at this hour is horrible, so you can walk there from your office."

"That's thoughtful of you. I'll see you at 6 then."

"Looking forward to it. Bye."

Sarah's call put a silly smile on his lips for the whole day, where he did no billable work. If the same behavior was shown by the other associates, they would be admonished. But he was Kim Junior and soon to be a partner in the prestigious Kim & Kim law firm.

5:30 in the evening. The walk from Citibank Tower to InterContinental Hotel at a leisurely pace took about six minutes. The meeting was scheduled at 6. Yet OJ's table was all cleared, and he was already walking out the office door, avoiding the raised eyebrows of his secretary Kimberly.

"You leaving for the day?" she asked as he walked past.

"Yes, calling it a day. See you tomorrow."

Sixteen quick long strides later, he was out the office's glass door and into the elevator lobby. For once, he was glad his office was the nearest to the main entrance of the Salt Mine. Waiting for the elevator, he kept glancing at his handphone screen for the time.

OJ made it to the hotel lobby with 20 minutes to spare. He scanned the entire lobby hoping to spot his *Juliet*. After two hopeful sweeps of the lobby, his heart sank. His *Juliet* was nowhere to be seen. *Perhaps she is already at Bentley*, he consoled himself as he headed for the bank of elevators. Halfway through the lobby, OJ felt a soft hand on his shoulder. Turning around, he was greeted by one of Sarah's tantalizing smiles.

"Thanks for coming. You're early," Sarah said, walking next to him.

"Am I?" OJ stuttered with a schoolboy grin.

"I like it when a man is early, doesn't keep a woman waiting," she teased playfully.

OJ beamed like a kid who had just won the first prize in a nursery's coloring contest.

"How was work? Did you sue any big-shot today?" Sarah asked, sensing OJ's tense vibes.

"No, we don't do trials, only corporate matters."

"I was teasing. Stop being so serious, will you."

Stepping out of the elevator, Sarah threaded her hand through OJ's arm as they approached the entrance to Bentley. OJ almost kicked his own leg and missed a step, but recovered quickly. He pretended her action was normal, expected; a natural act although they had just met.

The waiter ushered them to a table for two and waited patiently for their orders.

"What're you having?" Sarah asked, looking at him in anticipation. "Beer, or something stronger to wash away the day's stress?"

"Beer is fine with me, draft."

"Any preference?" the waiter inquired. "We've Tiger, Carl…"

"Tiger, thanks," OJ cut him short.

"I'll have a sweet martini, please," Sarah ordered.

"Anything light to eat?"

"No thanks," Sarah answered for them.

The instant the waiter turned to place their orders, OJ inquired, "So, Ms. Sarah, what's the legal assistance that you require?"

"Oh, can we at least wait until we sip our drinks first?" Sarah protested playfully. Then she quickly added, "Sorry, am I on the clock?"

"No, of course not," OJ blurted, embarrassed. "I just thought you … you might have other things to do after here."

"I told you, we meet in the evening so that we can have all the time to ourselves."

Their drinks arrived, and Sarah lifted her glass, toasting their acquaintance, "To lasting friendship."

OJ lifted his chilled beer, secretly wishing the toast had been 'to lasting relationship'. Putting down their glasses, an awkward silence took over. Sarah knew it was all up to her. She leaned forward and placed her hand lightly on OJ's hand, which was holding the beer glass a little too firmly. Instantly, she noted the sparkle in his eyes and the uneasy shift in his sitting posture. She inwardly smiled.

"Okay, I know your mind is clogged with the legal assistance I'm seeking. Unless we get them all cleared, you'll be as tense as a priest in a whorehouse," Sarah said, smiling.

The analogy made OJ blush.

"I need some legal contract or agreement, something that'll hold up in court here," Sarah started, then paused to sip her martini. "Something simple but binding."

"Sales?" OJ inquired.

"Services."

"May I know what services?"

"ADT," Sarah said laughingly.

"ADT, you mean the alarm system?"

"No!" Sarah laughed louder. "ADT — Any Damn Thing."

OJ, not understanding what she meant, managed a nervous smile.

"I provide my services to any individual, organization or corporation that needs it. Let's say, Mr. A wants something and engages me to source and secure it. I'll source for who has what Mr. A wants and persuade him or her to sell or off-load it. Normally, I'll arrange for them to meet, with me present of course, to watch over my interests. When the deal goes through, the parties will then pay for my services. Simple."

"And what are these services?"

"ADT. If Mr. A wants bananas, I'll source for who has and wants to off-load bananas."

"The salient points being?"

"Now you're getting all legal on me," Sarah laughed, touching OJ's hands.

Again she noted the sparks in his eyes. She liked what she was seeing and knew she had him under her spell.

"I mean, important points," OJ said, blushing again.

Sarah tilted her head like she was thinking hard.

"The person who engages my services will have to carry the engagement costs and expenses."

"What if the deal doesn't go through or you could not source the item?"

"There'll be a mutually agreed time period for sourcing. The extension is at the discretion of the engager. The fee term may be renegotiated and agreed by both parties, but the successful deal fee remains unchanged."

OJ nodded. "When do you need this agreement?"

"Soon as you can write it up."

"A deal is coming through?"

"Hopefully, I'm keeping my fingers crossed," Sarah smiled, holding up crossed fingers.

As Sarah predicted, once the legal matter was out of the way, OJ seemed more at ease. They ordered a refill each and started with small talk, Sarah doing all the asking and OJ the answering. When it was dinnertime, Sarah declined OJ's offer for dinner. Leaving the bar, she again threaded her hand around his arm. When OJ offered to drive her home, she gracefully declined, saying her fridge was empty and she really needed to do some grocery shopping.

No one except her best friend Lina knew where she stayed. When Sarah arrived in Kuala Lumpur, making her escape from the States, Lina was the first and only person from her previous life she contacted. She had asked Lina to lend her name for a tenancy agreement of an apartment, her excuse being that she was unemployed and the landlord insisted on a secured tenant. Lina agreed, and the lease was signed under her name. Lina was also made to promise not to tell anyone of Sarah's existence in the city.

Sarah never took a taxi directly to her apartment or from her apartment to her intended destination. She would take a taxi from her place to Shangri-La, Istana, Concorde Hotel or the surrounding malls, then change taxis from there on. Likewise, when going home, it was always to one of the hotels or malls and a change to another taxi to her place. She avoided using Grab for fear her data was recorded by them.

The guards and management staff at the apartment knew her as Lina, the name stated in the tenant's list. That served her fine. She, Sarah Jasmine O'Neil, was non-existent on their records as landlord or tenant.

9

✕

OJ was already waiting for Jeffri at the entrance when he arrived at SouledOut Ampang. They headed straight for the end of the bar away from the main hall. The pub and grill was filling up with after-office hour drinkers, mostly men, for several quick doses of alcoholic supplements before going home to face the challenges of real life: spouses, children, in-laws, and other tribe members. A few of them were accompanied by women, chattering cheerfully — *probably after fruitful business deals,* Jeffri thought.

Their Tiger draughts arrived. It had been a long time since they'd clicked glasses, in this case, mugs. Sipping the beers, memories of their romping days filled their conversation and they shared waves of laughter and smiles. Jeffri raised his mug, "To lost times."

OJ raised his mug chirpily. Their first mugs dried up fast, so OJ signaled for a refill.

"You said over the phone you needed to discuss something?" OJ asked, looking at his friend.

"Oh yes, the other day, Kenny said all he wanted was not to do jail time," Jeffri prodded. "How serious was he, I mean, about not doing time?"

"Very serious, I suppose. Why?" OJ asked, a bit apprehensively. "Are you anticipating a problem?"

Jeffri ignored his friend's anxiety. "He said he's okay with a fine."

OJ nodded, "I'm sure his family can manage the fine."

"How much do you think it's worth to the family for this to disappear?"

"I don't understand."

"If I can make it all go away, no court, no jail, no fine, poof, it's all gone. How much you think it'll be worth to them?"

OJ laughed. "Still the same old Jeff, several steps ahead of the game."

Jeffri laughed, "That's me all right."

They each took a swig at their draft, eyes locked.

"Can you?" OJ asked, putting his mug down.

"Maybe I can, maybe I can't."

"Will ten K make it all go away?"

Jeffri seemed to ponder the offer. "Make it fifteen to be sure it does go away."

"Deal," OJ said, extending his hand to shake on the deal.

Grabbing the hand, Jeffri said to himself, *This has to be the easiest fifteen thousand I've ever made in my life.* "Deal, will let you know in a couple of days."

They simultaneously took another swig. This time it was Jeffri who put down the mug and asked, "Is there something you want to talk to me about?"

OJ looked over his mug, avoiding his friend's gaze. Jeffri thought OJ's face showed misgiving, doubt. Jeffri waited. If OJ wanted to talk, he'd listen. Otherwise it was none of his business and he'd let it slip. OJ slowly turned his focus to his drinking buddy.

"My father is leaving," OJ said, then paused to sip his draft.

Jeffri already knew that. OJ'd told him so when they met during the not-so-coincidental meeting outside the courthouse at the Petronas station. He waited for more. He knew that was just the opening line.

"He's leaving next week. He told me this afternoon. My mom," followed by another pause, another sip of his draft to wet his dry throat, a lingering hesitation, and then the punchline, "she was diagnosed with lung cancer, stage two. They've made arrangements for her to be treated in China. My dad said China has the best care and facilities, and if she receives treatment now, her chance of beating it is good."

OJ gulped down the last trickle of his draft and signaled for another. Jeffri was unsure if he should say something or wait for his buddy to let it all out. Before Jeffri could decide, OJ continued.

"We had a meeting this afternoon between my dad, his partner Tan, and I. Tan had expressed his decision to leave and start on his own."

The draft arrived and OJ immediately took a sip.

"Clients will be informed and they'll decide who they want to handle their accounts. The associates too, they'll be given a choice to follow Tan if they wish."

"That's a very sensible and fair arrangement," Jeffri offered.

OJ nodded.

"Officially, when is this all taking effect?"

"The clients and associates are now being informed. Tan will start moving out tomorrow, the same day I'll be moved upstairs into my dad's office."

"Wow, that's fast."

"Yeah," OJ acknowledged, taking another sip.

"And your concerns are?"

OJ again stared blankly past his buddy to the end of the bar.

"Fallout?" Jeffri asked, gazing at his buddy's face.

The slight raise of his eyebrows answered Jeffri's question.

"I'm sure some of your key associates will stay put. They'll be able to keep the clients happy," Jeffri consoled him. "At the same time, your father would've given this a lot of thought and would've already done all the necessary lobbying for the clients to stay put and place their trust in you."

OJ remained quiet, his eyes now fixed on his drinking buddy.

"Most importantly, I'm certain your father is still available should you need him for advice or direction. *That* I'm sure will be the confidence bridge for your clients." Jeffri raised his glass, "You worry too much. Here, let's drink to your promotion to the partnership of Kim & Kim. Wait … there's no more partner, right?"

"Yes, just me for now," OJ said, lifting his glass.

"You know what? A saying by the Dalai Lama comes to mind. He said, 'If something can be solved, there's no need to worry, and if something cannot be solved, there's no point in worrying,' or something like that, because worrying won't solve it," Jeffri said laughing.

$$\times$$

They clicked mugs, and OJ's mood improved, most likely helped by the draft beers. Jeffri welcomed his buddy's mood shift. They started reminiscing again on their shared past: the pub crawls, the girls that shared a moment of their lives with them, the troubles they got into at university, and the sheer fun of living. Another refill was signaled for both. The atmosphere was sprinkled with laughter and countless endorsements of, 'Yeah, those were the days' and 'I really miss them.'

Feeling cheery, OJ could not hold back announcing his breathtaking new discovery: Sarah. The most beautiful woman he'd ever laid eyes upon, and who was seeking his, mind you, *his* legal assistance.

"What legal assistance could she possibly hope to get from you?" Jeffri asked, mocking him playfully.

"Legal stuff, definitely not *your* field," OJ said, grinning. "Anyway, that's not the issue."

"What's the issue then?"

"She, I mean, I've never seen anyone as gorgeous, and, and…"

"They always were and are with you. Remember the girl you fell head over heels for during one of our pub crawls? What was her name? Bunny or Bernice?"

"Bertie, but this is different. This is like, like…"

"Looove," Jeffri completed his sentence, dragging the word. "That was exactly what you said with Bertie."

10

After burning the phone line the entire morning, Juliana finally managed to track down Sergeant Mohd. Khalifah Budiman, the Assistant Investigation Officer handling Kenny's case. The appointment was set for 3 p.m. at IPD Dang Wangi.

In Jeffri's legal assessment, Kenny was a good — no, not good, but great client, and he would make a convincing witness. He was clean-cut, pleasant-looking, expressive and most of all, looked honest. In respect to clients handled by Jeffri & Associates, Kenny's qualities were rare. His street gut feeling said winning the case in court would not pose a problem, and if all of what Kenny told him was true, there was a good possibility the case would not even see the inside of a courtroom.

✕

Jeffri hated going to the police station. Police stations were supposed to be public-friendly for people to file their complaints in the form of police reports. A place where the public was summoned to present themselves to give statements either as complainants or witnesses. Yet, police stations in the city were not designed with the public in mind; usually there are minimal or no parking spaces for them. Whatever parking bays not allocated to police vehicles were taken up by the personnel's private vehicles. Most of the time, the main entrance guard would turn public vehicles away to park elsewhere, which in actual fact could be nowhere close.

To avoid aggravating himself, Jeffri decided to take the LRT from Ampang to Sogo Station and walk the 600 or more meters to IPD Dang Wangi. He took the elevator to level nine in search of Sergeant Khalifah's office. Halfway down the narrow corridor, he spotted the sergeant's name on the familiar blue door, knocked lightly a couple of times and pushed the door open.

"Sergeant Mohd. Khalifah Budiman?" Jeffri asked a rather tired-looking man seated behind one of the two desks.

"Ya," the white-haired man acknowledged, peering above his reading glasses.

"I'm Jeffri from Jeffri & Associates. My office called earlier for an appointment."

"Did it?" Khalifah asked, creasing his forehead. "Aah, yes, yes, sit. What's this meeting about? Your office didn't say why you wanted to see me," Khalifah said in detachment and closed the investigation paper he was working on, placing it on top of the stack of accumulated investigation papers to his right.

"It's about my client, Mr. Kenny Lim Loke Lai."

Again the wrinkled forehead as the sergeant's worn out brain searched for the name.

"The 324 case involving the mat salleh," Jeffri prompted, guiding the sergeant's mental search.

"Aah, yes," Khalifah said, riffling through the stack of investigation papers. He pulled one from the middle of the stack and laid it in front of him. "Lim Loke Lai, yes. What about the case, Encik, err, Encik..."

"Jeffri. My client's bail is expiring in six days. May I know where the investigation status is at this moment?"

Khalifah flipped the file open and pretended to read its contents, an act intended to be convincing when he answered the lawyers. Jeffri took the opportunity to sneak a peek at the contents and notes. He smiled inwardly when he noticed the investigation paper had not been forwarded to the sergeant's superior for instruction. The minute sheet was blank. As the sergeant flipped the pages, Jeffri saw a copy of the police report and one statement. He could not see the name of the witness. *Probably the complainant's statement*, Jeffri guessed.

"Yes." Khalifah flipped to the bail document, reviewing it. "Yes, we most likely will be charging him on the day the bail expires," he mumbled unconvincingly.

"Likely? And you said 'we'. Is that the instruction you received?" Jeffri asked, looking intensely at the sergeant.

Something about Jeffri's lawyer tone told Khalifah, *You could be dealing with someone who perhaps knows someone up the ladder.*

"I meant, that's what I'll be recommending to my SIO," Khalifah said, trying to sound confident, but Jeffri detected some nervousness.

"So you've not received any instruction as yet? It may be to your advantage."

Sergeant Khalifah gawked at Jeffri questioningly.

"You see," Jeffri said, pulling out an official-looking document from his backpack, making sure the sergeant saw the bold typeface **DEPOSISI** on it. "I've here a deposition from my client of the incident."

Jeffri noted with satisfaction that the sergeant's eyes widened, trying to get a glimpse at the content. He also noticed a flicker of anxiety.

"My client was accused of causing hurt with a dangerous weapon, a serious accusation indeed. According to my client, there was no dangerous weapon recovered by the police at the scene."

Khalifah opened his mouth to rebut Jeffri's claim, but was stopped by the lawyer with a raised open palm.

"My client informed you that his lady companion was molested. Your complainant grabbed her bottom, not once, not twice, but three times. My client informed you that he was assaulted with a kick to his left rib and thigh. He reacted to protect himself from further assault from the complainant and his two friends. He informed you that he was acting in self-defense of himself and his lady companion." Jeffri firmed his voice as he rattled on, making sure the sergeant was aware of his abhorrence at the sergeant's lack of professionalism. "He wanted to make a police report, but it was you, *you*, who told him it was not necessary as it will all be included in your investigation. My client was not sent to the hospital, which is, as you're aware, a standard procedure when an accused under arrest informs he was injured during the incident. Do you wish for me to continue?" Jeffri asked, staring at the sergeant.

Khalifah blinked rapidly, unable to respond.

"It's good that you've not made any recommendation to your SIO. Sergeant, may I suggest we see the senior investigating officer together and find out what he thinks?" Jeffri threw a dare.

Khalifah remained quiet. His forehead was wrinkled with anxiety and thought. Jeffri knew he had the sergeant cornered, and to continue pushing would only make him retaliate.

"I think there's still time for us to correct the situation," Jeffri said soothingly, pausing to read the sergeant's silent reaction. What he saw prompted him to continue. "In this case, my client, Kenny, was clearly the victim. He acted in self-defense and to defend his lady companion, who happened to be his fiancée," Jeffri lied. "I'm sure we all would have done the same, wouldn't we?"

Khalifah gave a slight nod.

"Yes, I'm sure we would. If there's anyone who should be charged in this incident, it should be the complainant and his two friends for outraging the modesty of my client's fiancée and causing hurt to my client. But I understand the complainant is a foreigner on a tourist pass," Jeffri threw in a wild guess.

Again Khalifah nodded.

"I also understand they'll be leaving in a couple of days."

"This coming Sunday."

Jeffri nodded. "And I don't believe the government needs to spend a load of money to bring them back here for the case because I can assure you, here and now, that my client is not going to plead guilty and we intend to take it all the way if need be."

Khalifah inhaled deeply.

"I've not sighted the medical report of the complainant's injury, but from my client deposition, it was a bruise, and at worst, a shattered white man's ego."

"Encik Jeffri." Khalifah finally found his voice. "What do you suggest we do?"

Jeffri liked what he heard, especially the use of 'we' and not 'I'. He took charge and, after 30 minutes, stepped out of IPD Dang Wangi smiling like a man who had just won at craps. The easiest fifteen thousand he had ever made.

11

A week after her arrival in the country, Sarah contacted the only family member she trusted: her father, James O'Neil. Before revealing her whereabouts and what had happened, she made him promise, under the threat of completely losing her and his beloved grandson, not to breathe a word about her to anyone. She then created a new email account and deleted or ceased being active in all her social media accounts.

She asked if James could bridge her financial needs until she could get back on her feet. He did. Through his network, James managed to hook Sarah up with a French company looking at the prospect of marketing its renewable energy technology in Malaysia. After several exchanges of emails, they placed Sarah on a retainer to do the footwork and establish the vital links, with the promise of a handsome bonus upon the conclusion of a deal.

Sarah had been working the trail for almost a year. Last week she finally made a breakthrough. Through one of the numerous political hyenas that made her skin crawl, she was promised to be introduced to Dato' Dr. Mohd. Tarmizi Lazim, the head of the Nuclear Power Commission. The catch was she had to be the political hyena's companion to a dinner where the introduction would be made. After one long year of chasing ghosts, she was desperate to make headway. She agreed.

At the reception, Sarah casually steered her political hyena companion close to her quarry, ever-mindful of the quarry's spouse's watchful eyes. When they were within talking distance, she insisted the hyena make the introduction. After making damn sure the head of the Nuclear Power Commission remembered her and her name, she gracefully stepped away to take her seat at the next table. All during dinner, she kept an eye on him. *Be patient, the moment will come,* she kept telling herself through the boring political ass-kissing dinner.

Sarah saw Tarmizi excuse himself to go to the washroom. Earlier upon arrival, she had checked out the distance of the men's washroom to the hall. At the right moment, she excused herself and headed for the powder room, bumping into Tarmizi in the concourse. She spotted his smile of recognition, politely stopped him and reintroduced herself. This time around, she categorically stated her profession and the principal she represented. The mention of her principal's name, Erava, caused Tarmizi's eyes to widen. He handed her his calling card, encouraging her to call for a more convenient and private discussion.

The appointment made during the dinner was fixed for 3:30 p.m. today. Sarah arrived early at Pullman Putrajaya Lakeside Hotel and selected a table overlooking the lobby. She ordered a cup of Earl Grey tea with lemon and honey, settled in and braced herself for a possible no-show. Watching the lobby, she replayed in her head how she was to handle this vital link. She had read everything she could get her hands on from the public domain about him: 57 – years old, holds a doctorate in political science, has been a civil servant all his life, at one time headed a division in Malaysian Administrative Modernization and Planning Unit (MAMPU), a government think-tank agency. That was when he managed to get close to the cabinet ministers and establish himself as a political stooge. His career from then on was smooth sailing with a strong wind in its sails. He was married with one daughter currently studying in Germany and, it goes without saying, on a full government scholarship.

Sarah decided to take the direct route. Play it like a man would: straight up. These people were so used to playing games, chances were they would not take offense. It could work out to her advantage, catch him off-guard. As an Asian woman, she was certain the seasoned Dato' would not expect her to be so daring and blunt. He would expect her to pussyfoot a little and leave the man-talk to the men from the power company.

A burst of horsey laughter from a group of women at a table in the middle of the coffee house distracted her. Turning away from the lobby, she glanced over in their direction. As her vision panned away from them, it stopped at another table where two men in their late twenties were taking their seats. At first glance, they seemed normal enough, but on a second look, she spotted one of them stealing anxious glances toward the main entrance. His partner was excitedly talking on the handphone through his hands-free ear-piece. Since leaving the Big Apple, Sarah had elevated her level of paranoia in observing her surroundings. The giveaway sign was when the man on the handphone reached over to the other man and excitedly indicated by tilting his head toward the entrance.

Sarah nonchalantly turned to look at the entrance and saw Dato' Dr. Mohd. Tarmizi Mohd. Lazim walking in. She calmly turned to observe the two men. One of them was excitedly tapping on his handphone. Sarah noticed that the man was not actually texting but following Tarmizi with his phone. Something told her he was secretly videoing Tarmizi's movements. Turning back to look at Tarmizi, she noticed another two men standing at the entrance. One gave a slight nod of acknowledgment to the two men seated at the table monitoring Tarmizi, then disappeared from sight.

*Shit. Is he under surveillance? But the two spooks were here before he arrived. Could it be me that's under surveillance?*

Sarah was suddenly overwhelmed with anxieties, the thoughts of the long arm of the Mafia and the safety of her son Imran invaded her head. Through the corner of her eyes, she saw Tarmizi slowly approaching her table.

Sarah stood flashing a big welcoming smile. They shook hands and took their seats. The waiter approached and Tarmizi ordered a cappuccino.

"Thank you for meeting me," Sarah started. "I'm sure Dato' is very busy and I really appreciate Dato' taking the time to meet."

Tarmizi grinned, gesturing for her to think nothing of it. As they talked, Sarah kept stealing glances at the two men who were noticeably very interested in them.

"You said you represent Erava," Tarmizi asked, "in what capacity?"

She was delighted at Tarmizi's directness. "I'm an independent agent under retainer by Erava. I'm sure Erava will be pleased to confirm my engagement and provide Dato' with my credentials," she replied confidently with an assuring smile.

"Yes, of course, I'm sure. Are you in the capacity to discuss the proposal?"

"If Dato' is referring to the power project, I'm sorry I am not. Erava is awaiting my call to send in their experts in the power and project management. I'm mandated to seek the key person-in-charge of the country's nuclear power initiatives and pave the way for Erava to further explore the possibilities of collaboration."

Tarmizi opened his mouth to say something, but Sarah beat him to it.

"I've informed my principal of this meeting, and they've given me their word that they're ready to jump on the next plane here to meet with Dato' if needed."

Tarmizi's eyebrows arched. "You know, there're several companies that have expressed interest in working with us. I don't mind telling you the Chinese are rather impressive, not to mention aggressively persuasive."

"I'm sure they are, but it's only fair to state that France, in this case, Erava, has established itself as a reusable energy forerunner in the world. Its technology and expertise are unmatched. At the same time, apart from being known for their romantic qualities, I assure Dato' the French are very accommodating too."

Sarah observed with interest the slight nod of acknowledgement of Erava's credentials, especially of the French being accommodating people.

"I don't think it's necessary for the technical people to come, not now anyway."

Sarah was quick to catch the drift. "Yes, I totally agree with Dato'. The team on standby are those that, how shall I put it to be diplomatically correct … are a part of the accommodation team."

Dato' Mohd. Tarmizi Mohd. Lazim smiled agreeably.

"Shall I inform them to book their flight? I heard Dato' is an excellent golfer. How about if I arrange for a round of golf over this weekend?"

"That sounds like a plan."

"Let me make some calls and arrangements. I'll keep Dato' informed on every detail."

"I look forward to it," Tarmizi said, standing without touching his cappuccino.

"Thank you again, Dato'. It has been a real pleasure dealing with a man of your caliber and integrity." Sarah added the last quality to draw Tarmizi's reaction.

As she expected, there was none.

As Tarmizi left, the two men observing them from their table spoke excitedly into their phones. One of them frantically waved to the waiter for the bill. *Amateurs*, Sarah said to herself as she walked to the cashier to pay her bill. She walked out and headed for the powder room. Walking along the mezzanine railing overlooking the lobby, she saw the two men who were behind Tarmizi earlier at the coffee house entrance, lingering at the hotel's main entrance. *Probably waiting for Tarmizi to come down from the coffee house.* She took the emergency staircase next to the powder room down to the lobby and positioned herself next to the newsstand.

From where she stood, Sarah was able to observe the hotel driveway through the glass wall. Tarmizi emerged from the elevator, nonchalantly crossed the lobby and went out the main entrance to a waiting car. The two men followed behind and got into another car with a driver waiting in it. Sarah noted down the car registration number and model.

Soon after, the two men from the coffee house appeared, looking lost and anxious. One of them spoke on the handphone, nodding several times, and to Sarah's relief they left.

Uneasy with what she just experienced, Sarah walked warily out of the hotel. She needed to be certain the men were really gone, not watching or following her. After about a hundred meters from the hotel, she crossed the road and walked on for another hundred meters before she popped into a 7-Eleven. She browsed through the goodies rack, keeping an eye on the entrance. After a couple of minutes, she felt confident she was not being followed. Stepping out, she waved down a taxi and headed for Istana Hotel, where she changed to another taxi to her apartment.

Once in the safety of her locked apartment, Sarah made a call to her best friend Lina. As the phone rang, she kept saying, "Pick it up gal, pick it up." The ring tone died and she immediately hit the redial icon, edgily repeating, "Please answer the phone, gal, please, please, please."

"Hi, gal, what's up?" Lina finally answered gaily.

"Lina, how's Imran?" Sarah blurted out tensely.

"He's fine. Why gal, what happened?" Lina asked, mindful of the urgency in Sarah's voice.

"You sure? When was the last you saw him?"

"Lunch time. What's wrong, gal?"

"You went home?"

"No, I watched him online. Sarah, what's going on? What's this Spanish Inquisition about?" Lina asked, annoyed by Sarah's tone and refusal to answer her inquiries.

"Online. Can I see him online too?"

"Yes, you can. Go to *www.Linaweb.com.my*. The password is Lina5191. Why won't you tell me what's going on? Look, Sarah, I hate to bring this up, but you told me when placing Imran with me that you'll one day tell me why. If Imran is in danger, then so are my mother, my boy and I. I need you to tell me what's going on."

"Sorry, gal," Sarah apologized, her voice calmer. "No, Imran is not in any danger, and neither are your mother, Jamal and you. You know I'll never knowingly put them or you in any danger."

"Okay, apology accepted. What's going on?"

"Just a mother's anxiety attack," Sarah said, giggling. "Hey, how about checking out the men tonight? I've a juicy bit to tell you."

"You slept with a gorgeous obscenely rich single hunk who is extremely good between the sheets."

"You're right on a few counts," Sarah laughed. "I'll tell you tonight, okay? Same place?"

"I can't wait. Okay, see you at 7."

Soon as she ended the call, Sarah surfed the net and logged onto the site given by Lina. The image of Imran playing in the living room with Jamal filled her handphone screen. She let out a sigh of relief, satisfied Imran was safe and well.

Peeling off her clothes, she stepped into the bathroom. Filling the bathtub with warm water, she poured in lavender aromatic bubble bath liquid soap. Waiting for the bathtub to fill up, she stepped in front of the full-length mirror, examining her naked body. Firm breasts, flat stomach, curves at the right places and firm butt. Smiling, Sarah said to herself, *You still got it, gal.* Strolling out nude into the living room, she selected Kenny G on the playlist and then proceeded to the kitchen, pouring herself a generous glass of Merlot and returning to the bathroom. Soon, Kenny G's magical saxophone, the slow swirl of warm water, the aromatic bubbles and red wine soothed her nerves.

Sarah shot off an email to Philippe, her overseer at the principal's office, updating him on her meeting with Tarmizi and his willingness to meet later. She made it clear it was to be an informal, casual meeting. She advised him to make the earliest possible arrangement to come over, for she wished to capitalize on the opportunity and not allow Tarmizi to have time for second thoughts. She also informed him to be prepared for a round of diplomatic you-lose golf.

The Pampas Reserve Grill & Bar, Bukit Ceylon, was crowded with diners when Sarah arrived. Standing at the entrance, she skimmed the place, looking for Lina. Failing to spot her friend, she peeked at her watch. It was 7:10 p.m. *It's not like Lina to be late.* As she looked up from her watch, she caught a glimpse of a man straightening up from bending over a table, revealing a gleeful Lina.

Lina noticed Sarah looking at her and waved coyly.

"I see you're already working on a substitute," Sarah jested, sliding into a chair.

"You're late. I thought you skipped," Lina said, grinning. "The least I could do for being stood up is get a free dinner from a willing buyer," she laughed. "Anyway, isn't he cute?"

Sarah turned to take a look at the man who almost became Lina's dinner ticket.

"Cute, but nothing close to the one I just hooked," Sarah swaggered.

The waiter arrived to take her order.

"Are we having dinner?" Sarah asked.

"Might as well, and since you made me lose my knight with a shining gold credit card, you're picking up the tab."

When the waiter left, Lina reminded Sarah of her promise to tell her the reason she came back to Kuala Lumpur. Sarah obliged by telling her almost everything, except that Imran's father might be linked to the Mafia. She gave the reason for leaving her toddler with Lina as she didn't want her mother involved. There were too many memories from her mother that she'd rather not revisit. Then there were the never-ending religious lectures, which she really did not think she could handle. Finally, and perhaps the most damning reason, was the imminent humiliation to her mother and family for Imran, her out-of-wedlock child.

"Okay, reasons accepted. Now, let's move on to more important matters. Who's the hunk you hooked?" Lina insisted, eager-eyed. "And when are you introducing him to me?"

"Meet you?! He's definitely not ready for you yet. I don't want you scaring him away," Sarah joked laughingly. "He's a lawyer, single…"

"Oooo, I'm beginning to like him already," Lina interpolated, "a lawyer, single and loaded. Second important matter, have you had sex with him yet?"

"A gal doesn't sleep with a man on their first date," Sarah replied mockingly.

"Which stupid gal said that?" Lina laughed. "But you're going to have sex with him, right?"

Sarah gave her a sly grin.

"Are you?"

"I'd like it to be a surprise, to me."

"How long has it been since you've been with a man, a year, more?"

"Let's order," Sarah said, avoiding the question.

In her mind, the question stuck like the honey badger to the actor's leg in the movie *The Gods Must Be Crazy*. It had been as long as Lina rightly pointed out. A healthy woman of her age needed sex, real sex. Climaxing by touching herself when the urge was unbearable wasn't satisfying enough. Superficial. But she reminded herself it had to be done for the time being. Perhaps she should get one of those mail-order sex toys, see if it could really satisfy her like the advertisements claimed.

12

Like on any other working day, OJ took the elevator to the sixteenth floor, the Salt Mine. Stepping into the general office, he sensed curious stares from the staff. He smiled awkwardly to a few of them, wondering what the hell was going on. Instinctively, his hand subtly touched his pants zipper to check. It was strapped, and he heaved a sigh of relief. Approaching his office, he noticed his secretary was not at her table. Odd, because Kimberly always was, unless of course she was on annual leave or had called earlier for an emergency sick leave or had an urgent errand to run before coming in. Then he noticed her desk was clear, absent of her usual stuff. "Shit," he cussed under his breath, "what the hell is going on?" Turning the doorknob to his office, it was locked. He felt the stares of the staff behind him. Turning around, he asked to no one in particular if they knew where Kimberly was.

"Kimberly said she moved up to seventeen," one of the staff replied, tipping her head upward.

"Right, right, thank you."

Embarrassed, OJ immediately headed for the emergency staircase. Once in the stairwell out of the view of others, he smiled. "How could you forget, dickhead."

Stepping into the lobby, Kimberly, who was standing beside his father's secretary Ms. Lim, greeted him. He nodded in reply, breaking his stride to a halt, unsure of where he was to proceed.

"I've moved all your belongings into the room," Kimberly said, coming to his rescue, gesturing to Kim Senior's office. "Ms. Lim had already sent all of Mr. Kim's personal items to the house."

"Thank you."

Kimberly noticed her boss's hesitation, stepped away from Ms. Lim, and led him into Kim Senior's office, which was now OJ's office. OJ stopped at the doorway. Not seeing his pug-faced father behind the large oak table felt weird to him. For years he had seen his father there; it was like him and the oak table were an item, like Pelé and a ball at his feet. Suddenly, he felt a cold shiver run down his spine; the absence of Kim Senior behind the table to bark instructions and make decisions was unnerving.

"Your things are all here," Kimberly informed, distracting OJ from his thoughts. "Do you want me to arrange them, or would you like to do it yourself?"

"I'll do it later," OJ replied, willing his legs to move, to step into the office and walk toward the chair. The chair seemed exceptionally huge without his father in it. For the first time, OJ noticed how black the black leather chair really was.

"Would you like a cup of coffee?" Kimberly asked as she moved to the door. "I brought your mug up."

"Yes please, thank you," OJ replied without taking his eyes off the empty black chair.

After Kimberly left, OJ turned around slowly to look at the office. Of course he had seen it before, but this was the first time he actually really looked at it. On the back wall directly above the black chair, there hung a large black and white portrait of his grandfather with its traditional gold-colored frame. His beady eyes fixed onto the door, scorning those who came with mala fide and welcoming those with bona fide intents. OJ stood beside the chair, staring at his grandfather. He could see the resemblance between father and son: the drooping edges of the lips, the constipated expression. His grandfather was in a black suit and cloak of the legal profession. *Why do they've to stand sideways with arms crossed when posing for a portrait?*

The left wall was adorned with framed certificates and photos of his grandfather and father, none of his. He stepped closer to look at them. Kimberly, who emerged at the entrance of the office with the mug of hot coffee, startled OJ. He walked around the table and stood next to the black leather chair, still unwilling to sit.

"Kimberly, I'd like to keep my schedule free today."

Kimberly placed the mug on the table, "I anticipated you would and I've rescheduled them."

"Thanks."

Kimberly looked at him hesitantly.

"Is there something you want to tell me?" OJ asked, noticing her expression.

"Ms. Lim told me she's leaving," Kimberly mumbled.

"Oh, did she say why?"

"She said she'd like to see a little of the world before she gets too old. Mr. Kim," Kimberly paused, "I think it's my moving up here that is making her…"

"Nonsense, Ms. Lim knows she is a valuable member of this firm, and she can always be of great assistance to you and me."

Kimberly sighed. "I really don't want her leaving because of me," Kimberly said. "Will you have a chat with her?"

"I will, and don't think too much of it. Ms. Lim was most probably telling you the truth, and she would've already made travel plans."

After Kimberly left, OJ tentatively pulled the black chair back, half-expecting his father to suddenly appear at the door asking him what the hell he thought he was doing. OJ smiled at his own foolish imagination and inability to step out of his father's shadow. Sitting down, he had to admit the old man knew how to pick a bloody comfortable chair that lovingly caresses the butt. *No wonder he could sit in here all day long, day after day.*

Feeling more sure of himself, OJ started checking the drawers. He found all of them unlocked and empty except the left bottom drawer. He pulled the stationery tray and found a bunch of keys. He tried them one after another and on the last key, the drawer unlocked. *Why must it always be the last key, not the second last, but the last?*

Opening the drawer, he saw several thick, worn-out brown manila folder files attached together by green tags. Green tags: something he himself had not seen or used for years. Something about the files made him feel apprehensive. The files were kept under lock and key in his father's table drawer and not in the file cabinets with other files. *Did Ms. Lim know of them?* The file covers were faded, discolored by time. The labels were handwritten. All these made OJ curious but yet uneasy. He tentatively lifted the files, making sure to support the bottom with his hand so they would not fall apart. He noticed the documents protruding from the files were turning dark brown with age. *What the hell is this?* OJ carefully placed the bundle on the table.

The first peculiarity was the absence of a client's name. The only writing on it was **2011** – written boldly in black marker pen. Carefully lifting the other files, he was shocked to note the file cover at the lowest was dated **1953 – 1960**, the second **1961 – 1970**, then **1971 – 1980, 1981 – 1990, 1991 – 2000, 2001 – 2010**. *Shit, these files go back for more than sixty years, from grandfather's time.* He gingerly turned the cover of the topmost file and read the latest document, which was dated February 20, 2014. It was a business acquisition agreement. OJ remembered reading about the acquisition in the newspaper. It was not handled by him, who was then not yet the firm's head of mergers and acquisition.

It was a hostile takeover with legal proceedings instituted by parties involved. If memory served him well, there were several police reports of criminal intimidation against the acquiring party and a fire at the company's premises which were suspected as arson. The acquisition finally went through for an undisclosed amount.

Curiosity gripped OJ and he flipped to the first file which was the bottom-most. The contents were either typed with a typewriter or handwritten. Some of them were in Chinese, which, as far as OJ was concerned, might as well be in Jawi or Sanskrit. OJ did not read Chinese. There was some sort of handwritten ledger listing names and numbers with decimals and zeros. The dates went back as far as 1957. OJ recognized some of the names: ministers, politicians, judges, senior government officers. His forehead wrinkled in bewilderment, but as he read on, his bewilderment turned to anger, which rapidly intensified into fury. "Damn you, damn you," OJ repeatedly swore under his breath. Unable to stomach what he read, OJ slammed the files closed, snapped the bottom drawer open and dumped them into it.

Leaning back in his chair, OJ's breathing was labored and his body trembled. Shutting his eyes, he inhaled deeply, letting it out slowly with the hope it would all go away. After several minutes, he reopened the drawer and hesitantly took the files out again. Placing them on the table, OJ stared at them, unsure of what to do, his thoughts racing in a thousand directions. It finally dawned on him about his father: *This's just fucking wrong. It's against everything you preached to me, everything you lectured me.* "What a bloody hypocrite," OJ swore, unaware of his grandfather's eyes glaring at him from the portrait behind him. "My righteous father, the man respected and envied by other legal professionals, always riding his high moral horse, is a bloody phony."

Opening the file, OJ searched for the client's name. David Lau, a name that seemed to be repeatedly listed in several correspondences. Oddly, most of the correspondences he flipped through were written on plain white paper without letterhead. In OJ's mind, the person whose name appeared in several of them must be the client or the client's representative and the telephone number was his contact number. With trembling hands, he made a call to the number using the office phone. After several rings, a male voice answered.

"Wey?"

"Mr. Lau, I'm Kim On Juan of Kim & Kim," OJ stammered. The instant the words left his mouth, he had second thoughts.

"Yes, Mr. Kim."

"I … I'm taking over the firm from my father, and I … I …"

"Oh, you're Kim Junior," the man said. "No wonder your voice sounded unfamiliar to me. You were saying?"

OJ detected a belittling tone in the man's voice. It angered him.

"I'm … I meant the firm has decided not to represent your interests anymore…"

OJ heard laughter on the other end of the line, causing him to stop mid-sentence.

"I'm sorry," the man said, followed by more laughter. "What did you say?"

"You heard me, the firm will stop representing you or whoever's interests you're representing," OJ blurted in one breath, trying very hard to hide the trembling in his voice.

"Junior, you're way out of your league," the voice said contemptuously, and the line went dead.

OJ closed his eyes and flopped back in the chair, which silently and effortlessly accommodated the sudden force. His throbbing head was now pounding like an old house being jackhammered. Taking deep breaths, OJ tried to calm his nerves while being disapprovingly watched by his grandfather's portrait.

OJ did not know how long it was since he closed his eyes, breathing heavily and trying all sorts of meditation exercises he could remember from when he was into the craze. His nerves were almost settled when the ringing phone startled him. "Shit," he cussed, bouncing upright, almost toppling onto the table. Picking up the phone, his secretary informed him there were two men waiting to see him.

"Two men?" OJ asked warily.

"They said you know and were expecting them," Kimberly answered.

"I do? I am?" OJ stuttered, puzzled. "Do I have any appointments for today? I thought you rescheduled all my appointments."

"No you don't, and yes I did reschedule all your appointments. I left today free for you to organize your moving in."

In the background, he heard an agitated male voice saying something in Cantonese to Kimberly, followed by Kimberly calling out, "Sir, you can't go in. Mr. Kim is not expecting you, and he's busy."

# 13

From the doorway, Jeffri tapered his eyes, adjusting them to the duskily lit pub. He surveyed the sitting area. There was only one group of three men sitting at one of the tables, and his friend was not among them. He turned his focus to the bar counter. OJ was half-slouched over the bar at the dark end, elbows on the counter, one hand cupping the back of his head. It looked to Jeffri like he was shielding or hiding his face, a whiskey glass sandwiched between his elbows.

Earlier, OJ had called, speaking erratically about gangsters, his father and people threatening him, all of which Jeffri could not make any head or tail. His friend sounded distressed and terrified. Then, OJ had asked if they could meet. Knowing his friend's hyper-apprehensive character, Jeffri thought it was probably nothing serious; OJ was most likely overreacting to something. But somehow, seeing his friend slouched over at 3:12 p.m. in a cheap scarcely lit bar staring into his drink, Jeffri knew his earlier assumption was wrong.

Jeffri snuck in, skirted the wall out of OJ's peripheral vision and stood facing the bar. He managed to attract the barman's attention. Pointing to his friend, he signed asking how many drinks his friend had had. The barman lifted two fingers and, gesturing with his eyes to the glass in front of OJ, held up a third finger. Jeffri nodded. From their uni-days' outing experiences, he knew three glasses of whiskey were way too much for his friend's alcohol tolerance level. Especially when it was consumed within an hour.

Stepping away from the wall, Jeffri made himself visible to his friend, who immediately swiveled around on the stool and let out a sigh of relief.

"Thanks for coming," OJ said, "I'm losing it, Jeff. I'm really scared."

Jeffri noted his friend's flushed face, probably from the whiskey, but there was also genuine fear in his eyes.

"Here, let me get you a drink?" OJ said, signaling for the barkeeper. "What'll it be?"

"What're you having?" Jeffri asked, motioning to the glass.

"JD, you want one?"

"No thanks, I'll stick to draft, Tiger."

After their customary cheers and a sip, Jeffri put down his mug and asked what had happened. Instantly OJ went into a sluggish rant, the same gibberish he blabbed during his call. Try as he might, Jeffri could not stop himself from grinning. After a while OJ paused, forehead wrinkling, to gaze intensely at him. Jeffri tried to wipe the grin from his face but failed miserably.

"What! What's so funny?" OJ asked, more puzzled than annoyed.

"You, I mean the way you were speaking, reminded me of Woody Woodpecker."

OJ puckered his lips. "Woody Woodpecker, seriously?"

Jeffri nodded, trying to keep a straight face and failing again. He broke into a grin. Then, like they were being simultaneously tickled, they laughed.

"Okay, let's start all over. This time let's try slowing it down like you're summarizing your case in front of a jury," Jeffri said, "or in your case, a corporate client's board of directors."

OJ started with him moving into his father's office, going through the drawers and discovering the old files. Then he deviated and vehemently griped about his father's lies and hypocrisies. About his father's unrelenting pressure for him to read Law and bury any interest in becoming an architect. About how he had pleaded, short of begging his father, then his mother, but to no avail. Jeffri listened patiently. He knew OJ wore his emotions like a brightly colored shirt. He allowed OJ to rant on for he knew the substance would eventually come.

OJ told of the visit by the two Chinese men without an appointment. How they had, in a threatening manner, reminded him of the obligation made by his grandfather: Kim's honor.

"What do you mean by 'threatening manner'? What did they say?"

"It was not what they said, nothing in words. It was the way they said it."

"I don't get you."

"You know, like in the Chinese movies where threats are made using insinuation and suggestive expressions."

"Are you thinking of lodging a police report?"

"And tell them what?"

"That you were threatened by two men with insinuations like in the Chinese movies," Jeffri jested, laughing. "That'll surely get their attention."

OJ made faces at his friend. "I'm serious, Jeff, you should've seen them. The big one kept cracking his knuckles, and all I could think of was my bones cracking, breaking. Then the other one said something about ancient Chinese honor, tradition, traitor and all sorts of shit."

The fear in his friend's eyes returned. OJ turned and emptied his glass with one swig, then held up his glass to signal for a refill. He unsteadily slid off the stool. Jeffri reached out, grabbing his friend to steady him.

"Are you okay?"

"Yes, yes, thanks, just need to take a leak."

OJ staggered off, holding the row of screwed-down stools along the bar counter to steady his walk. At the door leading to the back where the toilets were, he leaned against the wall and faced Jeffri, who was watching him with concern. From where Jeffri was seated, hampered by the poor lighting, he could not make out OJ's contorted expression and plea for help.

Without warning, OJ's knees jellied and he slithered against the wall, dropping hard onto his bum. Then his upper body toppled in slow motion to the side until his head lay on the floor. Jeffri jumped off his stool and rushed to his buddy. He helped OJ into a sitting position and propped him against the wall. Kneeling in front of him, Jeffri asked, "Buddy, you okay?"

OJ cracked his eyes open and immediately closed them back. Jeffri knew his buddy was smashed. The three glasses of whiskey had done their job. With the help of a waiter, they managed to half-carry OJ and plonk him onto the nearest chair. Jeffri did a cursory examination of his buddy's head but did not find any injury. The slow-motion toppling while leaning against the wall had probably saved him from serious head injury or concussion.

Satisfied his buddy was just plastered, Jeffri settled the bill while the waiter stood over him. With OJ's arm wrapped around his shoulders, Jeffri half-dragged him to the entrance.

"Okay buddy, I've got you, walk with me, move your legs."

OJ groaned, opened his eyes, flashed a half-smile and slurred the words, "Wherearewegoing, Ineedtotakealeak."

Jeffri made a U-turn and headed for the toilet. Holding OJ in front of a urinal, he told him, "Okay, do your thing."

To his amusement, OJ did but missed the urinal by several inches.

Once outside the pub, he sat OJ on the sidewalk against the wall. His car was parked about 50 meters away, and there was no way he could drag his buddy all the way. He needed someone to watch over OJ while he went to bring his car around. He thought of asking one of the passersby but decided against it as he feared his buddy would be robbed while he was gone. Poking his head back into the pub, he called for one of the waiters to assist.

When Jeffri pulled up in front of the pub, the waiter was nowhere to be seen. "Asshole," Jeffri swore under his breath as he climbed out of the car. He had to practically fireman-carry his buddy to the car — an act which drew curious stares from pedestrians of all genders and races, but not a helping hand was offered. *The city at its best, no one gives a rat's ass about anyone.* With all his remaining strength, Jeffri shoved his semi-comatose friend onto the back seat, grabbed his legs, bent them inward, and slammed the door shut. Walking around to the driver's door, he noticed a small crowd had gathered in the shade in front of a shop several meters away. Most, if not all, were taking shots or videoing the scene with their mobile phones. Pissed off with their unhelpful yet *kepochi* attitude, Jeffri took a bow and then gave them the middle finger.

With OJ sliding in and out of consciousness, mumbling incoherently in the back seat, Jeffri evaluated his situation. Traffic was building up in the after-office hour rush; he had no idea where OJ lived; OJ was in no condition to answer any question lucidly; and most importantly, he was in no condition to be left alone. Jeffri was faced with one huge problem. His apartment was located in a walk-up block, and he did not relish the idea of carrying his 60 kilogram semi-comatose friend up two flights of stairs. *What choice do I have?* he asked himself as he headed into the Jalan Ampang traffic crawl, hanging right to turn off onto Jalan Tun Razak.

After fifteen cusses that matched the number of times he had to slam on the brake for pea-brain drivers cutting queue, Jeffri finally reached his apartment complex entrance. Stopping at the guardhouse, he asked one of the Nepalese guards to lend him a hand. He informed them his friend had just been discharged from the hospital and was in no condition to walk. Parking the car, Jeffri and the guard supported OJ between them. With OJ's arms slung around their shoulders, they dragged his deadweight up the two flights to Jeffri's unit. After dumping OJ in his bedroom, Jeffri gave the guard 20 ringgit for his assistance, which in his opinion was generous.

## 14

OJ stirred, opening his eyes; outside through the window, it was dark. As he rolled away, the bright light from a florescent bulb directly above the bed stabbed his eyes and he reflectively shut them tight. Sharp pains shot through his head and multicolored pyrotechnics exploded in the blackness of his shut eyes. The display was fascinating but did little to clear his head. Opening his eyes, he felt the room spinning like he was in the pilot's seat of a crashing chopper. Queasiness took over. He desperately fought back the sensation of choking vomit in his throat, swallowing hard whatever nasty liquid pushed upward. Then, taking long deep breaths, he looked around, giving the bedroom a once-over.

A light brown double-door wooden cupboard stood against the wall at the foot of the bed. Beside it was a matching tiny table littered with magazines, men's cologne, a comb, a hair brush, phone charger and other manly junk. Turning his head in the other direction, he noted a slightly open door, which he was certain was the bathroom. A wooden towel hanger overloaded with clothes was next to the door.

OJ felt a chill, looked up and realized the bedroom air-conditioner was running at full blast and he was dressed only in his Snoopy boxers. Lying still, OJ wondered where the hell he was. He tried to recall, but his memory took him to the files and the scary visit by the two men who were like the Chinese movie characters. Fear overwhelmed him. "Ooh shit," he cussed under his breath and abruptly swung his legs over the side of the bed. The bed creaked under his weight from the sudden movement. With elbows on his knees, he palmed his face, breathing hard through his fingers.

From outside the bedroom, OJ could hear faint voices. The unfamiliar male voices further fueled his fears. His mind flashed back to the unscheduled visit of the two Chinese men. A cold shiver ran down his spine, his face a picture of utter fear. *Am I being held captive by the triads?* He jerked to a stand, causing the bed again to creak loudly back to its original state. Taking tentative steps, he approached the door. As steadily as he could, OJ placed his ear against the frame to listen. He heard mumbled sounds of people talking, but he could not make out what was said. Stepping to the side, he gingerly grabbed the doorknob. Gripping it tightly, he braced himself for any eventuality and turned the knob slowly, expecting it to be locked.

To his surprise, the knob turned smoothly. Turning it as slowly as he could, OJ tightened his grip, readying himself to put up a fight. As he slowly pulled the door to peek outside, he felt it being shoved inward. Freaking out, he pushed hard against the door, thinking it had to be his captors coming for him. The door burst inward with a sudden forceful thrust, its edge hitting OJ's face hard, splitting his left eyebrow. Blood spouted out, running down his face as he screamed in pain.

"What the fuck!" Jeffri exclaimed, pushing the door wider.

"Shit Jeff, why the hell did you do that?!" OJ barked, holding his face, trying to stop the flow of blood.

"What, what did I do?! And why the hell were you hiding behind the door?!"

"I was not hiding. I heard voices, male voices, and I was holding the door," OJ retorted, taking his bloody hand off from his head. "Now look at what you've done. Shit, Jeff," he groaned, gawping at Jeffri with his bloody face. "There's so much blood."

Jeffri grabbed a towel from the cloth hanger, handing it to him. "It was the television, and I was talking on the phone. Here, go wash your face then press hard on the cut for ten minutes. It'll stop the bleeding. By the way, who did you think was outside in the hall?"

"I thought it was them, and I was … never mind."

"Them? Them who?"

"Never mind."

After several 'arghhs' and 'holy shits', OJ emerged from the bathroom pressing the edge of the towel against his cut left eyebrow.

"Let me have a look."

OJ took the towel off from the cut and blood started trickling down his eye onto the cheek.

"Aww, it's just a small cut," Jeffri announced, "you'll live. Anyway, let's get you to a clinic and get it stitched up."

"You sure? There's so much blood," OJ asked doubtfully.

"It's the eyebrow, the easiest part to cut where you'll bleed like a woman having her period. I'm sure you've seen boxers getting cut there. Nothing a good cut man can't stop," Jeffri jested, laughing.

"Easy for you to say when it's not your face."

At the clinic, Jeffri sat in the waiting room while OJ was attended to by the doctor. For lack of anything to do, Jeffri watched the receptionist cum nurse cum dispenser. A Malay woman, probably in her early twenties, with the standard nurse uniform, but like most Malay women nowadays, instead of the nurse hat or whatever it is called, she had a white hijab. *Funny, how it's now the accepted dress code for Malay women in uniform. What a pity. She has such a lovely face and probably hair too, all distorted by the hijab. The glory and dignity of the uniform are lost.*

The examination room door opened and OJ emerged looking as upset as when he entered. Jeffri stifled a smile seeing his friend with a bandage patch over half of his left eye.

"The doctor said I've to leave this on for a couple of days at least," OJ stated, lightly touching his new facial gear.

"So, what's wrong with it? It does give you character," Jeffri jested.

"I can't go to the office wearing this," OJ declared, tapping his bandage softly. "The silly gossip will be murderous."

"Just tell them your girlfriend likes it rough," Jeffri said, laughing.

"I thought they didn't use bandages anymore, just clipped it."

"How many?"

"Four."

"Thought it wouldn't be more than two, oh well, four makes you look doubly macho."

Getting into the car, Jeffri asked where OJ lived. OJ instead asked him to drive to his office at Citibank Tower, saying his car was parked there and he needed to go up to the office to collect his bag.

"I hate to bring this up now, but have you decided what to do with the client?" Jeffri asked as he turned on to Jalan Ampang.

"Like I said, I'm dropping them. I became a lawyer because my father wanted me to, and now I know it was for all the wrong reasons."

He turned to look at Jeffri, who waited patiently without answering.

"To do his dirty work, that's why. Well, I became a lawyer, but that's it. He can do his own dirty work himself."

Jeffri detected the doggedness in OJ's words and decided to leave it at that. He knew his friend was hurting, and getting into a debate on the consequences of his decision would not be healthy for their newly reenacted gainful friendship. Stopping at the Jalan Ampang/Jalan Tun Razak traffic light, Jeffri again asked if his buddy was okay, if he wanted assistance to drive home. Again OJ declined, saying he was feeling much better and would be all right.

Pulling in to the Citibank Tower driveway, Jeffri glanced at the dashboard clock; it showed 20:11. OJ opened the door, stepped out, and before he closed it, Jeffri again asked, "Will you be okay?"

"Yes, thanks."

"Call me when you reach home, okay?"

"Sure. Hey, thanks for being with me."

Jeffri watched as his friend was swallowed by the tower's lobby before he pulled out of the driveway. He thought of waiting by the exit and then tailing his friend's car to make sure he arrived home safely, but decided against it. *OJ would call should anything happen to him.* Making a U-turn at the traffic light in front of the Petronas Twin Towers, he headed home, shoving aside all thoughts of his friend's predicaments.

OJ showed his tenant pass and signed in at the security counter as required by the tower's management for after 8 p.m. entry into the building. The elevator lobby was deserted, and within seconds of pressing the elevator call button, an elevator opened. OJ entered the empty cab and pressed seventeen, and before dropping his hand, he instinctively touched the bandage patch. It felt dry.

Stepping out onto the seventeenth floor, OJ turned left toward the tinted tempered glass door with **Kim & Kim (Advocates and Solicitors of Law)** boldly stenciled in gold lettering. A similar engraved signage on a black plaque was plastered on the side wall. Punching in his access code, the glass door clicked to unlock. Instantly, it hit him that the general office lights were on. *Probably Kimberly forgot to switch it off, being new in the office, or perhaps she noticed my briefcase and left them on thinking I might be coming back for it.*

Stepping into the general area, he noticed his new office's door was ajar and the lights were on too. *That's not like Kimberly,* he said to himself as he warily approached it. His first thought: the two Chinese movie characters had broken into his office looking for the files. This made him stop dead in his tracks. From outside the office, he could hear a faint sound of rustling paper but no voices. It was as if someone was flipping the pages of a book or a file. His heartbeat pounded in his ears as his brain scrambled for what to do next. He thought of calling Jeffri but was afraid he might be heard by whoever was ransacking the office. Then he thought of running out, but that would only be to the advantage of whoever was searching the office. He searched Kimberly's table for something, anything he could use as a weapon for self-defense. A six-inch steel ruler, several pens, pencils, highlighters in a mug was all he saw. He spotted a paper cutter among the pens and pencils in the mug. Arming himself with the steel ruler in his left hand and the paper cutter in his right, OJ found false courage.

# 15

Gingerly skirting the office contours with his MacGyver weapons, OJ stopped just before the door. Holding his breath, the sound of rustling paper from inside the office became more evident. A sudden thud of a drawer closing startled him, causing him to back away from the wall, uttering "Shit."

Before he could hide back into cover, a voice from inside the office called out, "Who's there?"

OJ leaned hard against the wall, holding his breath, wishing he could melt into the concrete. He swallowed saliva to wet his dried throat.

The voice called out again, this time more menacingly. "Who's there? Show yourself."

The voice sounded familiar to him. A voice he grew up with, the voice he respected, the voice of a hypocrite, the voice of his father, Kim Senior. His fear turned to curiosity, which quickly turned into anger.

With one lengthy step, OJ was off the wall and stood in the middle of the office doorway. In his left hand, a six-inch steel ruler and in his right, a blue paper cutter. Kim Senior was standing in front of his large table, in his right hand a leather-handled brass letter opener. Father and son were evenly matched in a pathetic standoff.

"What're you doing here at this hour?" Kim Senior demanded, being the first to recover his voice. His eyes zeroed in on OJ's hands. "What's that in your hands?"

"I may ask you the same question. What're you doing here, and what's that in your hand?" OJ stuttered.

Kim Senior ignored his son's question, looked at the letter opener in his hand, walked back around the table, and dropped heavily onto the lushness of his former chair. Placing the letter opener to its original place, he asked, "Have you any idea what you've done?"

Walking into the office, OJ plonked himself into one of the less lush leather visitor's chairs. He placed the six-inch steel ruler and blue paper cutter on the edge of the table, saying nothing in reply to his father's question.

"You've put the family at risk, all of us, your mother, sisters and yourself. You've dishonored the family name. You've gone against your grandfather's words," Kim Senior started. His words were harsh but laced with fear. "Your grandfather gave his word that as long as the Kims have a male heir, the Kims shall serve the Family. There's no two ways about it, none."

OJ remained silent, but internally his blood was boiling and the steam of anger building.

"I raised you with honor, respecting honor, and being honorable …"

"Honor! What honor? You think serving the triads and living on blood money is honorable? You forced me to be a lawyer, no, you cheated me into being a lawyer to serve your …"

"Why can't you get it into your head? It's not about me or you. It's about our family, our heritage, our bloodline."

"Yeah well, what was pledged or sworn by grandpa was his, and it has nothing to do with you or me. Grandpa has no right to bind you or me with this business. This is the twenty-first century, not the golden opium days."

"How dare you speak of your grandfather like that!"

"How dare he dictate my life before I was even born!" OJ seethed.

Kim Senior, and for that matter, OJ himself, was surprised at the words and manner that came out of the latter's mouth.

"Insolence is never and will never be tolerated in this family," Kim Senior retorted.

"But blood money, deceit, and hypocrisy are."

Wearily Kim Senior leaned all the way back in his chair, tilting his head at the portrait of his father directly behind him. His eyes fixed on his father's face, his lips moving as if in prayer or talking to the dead through telepathy. After what seemed like a lifetime to OJ, his father turned to face him. His face calm, his words controlled.

"Juan," Kim Senior started, then paused.

Kim On Juan was known to other family members and friends as OJ, but nevertheless, his father and mother never addressed him by that name. He was always Juan to them.

"You have to think of your mother, your sisters, and especially yourself. This's not something I'm proud of but neither could I walk away from it. What your grandfather did was something beyond your control or mine. It was well before we even existed, but it was made and it has to be honored."

OJ noticed his father's manner was one of resignation and regret.

"Then it stops with me."

"NO! Have you not heard a word I said?" Kim Senior snapped.

"I did, every single word and every single unsaid word," OJ snapped back. "Sadly, you have not heard a single word *I* said."

Kim Senior was not used to being talked back to by anyone, especially his children. OJ's harsh reproach stabbed his ego. He vaulted off his chair, pushing it violently backward, hitting the wall just below his father's portrait, causing it to drop to the floor with a glass-shattering crash. Freaked by his father's sudden move and the shattering, OJ reacted likewise. He leapt to his feet, knocking his chair to the carpeted floor with a muffled thud. OJ's action was met by Kim Senior's desperate dash from behind the table toward his son. Seeing his father's charge, OJ reacted the same. Their paths collided by the side of the table.

OJ, the smaller of the two body masses, was thrown backward, tumbling hard onto the floor flat on his back. Kim Senior then had his son in a bear hug, and OJ struggled to free himself from under him.

They tilted and rolled from side to side, knocking down a side table full of magazines and a glass figurine of Atlas holding up the Earth. Magazines were strewn to the carpet, and the fragile figurine centerpiece broke into three pieces: the body, the head and the Earth still attached to the hands.

"What in heaven's name did you think you were doing?!" Kim Senior hissed in OJ's ear, his arms wrapped tightly around his son's waist.

"What the hell do *you* think you're doing, coming at me like that?!" OJ replied breathless, struggling to push his father off him.

Kim Senior reeled onto his side, releasing OJ from being pinned down. In doing so, his arm scraped firmly against OJ's bandage, causing it to come off and reopening the cut. OJ, still lying on the carpet, yelped in pain. Blood started oozing from the opened stitches, down his left temple onto the carpet.

"Look what you've done," OJ snapped, holding his hand to the cut.

"Sorry, I didn't mean to. It was an accident," Kim Senior apologized, getting to his knees.

Kim Senior edged on his knees to take a closer look at his son's injury. OJ brusquely twisted away, getting to his feet. Warm blood seeped through his fingers, sparking his anger to flare again.

"Sorry! You were never sorry! You only say you are, but you never were and never will be," OJ blurted. "You ruined my life without even giving me a chance to live it. Were you ever sorry? No, Papa, you never were and never will be."

OJ pulled out his soiled handkerchief and pressed it onto his reopened cut.

Spurned by his son, Kim Senior sponged back to his lush black leather chair. He pulled the chair to its original position and gave an apologetic glance to his father, who lay on the floor covered with broken glass. Picking up the frame, he picked out the pieces of broken glass and placed them on the corner of the table, mumbling a silent prayer. Satisfied that his father's soul was pacified, he sat heavily and pulled the stack of old files from the lower drawer and carefully placed it on the table. Seeing the file, OJ's anger flamed.

"You can keep the clients. You can keep the firm and all the blood money. I made my decision, I'm not going to be a part of it."

"Juan, please listen to reason. Please sit and we'll work things out," Kim Senior pleaded, his voice frail. He seemed to have grown very old and very tired in the last few minutes.

"There's nothing more to discuss."

OJ turned toward the door. He half-expected his father to come charging from behind the table and pounce on him. His expectation did not materialize. As he reached the doorway, he heard his father's feeble voice.

"Please remember, I've always loved you and will always love you. I know I treated you imperfectly, but whatever I did, it had to be done for the family. If it's any consolation, I hated the life laid out for me by your grandfather."

Kim Senior watched as his only son walked out on him. With every step OJ took, his hope for his son to reconsider and turn around diminished. As OJ disappeared from sight, Kim Senior sunk deeper into the lush black leather chair, his favorite chair which he handpicked during one of his visits to Old Bailey, London.

He heard the front glass door click open, then click closed. With those clicks, his hope vanished.

## 1 6

✕

OJ, groggy with medication from his second visit to the clinic for re-stitching or whatever it was medically termed, stretched his arm across the bed, groping for his insanely ringing handphone. His hand felt the hard rectangular ringing object with its lighted screen displaying the word 'Mama'. His first instinct was to let the phone ring off without answering, thinking, *It had to be father asking mother to call, to persuade me to reconsider.* He knew his father and there was no way he was going to take the decision lying down. He would do whatever it took, morally or immorally, even perhaps illegally, to have things his way. The time on the phone screen showed 1:43 in the morning. OJ blinked several times to clear his vision and the cobwebs in his head. It was probably the medication, but his instinct sensed something different about the ringing, some urgency, like it was begging or urging him to answer. Picking up the phone, he swiped the answer icon.

Before he could answer, his mother's desperate voice asked, "Juan, where are you?"

"At home, why?"

"Papa is … is … Papa is dead." His mother went into uncontrollable sobs.

"Ma, what did you say? Papa's what?" OJ sat upright, veering his legs over the bedside. The cobwebs in his head cleared and so did the stinging pain at his brow.

"Papa is no more," his mother managed in between sobs.

"What happened? Where're you?"

"We're at the morgue."

"Where?"

"HKL."

"I'll be right there."

OJ put on a pair of jeans and pulled a T-shirt over his head. The collar rubbed against his new bandage, but he didn't even notice the pain. As the T-shirt collar cleared his head, his eyes searched the dressing table. Panic swept over him when he did not see his car keys. "Oh shit, did I leave them in the car? Ooo, you idiot." Frantically racking his brain, he remembered the wallet and car keys were in his work pants.

On the way down to the car park, he called the one and only person on his mind. After several rings, Jeffri's sleepy voice answered.

"Jeff, my father is dead," OJ blurted out. "He is at HKL morgue."

"What? Your father's dead? How?"

"I don't know, my mother called and I'm on my way to the morgue. Can you come, please?"

"Sure, HKL right?"

"Yes."

"Hey, OJ, I'm sorry."

Driving out of his apartment's car park, OJ was confused as to which route to take to Kuala Lumpur Hospital. Although he knew the general location, he had never been there. Being a true Malaysian, he multitasked and pulled out his handphone to Waze the route while driving. Waze directed him to go through Sungai Pencala to Mont Kiara, then into the city center. Hitting the city center, he turned onto Jalan Raja Laut, a road he was familiar with, then onto Jalan Pahang and KLH. Once in the hospital compound, he stopped to ask for directions to the morgue.

When OJ arrived at the morgue, Jeffri was already there, but he kept his distance from the mourning family members. OJ noticed Jeffri standing by the car shed; he gave his friend a perfunctory nod and walked straight to his mother.

She was seated outside the morgue flanked by his uncle and aunt. Approaching them, he was puzzled by his uncle's disgruntled expression, but he attributed it to him losing his elder brother.

Kneeling in front of his mother, OJ asked, "How did Papa…?" His question hung in midair.

His mother shook her head and started sobbing, "The police called. They said Papa was…" She paused, taking a deep breath "… found by the building security."

"Where? Found where?"

"At the pathway, beside the office building," she managed and broke into shattered sobs.

OJ stood to hug his mother and was immediately stopped by his uncle's arm stretched across his chest. OJ gawked at his uncle, puzzled by his action. Confused, but he did not want to make a scene, not here, so he incredulously stepped back.

"When?" he asked, staring at his mother.

"The police called around midnight. They said they got the house number from the security emergency contact number list."

OJ opened his mouth to say he was with his father in the office until about ten plus or eleven at night. That his father was alive when he left. However, when he saw his uncle's knotted expression, he decided not to say anything. Instead he asked, "Where's Papa now?"

She stopped sobbing and turned to indicate the morgue.

Stepping away from his mother, OJ beckoned for Jeffri and waited for him in front of the morgue entrance. They had never set foot into a morgue and they didn't know what to expect. Jeffri, however, had seen the inside of Western morgues in several TV crime series, and he was in for a huge disappointment.

The morgue two-leaf door felt cold, thick and heavy to their push. A stream of cold air rushed out, engulfing them as they stood in the doorway. It was like they were stepping into a refrigerator. Two men standing beside a stainless steel table stared at them questioningly.

"Sorry," Jeffri said, "we are here to see Mr. Kim. I mean, the late Mr. Kim."

One of the men stepped forward while the other told them to close the door.

"I'm Sergeant Hussien, the AIO (*Assistant Investigating Officer*), and you are?"

"Kim, Kim On Juan, and this is my friend, Jeffri," OJ replied, extending his hand.

Sergeant Hussien took his hand, offered his condolences, and asked how he could be of assistance. "I've spoken to your mother, and she had already made the identification."

"What happened?" OJ asked.

"As I told your mother, we received a call from the building security, and when we arrived, we were shown the deceased. We're told the deceased had an office on the sixteenth and seventeenth floors. At this moment, we believed the deceased had fallen from the building, but we've yet to complete our investigation."

"Do you suspect any foul play?" Jeffri asked.

"I'm not able to comment. The IO (*Investigating Officer*) has been informed and will conduct the investigation."

"Can I see him, I mean, my father?" OJ asked.

"I don't recommend it. It's not a pretty sight. Anyway, your mother has made the identification, and all the deceased's ID was recovered from his body. But if you insist."

Jeffri touched his buddy's arm and shook his head. OJ hesitated then nodded.

"Sergeant, you said the IO will conduct the investigation?" Jeffri asked.

Sergeant Hussien nodded.

"May we see him?"

"I think she may have gone to the scene. Why don't you see her there?"

"At my office?" OJ asked.

"The Citibank Tower. I don't know if she will go to your office as I'm sure there is no one there at this time."

"Okay, thanks."

## 17

$\times$

They took OJ's car and headed for Jalan Pekeliling in silence, then turned onto Jalan Ampang. OJ drove straight into the basement parking. At the lobby, they stopped at the security counter and checked in. Jeffri asked the security guard if the police were here.

"They left with the body," the Nepalese security guard replied.

"Who found the body?"

"My friend SG Golbargu."

"Where is SG Golbargu?"

"The police took him to the police station."

In the elevator, Jeffri asked his buddy why they were going up to the office. OJ did not reply. He seemed to be engrossed in his own thoughts, like he was acting on auto-cruise: looking but not seeing, listening but not hearing.

"OJ, why are we going up to the office?" Jeffri asked again.

"Emm, oh, sorry. I don't know. Didn't the sergeant say the police were going to the office?"

"Yes, but he said perhaps tomorrow, because there's no one at this hour. So why are we going there now?"

"I just need to see it."

"You think it happened at the office?"

"What? What happened at the office?"

"Whatever it was that led to your father's death."

"I don't know. I left him at the office last night."

"What do you mean you left him at the office last night?"

The elevator door opened and they tentatively stepped out into the lobby. OJ noticed the office lights were on and stopped in his tracks.

"Why, what is it?" Jeffri apprehensively asked. He followed OJ's line of vision. "What's wrong with your office?"

"When you sent me here last night, my father was here in the office."

"You mean he was waiting for you?"

"No, I don't think he knew I was coming back. I found him at his ... my table. We had ... Well, we talked about the client, and I told him that I made my decision."

OJ walked toward the office door with Jeffri close by his side. He punched in the code and the glass door clicked open.

"Then what happened?"

"When I left, he was seated at his ... my table."

Standing at Kim Senior, or now OJ's office doorway, Jeffri exclaimed, "Holy shit, what the hell happened in here?"

OJ's eyes were fixed to the oak table and his face went pale.

"Somebody broke into the office after you left?"

OJ whispered, "It's gone."

"What, what's gone?" Jeffri could see his buddy starting to tremble.

Just then they heard the front doorbell. They looked at each other, bewildered. The doorbell rang again repeatedly. Then a firm voice called, "Encik Kim, polis, buka pintu."

They let out a sigh of relief and OJ stepped away to open the door. Jeffri turned to give the office another look and digest the scene. There was an overturned chair, an overturned coffee table, scattered magazines, and a broken something — a ball or bronze statue. On the wall behind the desk he noted faded markings, like something was taken from it. He looked for signs of ransacking but saw none. All the drawers and cabinets at the book shelves were closed, and the sofas were not in disarray or ripped open. *What happened in here? What was gone? What was stolen?*

"Mr. Kim?" the woman among the men asked, extending her hand.

OJ took her hand, nodding. Jeffri gave the inspector a once-over: slim, about five feet four, clear sharp eyes even at this hour of the morning, sweet oval face with no makeup. She looked very elegant in her uniform. *Never dated a policewoman before, never knew they had good-looking women officers, or I would have gladly enlisted*, Jeffri fancied.

"I'm Inspector Ruby, my condolences on your loss."

"Thank you. How did you know we were here?"

"The security guard informed the station when you checked in. I thought of coming in tomorrow, but since you're here, I decided to come over now. And who is this?" Ruby asked, referring to Jeffri.

Stepping forward, Jeffri introduced himself.

"Ahh, a lawyer. Do you need to bring a lawyer?" Ruby asked, flashing him a smile.

"No, no, he's a close friend, and we were at the morgue. I asked him to accompany me."

Jeffri counted six of them: the inspector, a man in plainclothes, and four men in uniform with **Team Forensik** written on the back of their vests. They started moving toward the office and stopped in the doorway.

"What happened here?" the plainclothes man asked no one in particular.

"Mr. Kim, did you enter the office before we arrived?" Ruby asked.

"No, no, we just stood exactly where you are."

Ruby and her team members gave OJ and Jeffri an unconvinced long stare, then carefully proceeded in. OJ and Jefrri followed.

"Please sit over there," Ruby instructed, pointing to the sofas. "Let my team do their work, then we can have a little chat."

Glancing at each other like school children at the principal's office, OJ and Jeffri mutely obeyed.

They observed as the forensics team snapped photos of the overturned table, chair, scattered magazines, broken ornaments, and shattered frame of OJ's grandfather's portrait. Snapping on a rubber glove, Inspector Ruby carefully made her way around the table. Jeffri noticed his buddy's face; there was anxiety as the inspector started pulling the drawers. *What's he afraid of?* When the inspector finally moved away from the table, he noted relief on OJ's face.

Suddenly one of the forensics team members pushed the window curtain aside, and a gust of wind blew in. Ruby immediately moved to the window. One of its panes was opened. She signaled the forensics member who was dusting the coffee table for prints to dust the window. She bent down to examine the floor next to the window, then carefully stepped to one side to examine the window ledge.

After a few minutes, she proceeded to where OJ and Jeffri were seated and asked, "Is the window always open?"

"I didn't even know it could be opened," OJ answered sincerely. "I just moved into this office yesterday."

"Oh." Ruby took a seat facing them, looking straight at OJ, and asked, "Can you tell me what happened here?" She indicated the mess.

Jeffri sat on the edge of the sofa. "I'm sorry, Inspector, are you interviewing Mr. Kim?"

"We're just having a chat," Ruby replied smilingly. "That's if Mr. Kim doesn't mind."

OJ turned to face his friend questioningly.

"So, this is just a casual chat and won't be used in any manner against Mr. Kim?" Jeffri stated.

"Why, are you afraid Mr. Kim will incriminate himself?"

"No, but just to be clear and on the safe side."

"Are you representing Mr. Kim?"

"Does he need a lawyer?"

Ruby laughed, and she had a lovely smile. Jeffri joined her.

OJ told the inspector what had happened between his father and him and the mess they made. He left out the files.

"I don't get it. What was the heated argument all about? Who was the client that caused all this?" Ruby asked.

"An old client," OJ replied evasively.

"And why don't you want to represent this client?" Ruby inquired.

"I don't know them. They were my grandfather's client."

"Hmmm."

It was clear to Jeffri that the inspector was not convinced by OJ's explanation. That bothered him; unconvinced investigators can be dangerous, relentless snoopers.

"Why did you hide your face when you left the building?" Ruby changed the subject.

"I did not. I was holding the cut to stop it from bleeding." OJ instinctively touched his left eyebrow.

"Well, I've viewed the CCTV recording from the security cameras, and for the moment your story checks out. However, I may need to speak to you again should there be any new development."

"In other words, you're telling Mr. Kim not to leave town," Jeffri jested.

"They only say that in movies," Ruby replied with a sly smile.

"Have you classified the case?"

"For the moment, it's still an SDR, 'Sudden Death Report'."

"But it may change?"

"In an investigation, nothing is cast in stone until the case is concluded or CFF. That's 'Closed For Filing'," Ruby explained.

"Are we free to leave?"

"You were never under arrest."

"So that's a 'yes'?"

"Yes, but might I suggest that you hang around until my team is done? You don't want us to be here all by ourselves, do you? Things might grow legs and walk away," Ruby smiled and swaggered to the window. "Or chocolates might go missing as our ex-PM claimed when his rented premises were searched by our Commercial Crimes officers."

"She is cheekily cute," Jeffri whispered to OJ.

When Inspector Ruby and her team were done, it was almost 3:45 in the morning. She thanked them for their cooperation and patience, smiled teasingly at Jeffri, and left. After OJ let them out, he asked Jeffri, "Now what?"

"Now we go back and get some sleep."

"I don't think I can."

OJ pulled out his handphone and called his mother. Jeffri stepped aside to give him some privacy, but he was eavesdropping on their conversation. His mother, uncle and aunt were at home; the body would be released after the forensic pathologist completed the autopsy, probably between 3 to 4 in the evening. His uncle had contacted a funeral home to arrange for the body to be picked up. OJ terminated the call and looked at Jeffri.

Jeffri looked at his buddy. OJ told him what transpired between him and his mother.

"You're probably right. I should go home and get some sleep, but I don't think I can. I kept seeing his saddened face when I walked out on him tonight. It will be the last image of him etched in my head. I regretted not having the courage to see him at the morgue."

"It was better that way. Your father was probably badly disfigured from the fall."

OJ remained silent for a while. "The police said the body will be released late afternoon. Perhaps I can still see him if I go back to the morgue."

"I suggest you see him at the funeral home, after they clean him up. For now it is best if you get some rest. I'm sure tomorrow is going to be a long day for you."

"Guess you're right. Come, I'll send you back to the hospital for you to pick up your car."

"Don't bother, I can call a Grab."

18

Outside the morgue, Jeffri made a call to Shah, one of the street-pack members who stayed true to the lifestyle he grew up in. From his days on the street, Jeffri could see Shah's entrepreneurial qualities. He was fascinated by how easy it was to make money through racketeering. Money — the love of every man and woman; what they worked and would die for; what they dreamed of having. Money, a language that criminals, enforcers, politicians, judges, religious preachers, basically everyone understood. After leaving school, Shah decided racketeering was his career path. He formed his own outfit and slowly muscled his way into the scene. He carved out his territory, covering the entire Pandan area operating car washes, protection services, loan sharking, bookies, fencing, contraband, social escorts, security escorts, anything and everything that generated money. However, no matter how lucrative the drug and robbery business were, he stayed away from them. He remembered what Jeffri had told him: *Drugs destroy everything you love.* Shah also operated a kickboxing gym, which doubled up as his recruitment center. Jeffri kept in touch with Shah from time to time, and he knew the latter had made it good and was a respected figure in that circle.

Jeffri was worried about OJ, about the sequence of events from the time he discovered the files and was visited by the two Chinese movie-like characters. He figured they might be involved in Kim Senior's death, but he was unsure how. At the back of his mind was the thought that the death was their doing, but he knew it was a dangerous assumption. But one thing he was certain of: OJ was in trouble. Exactly what and how, he had no idea just yet.

"Shah, sorry to call you at this hour," Jeffri apologized.

"Jeff, it's okay, I'm still up and about. What's up?"

"At this hour?"

"Nights are my business hours," Shah laughed. "So, what's up?"

"Shah, I need you to keep an eye on one of my friends."

"Keep an eye like how?"

"Put a tail on him, keep him safe."

"What kind of mess is he in? Loan shark? Gambling?"

"No, nothing of that sort."

"Pissed off somebody's husband?"

"No, I can't tell you now, but I need you to keep an eye on him for me. I'll give you details when I get them later of where to pick his trail from."

"Okay."

"Thanks, Shah."

Terminating the call with Shah, he made another call.

"OJ, are you home yet?"

"Just arrived, why?"

"Nothing, only checking. What's your plan for tomorrow, or rather this morning?"

"I thought of going to the office to sort things out. I'm sure the staff will be anxious and frightened. Hopefully, I can get all that done before 3 pm. Then I'll go over to the morgue."

"What time will you be in the office?"

"I'll try to get a few hours' sleep and should be there around 10."

"Do you need me to come along?"

"Thanks, but I'd rather handle it myself."

"Okay buddy, call me if you need any assistance. There's nothing much you can do now, might as well get some rest."

"Thanks, Jeff, for being there for me."

"No problem. I know you would do the same for me."

Jeffri called Shah and passed on the information of OJ's whereabouts at ten a.m. and his car make, model and registration number. On his way home, he stopped at a roadside stall for a glass of much-needed teh tarik.

1 9

✕

Kimberly was at her desk in a state of shock when OJ arrived at the office that morning. The moment he stepped in, she shot up from her chair wide-eyed. She just could not believe it.

"How did it happen? Was he…?" Kimberly could not bring herself to say the word 'murdered'.

"The police are not saying, but they're not ruling out anything either."

"I'm so sorry for … for …" Again, she could not complete her sentence. "Do you think it had anything to do with the visitors you had yesterday? I mean…" She indicated the state of his office.

"I really don't know."

OJ stopped in front of his office, then turned toward the conference room.

"Kim, can you get the cleaner to clear the mess? The police said they were done."

"I'll get on it right away."

"Thanks. For the time being, I'll work in the conference room."

"By the way, Mr. Tan said he'd like to see you the moment you come in."

"Please tell him I'll be in the conference room."

"Ms. Sarah called and asked if you could return her call."

"You got her number?"

Kimberly nodded.

"Pass it to me, I'll call her myself. And, Kim, can you get me a cup of strong black coffee? Thanks."

After a brief Q&A with the outgoing partner on the incident, the answers to which were still mostly unclear or unknown, OJ called Sarah.

"Sorry for the delay in returning your call. Is there anything I may assist you with?"

"No problem. Is the timing right? I mean, can you talk?"

"Yes, yes, of course."

"You sound a little … hmmm, how shall I put it? Formal. Is everything okay?"

"Yes, sorry, everything is fine. Just that I was out a bit late last night," OJ lied, uncertain if he would like to tell her what had happened.

"Hmmm, she had to be someone special," Sarah jested.

"No, no, not that kind of late night," OJ was quick to reply.

He heard Sarah chuckle. "Mr. Kim, there's something I need your assistance with — that is, if you can."

"Anything."

"I need to find out the owner of a car."

"Oh."

"I've the car number and make. Can you?"

"Yes, I'll get my staff to check with JPJ."

Sarah gave him the details. OJ thought of asking the purpose but decided it was not the right time. Perhaps later, after he obtained the information she needed.

"When do you need it?

"At your convenience, but the sooner the better," she replied.

"Okay, I'll call as soon as I get the details."

"Thanks, you're such a dear."

Terminating the call, OJ was unsure if anyone could just go to JPJ to check on a vehicle's record. Deciding against embarrassing himself in his ignorance, he sought the assistance of a person who would surely know what to do.

"Jeff, can you talk?"

"Hey, buddy, how are you holding up?"

"Okay, I guess. Jeff, I need your assistance. Can you find out who the owner of a vehicle is if I give you the number and make?"

"Yes."

OJ gave him the details.

"Why do you need it?" Jeffri asked skeptically. "Does it have anything to do with your father?"

"No, no, nothing of that sort. I'm doing it as a favor for a friend."

"Who may this friend be?"

"Tell you later after I get the details," OJ replied with a soft laugh.

Jeffri was delighted to hear the soft laughter. "Okay, will get back to you soon."

Kimberly poked her head into the conference room and informed OJ that Inspector Ruby was waiting to see him. OJ was surprised. He did not recall her mentioning anything about coming back this morning when they left earlier. *Did she find something amiss in her investigation? Had she reclassified the sudden death to murder? Am I a suspect? Is she here to arrest me? Will I be thrown in the lockup? Should I be calling Jeff?* A thousand questions played in his head.

"Shall I show her in?" Kimberly asked.

"Is she alone?"

"There is a man with her."

"Shit," OJ hissed in near panic. "Did she say what she wants?"

"No, she just asked to see you."

"Okay, give me a couple of minutes. I just need to make a call."

After Kimberly left, OJ called Jeffri.

"OJ sorry, I haven't got the car owner's details yet."

"Jeff, the police are here," OJ whispered, freaking out.

"What? I can't hear you. Why are you whispering? Is someone there?" Jeffri asked, thinking of the two Chinamen movie-like characters.

"No, she is waiting outside."

"Who, the beautiful girl you're madly in love with?"

"No, not her, the cute police inspector, Ruby."

"What does she want?"

"I don't know. All she said was that she wants to see me. I think she found some incriminating evidence and is here to arrest me."

"Did she? Is she?"

"I don't know. Can you come over, please?"

"Stall her, say you're putting the finishing touches to an urgent report and will be with her in fifteen minutes. I'll be there as soon as I can. Do not say anything to her until I arrive."

"Okay, please hurry. Thanks."

# 2 0
✕

Sarah checked her email. She opened the eagerly awaited email from Philippe, her overseer at Erava:

*Dear Sarah,*

*Excellent news, good touch about the golf, great job. Will arrive Friday and will be staying at Hilton Sentral, Roger is accompanying me. No need to arrange for pickup. Can we meet for brunch at 10 a.m. at the coffeehouse?*

*Looking forward to the meeting.*
*Regards, Philippe*

Sarah beamed at the reply and felt good about herself. Finally she was making headway, and if Philippe played his cards well, she was looking at a handsome reward for all the footwork and time she had invested.

She still had a few things to arrange and set up: dinner for the introduction, a round of golf at a reputable club, and to get some practice herself. She had not touched a golf club since stepping foot in Kuala Lumpur. Back in the States, she used to golf almost every weekend with James and his beer-drinking buddies. James was the one who encouraged her to take up golfing, stating, apart from her being a natural at it, golf was also a great way to network.

Searching the net, she decided on two golf clubs that suited her purpose: Kuala Lumpur Golf & Country Club and Glenmarie Golf & Country Club. Both clubs were of international competition standard and with prestigious standing. Checking with the clubs, she was told there were no walk-ins for weekends and all bookings must be through a member.

She thought of calling Dato' Tarmizi to inquire if he was a member of either club but thought better of it. He might think she had no capability, connections or clout to even arrange a round of golf. Then she thought of OJ, but he didn't seem to her like a golfer. Having no other alternative, she called the political hyena.

After several promises of future golfing and dinner with him, the hyena agreed to get her a booking at Glenmarie. Sarah knew the promises she made were never to be honored. He was a politician, and politicians broke their promises to the people on a daily basis. So he had no right to insist she keep hers.

That afternoon she went to Darul Ehsan Golf Club, rented a set of clubs, and paid for a hundred balls at the range. The range was built on an old mining pool, and balls, known as floaters, were hit into the water that stretched about two hundred meters toward the golf course. She started with her seven iron and moved on to longer irons before giving the woods and driver a go. Then she went back to the short irons, pitching and sand wedges. Satisfied she still had the swing, she walked to practice putting at the green and bunker shots. After working out a good sweat and feeling every muscle in her body aching like they had been turned and twisted by a skilled woman, she stopped. Returning the clubs, she stopped at the golf terrace for refreshments, drawing stares from sweaty, middle-aged, horny male golfers.

2 1

✕

After fifteen agonizing minutes of hiding in the conference room, OJ poked his head out, smiled to Inspector Ruby and offered his apology for keeping her waiting. The inspector was dressed casually in jeans and a blouse. She smiled back, replaced the magazine, and rose to her feet. OJ greeted her, extending his hand.

"To what do I owe this pleasure?" he added, trying to act and sound calm.

"Mr. Kim, I'm sorry for this unscheduled visit," Ruby said, taking OJ's proffered hand. "This is Detective Halim," she said, turning to the man next to her.

"Detective," OJ greeted.

"I've been instructed by my SIO, that's Senior Investigating Officer to record a statement from you before he classifies the case."

"Statement from me?" OJ repeated with a hint of panic in his voice.

"Yes, is there a place where we can do it?"

"Yes, please come with me. I'm temporarily using the conference room until my office is tidied up. I can tidy it up, right?"

"Yes, of course, we're done with it."

Ruby told his detective to wait there while she followed OJ to the conference room. With every step, OJ was silently praying for Jeffri's arrival.

Jeffri, having heard the desperation in OJ's voice, decided to take a Grab ride instead of driving to Citibank Tower. It would be much faster as he need not look for parking space, but definitely more costly.

Seated, Inspector Ruby dug out some formal-looking forms from her oversized handbag and placed them on the table. She looked up at OJ and noted the fear in his eyes. Fear always worked to an investigator's advantage. You can gently stoke fear to make a person believe that you were on his or her side. Once you have their confidence, the tongue is loosened.

"Mr. Kim, for the record, may I have your full name?"

"Kim On Juan."

"Any alias?"

"No, but my friends call me OJ."

"Is that official, I mean, is it recorded in your IC?"

"No."

"Your date of birth and IC number."

OJ read it out to her.

"Address?"

OJ gave her his apartment address.

"Is that you permanent address, listed in your IC?"

"No, my IC address is my parents' house," OJ answered, and gave her the address.

"Okay, shall we begin?"

"Is this necessary? I mean, I already told you what I knew of the incident."

"Yes, and I told you that was not an official interview. This is official in the form of a statement."

"Am I a suspect?"

"Like I said before — no you're not, but you're the last known person to have been with the deceased. Your account of what happened before the deceased was found is important to the investigation."

"May I go to the washroom for nature's call?" OJ asked, surprising Ruby.

"Yes, of course," Ruby answered with a smile. As OJ stood, she added jokingly, "You're not thinking of running, are you?"

"What? No, no," OJ murmured, forcing a grin.

Stepping out of the conference room, OJ pulled out his handphone and called Jeffri.

"Jeff, where are you?"

"Just arrived, will be up in a minute. Have you started?"

"Just about."

"Just hang on a minute or so. I'll be right up."

"I just excused myself to go to the washroom."

"Good ditch," Jeffri complimented with a chuckle.

"Learned it from the best," OJ replied, relieved that his rescuer had arrived.

OJ turned back and headed for his office; magically, the urge to answer nature's call had suddenly vanished. Stepping into the conference room, he was greeted by a curious stare from Inspector Ruby.

"That was super-quick," Ruby lampooned, narrowing her eyes at him.

Unsure of a plausible reply, OJ grinned and took his seat. Ruby eyed him closely. She noted the change in his body language; there was confidence where once was fear and uncertainty. *What had he been up to?*

There was a light knock on the door, and Kimberly poked her head in to inform them Jeffri from Jeffri & Associates was here. OJ immediately asked her to show him in.

Jeffri entered, and OJ immediately stood to introduced him. "Inspector Ruby, you remember Jeffri from your earlier visit?"

"Yes, another lawyer," Ruby replied with a cute smile without standing up. "Pleased to meet you again, Encik Jeffri."

"The pleasure is all mine," Jeffri said, extending his hand. Taking a seat next to her, he asked, "Are you recording OJ, I mean, Mr. Kim's statement?"

"Yes."

"Is he a suspect?"

"For now he is a witness, but being the last person who was with the deceased, there's a high probability he will be, that is, should the case take a turn and be reclassified as murder," Ruby answered. Her eyes twinkled with amusement at the reactions of the two lawyers.

"Will the case be reclassified?"

"I don't know. It all depends on Mr. Kim's statement and my SIO's instruction."

"So this is a 112 statement and not 113?"

"Yes."

"Have you informed Mr. Kim that he need not answer any question which may incriminate him as expressed under section 112?"

"We've not come to that part yet. Mr. Kim was quite good at delaying matters," Ruby said, smiling. "Now, I know why."

"I'm sorry," OJ apologized.

"No need to apologize. I would have done the same if I were in your position. Shall we begin?"

"Can Jeff be present?"

"If he feels the need to, yes."

Jeffri felt compelled to, not because he feared OJ would make an incriminating statement, but because he took a fancy to Inspector Ruby.

## 2 2

✕

While Inspector Ruby was recording OJ's statement, Jeffri received a WhatsApp message informing him the vehicle OJ inquired about was registered to a security company specializing in private investigation. The company Alpha Security was located in Petaling Jaya.

Jeffri forwarded the text message to OJ. He noted with interest OJ's wide eyes when he read the message. Then OJ looked at him askance.

Jeffri shot a Whatsapp message: *want to talk about it?*

OJ read the message but did not respond.

After OJ was done giving his statement, reading and signing it, Ruby thanked him for his cooperation. Jeffri stood, thanked the inspector and they exchanged name cards.

"May I call you to get updates on the case?"

"You may, but it does not necessarily mean you will get one," Ruby teased.

"In that case, may I call you after all this blows over?"

"You may, but then again, I may not answer."

"I'll take my chances."

"Thank you gentlemen, it has been a long day for me, and I need to get some shuteye."

✕

After Inspector Ruby left, OJ asked Jeffri about the WhatsApp message on the vehicle owner.

"What does it mean?"

"The car is company-owned. Want to tell me why your friend is interested in a vehicle owned by a security company?"

"I don't know."

"Okay, I'll leave it at that. Aren't you supposed to be going to the morgue?"

"Yes, I should be leaving."

Leaving the office, Jeffri called Shah and told him OJ would be leaving the building soon.

Stepping into his office, Jeffri saw a thick package on his desk. It was from Kim & Kim and was addressed to him by name. Juliana told him it arrived just before lunchtime. Since it was addressed to him, she did not open it.

"I was with OJ earlier. He didn't mention anything about new farm-out cases," Jeffri remarked. "Probably slipped his mind with all that's going on."

"Open it," Juliana pestered. "By the size of it, there could be several cases and lots more money for us."

Jeffri sat and pulled the package closer, reading the label. Intuition told him the package was not from OJ. The clue was the address, handwritten, and the return address was level seventeen, which was the partners' level. Something about the package looked suspicious, like it was wrapped in brown paper by an unskilled individual, lots of tape binding too, as if to ensure the content was really secured. Jeffri felt uneasy, and to get Juliana out of the office, he asked her to get him some lunch.

Alone, he unwrapped the package. There were several old files and an envelope. He instantly remembered the files which had terrified OJ. Instinctively, he pulled out the envelope and opened it. It contained a letter and a check for RM500,000 payable to his name.

His hands started shaking. Jeffri took several deep breaths to calm himself and steadied his hands. The letter was handwritten.

*Dear Jeffri,*

*You have been spoken of by Juan in an endearing manner ever since he went to university. From what I have heard of you, I've no doubt that your friendship with Juan is pure and true. It was my loss that I did not make an effort to get to know you as my son's best of friends.*

*In time of my and my son's need, I turn to the one person who I know will, without hesitation, come to our aid. My son's life is in danger, not of his own doing but by my lack of courage to put an end to something that was done before my time.*

*The files will enlighten you of my weakness, wrongfulness and my son's unquestionable integrity. Juan's integrity is something that I can be proud of. I love my family, my son included.*

*I hope with my sacrifice Juan would be free from the bond made by my father. I know with all my heart that you will do everything possible to protect him, so he can live a full and fruitful life of his own choosing. Please do not let my son meet a fate similar to mine.*

*Thank you.*

Sincerely,<br>
Kim Jong Yi

Jeffri's hands trembled as he reread it. Putting it down, he picked up the check. It was a personal check from Kim Senior, dated the day he flew without wings. A letter from a dead man he had never met. He heard Juliana coming back and hurriedly put the files, letter and check away into his drawer.

"Here, bought you a burger, easy and not messy," Juliana announced, placing the goodies on his desk.

"Thanks." Jeffri took a sip of iced tea but skipped the burger.

"Have you opened the package?" Juliana asked, turning around to scan the office. "Where is it?"

"Not new cases, just my personal documents."

"From Kim & Kim?" Juliana remarked. "What's going on here?"

"Something OJ kept from our uni days."

"Yeah, right."

"Ju, can you get me a large plastic bag?"

"What for?"

"Just get it for me, okay," Jeffri said rather firmly. "And can you give me some space? I need to work something out."

"Hmmm. As you wish boss," Juliana said, displeased at being told to mind her own business.

Jeffri needed time to review this new development; he needed to be alone. Putting the files into the plastic bag given by Juliana, he left with the excuse that he needed to go to Dang Wangi Police Station.

OJ called his mother and was told his father's body was released earlier than expected. Nirvana Funeral Service had taken it to their place in Salak South. OJ Wazed the location. He drove out to Jalan Ampang and turned onto Jalan Tun Razak, heading for Jalan Sungai Besi. The traffic was heavy and slow. Without him knowing, two motorbikes noticed him as he emerged from the Citibank Tower basement car park.

OJ made a call, and after three rings, a woman answered.

"Mr. Kim, nice to hear from you again," Sarah said.

"Ms. Sarah, I have the details you wanted of the vehicle."

"Great."

"Have you got a pen and paper?"

"Hang on … okay, shoot."

OJ gave her the details as provided by Jeffri.

"Private investigator, are you sure?"

"That's what the record said. Why? Are you in some kind of trouble? I mean, the PI was tailing you or something like that?"

"No. Not that I'm aware of, and I hope not."

"Good."

"Are you free for a drink later, say around six?"

"I don't know if I can. I've some urgent matters to attend to. In fact, I'm on my way there." However, not wanting to miss the chance of seeing the woman he was crazy about, and certainly not wanting to disappoint her, he said, "Let me call you back as soon as I know if I can make it or not."

"That'll be great."

## 23

Jeffri went straight home, made himself a cup of coffee, and went into his bedroom. Turning on the air-conditioner, he dropped the files on the bed and changed into a pair of shorts and a T-shirt. Seated cross-legged on the bed, he carefully started on the files. Most of the early entries were written in Chinese, with sporadic numerical and legal terminology in English. Tried as he might, he could not make any sense of what the entries were about. His street sense told him these were records of dealings, shady dealings.

In the third file, he discovered some form of ledger. There were names, dates and amounts, but no mention of any deeds. There were hundreds of names. Some of them he knew but only by reputation. Others sounded familiar, but he was not sure if they were the same individuals. Names are not exclusive, so there was no way of knowing if the names were the same persons he knew of politicians, high-ranking civil servants, and judges. Some were already deceased, some retired or no longer held portfolios in politics, some still active. The first entry went way back to 1953 and the latest was 2018. The amounts were not staggering, but enough to raise suspicions of payoffs.

His handphone rang; it was OJ.

"Jeff, are you free to meet?" OJ asked. He sounded agitated.

"When? What's up?"

"Say around five, five-thirty. I'll tell you when we meet. By the way, can you find out more about the PI?"

"More like what?"

"Like who are they investigating, or who hired them?"

"I don't know if I can. Let me make a few calls and get back to you on that."

"Okay, meet you at No Black Tie. You know the place?"

"Bukit Bintang, right?"

"Yes, see you there."

OJ arrived at No Black Tie at 4:45 pm, and Sarah was already waiting for him at the bar. On seeing OJ, she got off the stool, picked up her glass and moved to a table at the far end away from the bar. Passing the bar, OJ ordered a beer and sat facing her.

"What happened to your face?" Sarah asked, staring at the stitches over his eyebrow.

"A minor accident."

"Hmmm, wild night," Sarah joked.

OJ just gave her a wan smile.

"Is everything okay? You look like something is weighing you down. Like your world is falling apart."

Hearing Sarah's words, it struck OJ that his world was indeed falling apart. He had just lost his father in the most tragic manner, and he was just told by his uncle that he was not welcome to his father's wake. When asked why, his uncle just said, "You know the reason." His mother, his dear mother, just sat there and sobbed. When he tried to approach his mother to protest, his uncle firmly stood between them.

"Hey, are you okay?"

Suddenly, OJ realized he had not shed a tear for his father. He had bottled it all up and now, in the presence of the woman he loved, all the anguish and sorrow started to swell. OJ cupped his face and broke down, letting it all out.

Caught by surprise, Sarah moved next to him. Hugging him she soothed, "Shhhh, everything's going to be all right."

The hug, the soft feel of her breast against his arm, the sweet smell of her perfume and her soothing whisper calmed him. His body stopped shaking, and he drew in several deep breaths. He felt the pain ooze out with every slow breath he exhaled. Sarah handed him some tissues, and stroking the back of his neck she asked, "You want to talk about it?"

"My father, he … he passed away last night," OJ blurted out.

"What? What happened?"

"He fell."

"Fell! Fell how? Where? Why didn't you tell me? Have you got to be somewhere? We can meet some other time."

"But I want … I need to be with you." OJ started to sob and Sarah hugged him tightly.

"Shhhh, I'm here for you."

OJ spotted Jeffri entering the bar, and broke away from Sarah's hug.

"Sorry, I asked my good friend to join us."

"Who?" Sarah asked.

"Jeff. He may have some additional information on the vehicle's owner."

"Oh."

OJ waved to Jeffri, who was standing at the entrance, scanning the bar. Jeffri acknowledged OJ's signal and walked over to join them.

"Thanks for coming. Can I get you a drink?"

"Coke, thanks."

"Jeff, this's Sarah," OJ introduced, pride written all over his puffed face.

"Pleased to meet you," Sarah said, shifting a little apart from OJ.

"Pleasure's all mine," Jeffri replied, taking her hand. "Sorry, am I interrupting?"

"No, it's not like what it seemed," OJ said.

"Mr. Kim just told me of his loss," Sarah said.

"Oh."

"Mr. Kim did not say what happened. What really happened."

"Perhaps OJ will tell you when the time is right. By the way, why are you calling him Mr Kim and not OJ? I was sure by now you would've moved on to OJ," Jeffri said, smiling.

OJ smiled, liking what his friend was implying. Sarah blushed.

"What is it that you wanted to talk to me about?" Jeffri asked OJ.

OJ described what had happened at the funeral house. Walking in, he was stopped by his uncle, who in no friendly terms told him he should leave. As it was a wake, he did not want to make a scene. He politely tried to sidestep his uncle to speak to his mother, but the man adamantly blocked his path. Two men he had never seen before came forward and close to him. Both looked menacing but said nothing. His mother, seated about three meters away, did not even look up, although he was certain she saw him coming in and heard them.

"What did your uncle say, exactly?"

"That I'm not welcome and to stay away from the family."

"Anything else?"

"That this was all my doing and that I was ungrateful for all the sacrifices my father had done for me."

Jeffri recollected the contents of Kim Senior's letter and strongly suspected he would have spoken to his brother before his death. *Did he blame his son — OJ? In the letter, he admitted his action was his choice to protect his family and son. Is it possible his uncle blamed OJ out of anger for losing his brother?*

"What about your sisters?"

"They're on their way back from abroad."

"He had no right to do that to you. It's your father," Sarah remarked.

"My family is very traditional. He's a Kim and the most senior now. I guess he has the right," OJ said defeatedly.

"Okay, let's leave it at that for now. What are your plans?" Jeffri asked.

OJ shrugged, his face dejected. Jeffri felt sorry for him. He knew the truth or part of it, but he was not able to tell him, to console and exonerate him of all the blame. Not now. Just then, Jeffri's handphone beeped, signaling an incoming WhatsApp message. He read and then forwarded it. OJ read it and looked to Jeffri.

"You want to talk about it?" Jeffri asked.

"The information was requested by Sarah."

Jeffri looked straight at Sarah. "You wanted to know the vehicle owner because...?" he addressed his question to her.

"I was doing a favor for a friend. She thought she was being followed," Sarah said smoothly.

"Oh, is your friend married?"

"No, why?"

"Is your friend seeing a married man?"

"Nooo."

"Then I think your friend was just paranoid," Jeffri said.

"Why do you think that?"

"The PI your friend thought was tailing her specializes in marital cases — divorce, affairs, so on. Since your friend is not married and is not having an affair with a married man, I don't think she's under surveillance. That is, assuming your friend is telling you the truth."

"You are a cut and dried person, straight to the point," Sarah said with a tiny smile. "I like that in a man."

"I thought women liked romantic men," Jeffri jested.

"Women love romantic men but like cut and dried men in dealing with daily matters," Sarah replied with a tiny chuckle.

"OJ, may I suggest you stay away from the funeral? I know it's not easy being the son, but let's wait until the storm blows over."

"You think?"

"Yes."

"I think Encik Jeffri is right," Sarah agreed.

"Let's drop the Mister and Encik, shall we? If we're to be friends, which by the looks of it we are, call me Jeff and him OJ."

Sarah agreed and they clicked glasses.

# 24

Leaving the two to discover each other more intimately, Jeffri made a call to Shah. He asked if anything unusual happened when his men were following OJ. Shah told him nothing out of the ordinary happened. OJ was followed to Nirvana Funeral House, Salak South. He was there momentarily and then left. He headed straight to No Black Tie and met up with a woman. About half an hour later he, Jeffri, arrived. According to his men, Jeffri had just left and the two of them, OJ and the woman, were still in the bar.

Jeffri was delighted. He knew that Shah's men were up to the mark and were keeping a close eye on his buddy.

"Great job. Shah, I need round-the-clock monitoring on him. Can you arrange it?"

"Sure, but it'll cost you. I need to get in some backups."

"How much?"

"Give me five K for a start, and we'll work out the actual cost when it's over."

"I don't have that much cash now, but let me work it out. Can it wait until tomorrow?"

"Sure. Hey, what's going on with your friend? I mean, why does he need 24-hour monitoring?"

"Maybe it's nothing. I'm just taking precautions."

"You've always had a good nose to smell out shit. Nine out of ten times you were right."

"The streets taught me well," Jeffri said, laughing.

Back in his apartment, Jeffri deliberated on the predicament he was drawn into by the late Kim Senior. He reread the letter, trying to figure out what had happened. The last paragraph: *I hope with my sacrifice Juan would be free from the bond made by my father. I know with all my heart that you will do everything possible to protect Juan, so he can live a full and fruitful life. Please do not let my son meet a similar fate.*

What 'sacrifice'? Managing the triad accounts? Didn't OJ say his father deemed it an honor to carry the family's torch? *So what sacrifice? Oh SHIT, the ultimate sacrifice … his life. He killed himself, didn't he? If he did, this letter cleared OJ of any suspicion. No wait, I can't show this letter to the police. If I did, they'd want the files. Giving the police the files is as good as signing OJ's death warrant.*

"FUCK! What do I do?"

He picked up the check. Half a million ringgit to his name, an amount he had never seen or even dreamed of having. He could not bank in the check; it was a personal check of the deceased dated on the date he died. He was sure the bank would notify the police, and he would make the number one spot on their suspect list. *For what? Extortion maybe, and knowing how the police think, they would certainly cook up some other charges.*

Jeffri let out a long sigh. *I could really use some of the money now to protect OJ.*

He thought of talking to Shah; perhaps Shah could show him how he could get some cash until he was able to sort matters out. On second thoughts, he did not want Shah to be directly involved in the case, what with his tainted business. That would only complicate things with the police, should the case make it to them. Shah would be more useful in the background.

×

It was almost 10 at night when he pulled up in front of his mother's house in Jalan Reko, Kajang. It was one of those single-story, two-bedroom, low-cost houses built by the council. After he graduated, his mother decided it was time for her to retire and live a quiet life. Through one of her regular patrons at the KTV where she used to work, she managed to secure a unit by paying a few thousand ringgit under the counter. Now she survived on what little she made through sewing clothes for the surrounding people and the miserly amount Jeffri managed to set aside for her.

The lights were still on in the living room and Jeffri knocked lightly on the door.

"Who is it?"

"Me."

His mother opened the door, "Jeffri, do you know what time it is? Is something the matter?"

His mother always called him Jeffri, never Jeff. Stepping in, Jeffri saw that his mother had been sewing in front of the television, which was airing a Malay drama.

"Are you okay?" his mother asked again. "Have you eaten?"

Jeffri suddenly realized he had not eaten since the afternoon. The burger bought by Juliana was at his office. He was suddenly starving.

"Let me warm up the curry," his mother said without waiting for his reply. "You want fried egg?"

Jeffri followed her into the tiny kitchen, which was in actual fact part of the living room, and sat at the foldable dining table. His mother made a glass of hot tea and busied herself frying bullseye eggs and warming the leftover fish curry.

"How long has it been since you came home?" his mother asked, making small talk.

"Don't know, one month maybe."

"More like three. How's business? Are you doing well?"

"Surviving, how about you?"

"Enough. What brings you here?"

"I was around the area, so I just stopped by."

"Hmmm, you're such a bad liar," his mother laughed. "What's bothering you? I know something is weighing heavy on your mind. Is it a girl? I hope it is. You need to start thinking about settling down. Start a family and give me grandchildren to spoil."

"Not ready to settle down yet," Jeffri answered with a smile.

"You're never ready, but that shouldn't stop you. Once you commit, all will work out fine," his mother said, laying a plate of rice, warmed up fish curry and fried eggs. "Do you want soy sauce?"

"Please."

It had been a long time since Jeffri tasted his mother's cooking. The fish curry tasted just as delicious as it did when he was growing up, even the fried egg. Nothing like what he got from the mamak restaurants or roadside stalls. He wondered why his mother was not selling mixed rice in front of the house. He was sure she would do brisk business.

After Jeffri finished his meal, his mother asked, "If it's not about girls, tell me what's on your mind."

"It's work. I have this case and I need to use a lot of money."

His mother looked at him. He'd never once asked her for money, not even when he was at university. Something must be serious for her son to come home and talk about money.

"Tell me the truth. Are you in some kind of debt trouble?"

"No, nothing like that."

She let out a sigh of relief. "What's the case about?"

"I can't talk about it. It's lawyer-client confidentiality."

"Don't you give me that bullshit. I'm your mother."

"It applies to mothers too," Jeffri laughed, "especially mothers."

His mother made a face and laughed. "I don't have much savings, but how much are you talking about?"

"A hundred thousand, at least."

"A hundred thousand! Where're you supposed to get that kind of money?"

Jeffri shrugged. They were both silent, lost in their thoughts. After what seemed like ages, his mother wearily stood up, took the plates, and placed them in the kitchen sink. She disappeared into the house, while he sat sullenly at the dining table. Jeffri heard her talking over the phone, but paid no attention to it. Then she appeared with a smile and told him to go see a man. She said his name was Yusof, and gave the address.

"He's expecting you."

"Who is he?"

"A friend, a dear friend. If anyone can help you, he'll be the one."

Guided by Waze, Jeffri drove to Damansara Utama. The address was a double-story, semi-detached house. Jeffri parked by the roadside and observed the house. The porch light was on, but the house interior was dark. Driving here, he wondered who this Yusof was, how he could help, and what his mother had told him. By the look of the house and the luxury car in the porch, he must be wealthy. Perhaps he was a money-lender who used to be his mother's regular. He might even recognize him as one of the many uncles that passed through his young life.

Then the lights in the upstairs bedroom came on, followed by the living room lights. Through the thin curtains of the living room sliding glass door, he saw a person's silhouette. The front gate slowly swung open, and a man emerged at the front door. Jeffri remembered his mother told him the man was expecting him. The man must have heard the car stop by the roadside.

Jeffri got out of the car and walked over to the open gate. The man waited at the front door and, as he approached, asked, "Jeffri?"

"Yes," Jeffri answered, extending his hand. "Encik Yusof?"

Yusof grabbed his hand and pulled him into a hug.

"It's so nice to see you again," he said. Holding Jeffri at arms' length, he added, "The last I saw you was when you were about this high," he said, indicating his waist. "Come in. How's Katty?"

Jeffri looked at him, puzzled.

"I meant your mother. That was the name she used to go by," he said with a tiny smile.

"She is fine, thank you."

"Your mother told me you're a lawyer. I always knew you were special and would make it in life."

Jeffri nodded.

"She also told me you're handling a big case and needed some funds to kickstart it."

Again Jeffri nodded.

"After Katty called, I made some calls and managed to secure the funds you needed. Sorry, can I get you a drink?"

"Thanks."

"Coffee or tea?"

"Cold water's fine."

Yusof left to get the drink. Jeffri did a cursory check of the living room. There was a framed black and white photo of a young man with crew-cut hair in uniform on the side table. His height was about the same as Yusof, but he was slimmer. The uniform looked like some police or army officer's, with pips or stars on the shoulders, Sam Browne belt, high cut shoes, peak cap and a cane or baton or whatever they called it under the arm.

Yusof came back with a glass of cold water and handed it to Jeffri.

"Do you know Lim Kee Seafood Restaurant at Lorong Haji Taib?"

"Sorry, I don't think so."

"Do you know the Hong Leong building along Jalan Raja Laut? It used to be the EON building."

"Yes."

"The road next to it is Jalan Sri Amar. If you come from Jalan Raja Laut, Lim Kee Restaurant is across the road just after the Hong Leong building. You cannot park along the road, but if you come in from Jalan TAR, you can park right in front of the restaurant or along Lorong Haji Taib."

Jeffri could picture the Hong Leong building and the roads mentioned, but could not say he knew exactly where the restaurant was.

"Ah Meng will be there waiting for you. You cannot miss him. He is a midget, but don't mention it to him or stare," Yusof laughed. "Short people are very sensitive about their lack of height."

Jeffri just nodded.

"He'll assist you with your needs." Standing, Yusof said, "It's late. I think you should go now. We don't want Ah Meng to be waiting too long."

Jeffri stood, extended his hand and said, "Thank you."

"There's a lot for me to catch up with you. Please call me, and we can go for coffee or tea and chat. Say hi to Katty."

Leaving Damansara, Jeffri hit the Sprint Highway all the way to Jalan Parlimen onto Jalan Tuanku Abdul Rahman. It was late and the road was devoid of traffic. It took him only 18 minutes to reach Jalan Sri Amar. Immediately he spotted Lim Kee Seafood Restaurant to his right, a corner shop at the junction of Lorong Haji Taib 4 and Jalan Sri Amar.

Jeffri was mindful of the surrounding areas. Back when he was running the streets, these places — Chow Kit, Haji Taib, Tiong Nam and Tamboosamy, generally known as Belakang Mati — were gangs' hotbeds. It was the playground and haunt for triads, or known locally as secret societies like Wah Kee, Ang Beng Ho, 21 Immortals, Gang 08, Gang 04 and many others. His street-pack stayed clear for a good reason: as street urchins, they were no match for the notorious secret societies or gangs.

The area had undergone massive development, tall buildings everywhere, but somehow it was not able to wash away its reputation. The people were still the same, the triads and hoodlums. Add an influx of Indonesian migrants, some aggressive and violent, and of course this area would retain its colorful reputation.

Parking along Lorong Haji Taib 4 at this hour of the night gave Jeffri the shivers. Seated in his locked car, he surveyed the immediate surroundings and pulled out his handphone, ready to call Shah should he need him. The street and area around it were dimly lit, quiet with numerous shadowy spots. Almost all the shops were closed and the sidewalks were barren of pedestrians. He noticed a three-legged dog on the sidewalk staring at him. *Shit, even the dogs here are freaky.* Suddenly he remembered a caution by one of his street-pack members: *If you have no business here, there is no reason for you to come, unless of course, you are looking for trouble.* Satisfied there was no one hiding in the shadows or parked cars to ambush him, Jeffri felt safe enough to get out. The strays probably decided he was not a threat, and continued whatever they were doing. Vigilantly, he crossed the road to Lim Kee Seafood Restaurant.

The restaurant was a corner unit of a double-story shophouse. It had two frontages, one looking out to Jalan Sri Amar and Jalan Tuanku Abdul Rahman and another to Lorong Haji Taib 4. Strategically located for gangland powwows or table-talks, where they can easily detect threats coming from both directions. The restaurant's setting exuded the typical old Chinese ambiance, furnished with dark brown upright wooden chairs, and tables wooden with gray marble tabletops. Almost all the displays on the wall were written in Chinese calligraphy. A very red-faced, beer-bellied deity statue sat on a very red altar with half-burnt joss sticks sticking out of a very red pot against the back wall of the restaurant.

There were a few Chinese men seated at one of the tables drinking beer. They practically stared at him without concealment as he entered. He sat at the table nearest to the sidewalk, a precautionary measure just in case he needed to make a quick escape for whatever reason.

An elderly man approached and took his order for iced coffee. Jeffri had always loved Chinese coffee shop iced coffee. Unlike the mamak's watery and super sweet iced coffee, the Chinese made theirs thick and strong. After the waiter placed his drink, the Chinese patrons continued their beer-drinking, smoking and conversation, but Jeffri could feel their eyes on him. They probably thought he was a dirty cop waiting for his unofficial salary from a massage parlor operator, gambling den or something like that.

A moment later, through the corner of his eye, Jeffri saw a short, a very short, man appear from the darkness of Lorong Haji Taib 4. He wore shorts and a T-shirt with flip-flops, and his small hand held a black plastic bag. *Freaky*, Jeffri thought to himself, but dared not show any reaction on his face. He entered the restaurant to hearty greetings from the men at the table. He replied likewise, but walked straight to Jeffri's table and literally lifted himself onto a chair.

Without formality he asked, "You Tuan Yusof's nephew?"

"Eh?" Jeffri asked, but recovered fast enough to add, "Yes." He figured Yusof must have told Shorty he was his nephew to call on the favor.

"Okay, one hundred thousand, no interest for thirty days, after that ten percent per month."

Jeffri opened his mouth to protest about the thirty days, but thought better of it. He swallowed and nodded. Shorty placed the black plastic bag in front of him, literally jumped off the chair, repeated, "Thirty days," and went to join the group of Chinese men.

Jeffri was stunned at how fast things went down. A hundred thousand ringgit in a black plastic bag that Shorty probably recycled from his packed dinner, dumped right in front of him, just like that. No questions asked, no collateral required, no agreement signed.

Jeffri called to the waiter to pay for his drink, but one of the Chinese men waved him off. He sensed the men watching him as he walked to the car. *Do they know about the money? Most likely. Am I walking into a trap? Am I going to be stopped and robbed by their gang members? Not here; perhaps they'll wait until I'm out of their playground.*

Earlier, when he arrived, he had cold shivers; but now on leaving, he was shaking. Putting the car into gear, he reversed back onto Jalan Sri Amar and headed for Jalan Tuanku Abdul Rahman. His eyes darted side to side and to the rear view mirror, trying to spot anything suspicious. His heart was racing, but he knew he had to keep within the speed limit so as not to draw attention. He made a left to Jalan Tun Dr. Ismail and headed for Kampung Pandan and on to Ampang. When he reached his apartment building with the bag, he took the stairs two at a time, entered his unit, and locked the door.

Jeffri lay on the bed as he calmed his nerves. Never before had he been so terrified, and he blamed it on the money: the large amount and the manner it was gotten. Ironically, he would be using triad money against the triads. He took his handphone, scrolled to the calendar, and keyed in the date the money must be returned, typing 'Return Money to Shorty'.

He started to wonder: *What if I can't make the payment as scheduled? Ten percent of a hundred thousand is ten thousand. Where can I get my hands on that kind of money? Could OJ come up with it? Probably, but then I'd have to tell him the whole story.* Thinking of OJ, his mind wandered to him and Sarah. *Where are they? Most likely at his apartment, making passionate love.* Thinking of sex, his thoughts moved to Ruby, the cute inspector. How he wanted to get to know her. Apart from being cute and having a sensual figure, she was sharp and witty, qualities in women that aroused him. He'd always considered himself to be witty and quick on his feet, and when a woman displayed similar characteristics, it was a challenge to him, mentally and sexually.

Mental exhaustion took over and he fell asleep with a hundred thousand ringgit next to him.

# 2 5

Jolted from his sleep by the ringing of his handphone, Jeffri's head throbbed. He groped for the phone next to his head and peeked at the screen. It was 9:15 am, and the caller was OJ. Before he could answer, OJ went into verbal hysteria; "They broke into the office, the whole place was ransacked. Shit, Jeff, I'm scared."

"OJ, OJ, calm down. Take a deep breath and tell me what happened," Jeffri said, sitting up.

"They …"

"They who?"

"I mean, someone broke into my office and turned the place upside down. Kimberly came in this morning and found my office in a mess."

"Have you called the police?"

"No, I don't know what's missing yet."

"Okay, don't touch anything. You can do it later after the police check the place out. Call the police, I'll be there shortly."

"Okay, okay."

"And OJ, don't talk to anyone, even the police, until I arrive."

✕

Jeffri realized he had slept in yesterday's clothing. He called for a Grab, washed his face and changed. Then he took the files and cash and stashed them into the kitchen cabinet behind some stacks of plates and cups. By the time he walked downstairs, the Grab driver was already waiting for him.

When he entered the Kim & Kim office, Jeffri found a devastated OJ seated at the waiting area with his secretary. Both were staring at his office door. Seeing Jeffri, OJ sprang to his feet, his face ashen with fear.

"Can we go into the conference room?" Jeffri asked.

"It's in a mess too."

Jeffri walked to the office door to see for himself. The room looked like several water buffaloes with razor-sharp horns had decided to hold a wild orgy in it. Every cabinet was wide open, books and files thrown to the floor. Drawers scattered with their contents spread beside them. Framed pictures, certificates and displays taken off the walls and thrown on the floor. Sofas dragged away from walls, the rears ripped open. *These guys must be desperately looking for the files,* Jeffri thought. Turning away, he walked to the conference room. *The same buffaloes must have decided to have a go in here too. Whoever did this must believe the files are still with the firm. That puts OJ in real danger.*

"Anything taken?" Jeffri asked.

"I don't know, it'll take time to check."

"Any valuables or cash kept in the office?"

"Not that I know of."

"Have you called the police?"

"Kimberly did."

"What about the other partner's office?"

"Not touched. Anyway, he had already cleared all his belongings."

"Was it broken into?"

"No."

Now Jeffri was certain that, whoever they were, they were after the files. They knew the files were kept by Kim Senior; that was why the other partner's office was untouched.

"OJ, do you have any idea what the intruders were looking for?" Jeffri whispered.

"Remember I told you about the files? When I left my father that night, they were on his table, I mean, my table. He took them out from the drawer and placed them there. Then when we came back that morning, they were not there. Gone. I don't know what he'd done with them."

Jeffri nodded. He knew what Kim Senior had done with them, but he was not able to enlighten OJ for the moment.

"Jeff, I'm scared. My father said I was putting my family in danger. What should I do?"

Just then Inspector Ruby and her team arrived. They were let in by Kimberly. She greeted them and walked straight to the office, stopping at the doorway. OJ and Jeffri followed close behind.

She nodded to her team to start and beckoned for OJ, Jeffri and Kimberly to follow her as she headed for the conference room.

"Sorry, Inspector," Kimberly said, "the conference room was also messed up."

"Oh, then we'll sit over there," Ruby said, pointing to the waiting area.

With his eyes fixed on Ruby, Jeffri listened intensely to each question asked and each answer given by Kimberly and OJ. *She's really cute and sharp*, Jeffri confirmed to himself. When OJ and Kimberly were done telling her what they possibly could of the break-in, Ruby asked if they would answer a few preliminary questions. They both nodded.

"Do you have CCTV in here?"

"No," they answered in sync.

"What about in the corridor?"

"No," Kimberly answered, "only in the lift and the lobby."

"What about the access code for the front door?"

"Each of us has our own code."

"Different codes for each of you."

"Yes."

"Interesting."

"Why's that?"

"There was no sign of a break-in, no tampering of the front door. It means the door was opened using an access code. Is there any way I can find out who was the last person that came in?"

"Yes, I just need to call the system provider to read the history." It was Kimberly that answered.

"Can you do that for me? It'll be helpful."

Kimberly left them to make the call. Jeffri took the opportunity to get some feedback from Ruby.

"Inspector, please excuse my ignorance, but are you specifically assigned to the Kim & Kim cases or incidents?"

"No one is specifically assigned to any particular company's cases or incidents. When we received the report of a break-in here, my SIO told me it may be linked to my current case, so here I am. May I ask why, I mean, why you are asking if I'm specifically assigned? You don't like the way I'm handling the investigation?"

"No, not at all, I mean, you're doing a fine job, very professional."

"Thank you."

"Does this now mean the sudden death will be reclassified to ...."

"The likelihood has increased tremendously," Ruby answered with a heavy sigh.

"I sense that it bothers you. Can you enlighten us?"

"Okay, this is just between us. I can feel that the loss of his father weighs heavy on Mr. Kim, and it's only fair he should not be unnecessarily burdened by the thought of him being a suspect."

Jeffri nodded. His fondness for the inspector just doubled.

"When we closely examined the window, there was no indication of scuffle below it. There were foot markings, depressions on the carpet, but they were clear, not messy like if two or three people were wrestling with each other. Then the fingerprints we recovered from the window itself were of only one person. The deceased. On the outer ledge we also managed to lift shoe prints. They too were from one pair of shoes, the deceased's."

Ruby paused, looking at OJ.

"What does all that mean?" OJ asked.

"It was evidence that the deceased was by himself. There was no indication he was helped or forced by any individual to the window. It also indicated the deceased sat on the window's frame, held onto the window with his feet planted on the ledge."

Again Ruby paused. Jeffri saw it was not easy for her to tell OJ what she had concluded.

"You believed Kim Senior took his own life, there was no evidence of foul play involved," Jeffri said it for her.

'Yes," Ruby concurred softly, eyes fixed on OJ. "I'm sorry."

OJ's face went white. He looked like he was going to throw up. He abruptly stood, held his hand to his mouth and dashed to the front door. Jeffri sprang to his feet, said, "Excuse me," and ran after him.

OJ was bent over a sink, crying "I killed him" repeatedly when Jeffri entered the washroom. He stood by him with his arm on his back.

"No, you didn't."

"I did. I was the one who made him jump. I killed him."

"Stop it. You didn't know what he was going to do. Did he tell you that he was going to, you know," Jeffri left the cursed word out, "when you left? Did he?"

OJ shook his head.

"Did you at any time think he would do what he did?"

Again OJ shook his head.

"Then how come you're blaming yourself for something you had no idea was going to happen? Look, blaming yourself will not bring him back. Rest assured, he never blamed you for his actions, so you shouldn't either."

OJ washed his face, wiped it with paper towels and looked at Jeffri. "I just cannot forget the look on his face when I walked out that night. He looked dejected, lost and defeated."

"Remember him during your happy moments, soon that'll be what you remember."

Inspector Ruby's team had moved to the conference room when OJ and Jeffri returned to the office. Ruby came out on hearing their return and continued with her inquiries.

"Mr. Kim, you said you don't know yet what was taken, but do you have an idea of what the intruders were looking for?"

"No, I'm sorry. I just moved up here. I really don't know what was kept here."

"Any cash or valuables? Could it be something related to any major case your firm is currently handling?"

"I really don't want to speculate."

"I understand. However, when you discover what was taken, please inform me. It may give a clue as to who the culprits were."

"Yes, of course."

"Inspector Ruby, does this mean my friend, Mr. Kim, is off your suspect list?" Jeffri asked.

"He never was on it," Ruby answered with a warm smile.

"That was when you came to your earlier conclusion, but now with this break-in and the likelihood of the case being reclassified, would Mr. Kim be on the list?"

"In my opinion — but you cannot hold my opinion as conclusive. I believe the two incidents may be connected, but the break-in was more of an after-the-fact action. A consequence of the first incident, but that is yet to be established."

"Interesting," Jeffri complimented.

Ruby's team emerged from the conference room and told her they were done. She stood, thanked OJ and Jeffri, and reminded Kimberly to contact her when she got the feedback from the door access system provider.

OJ and Jeffri walked them out, and while waiting for the elevator, Jeffri again asked Ruby if he could call her for updates on the case.

"Yes you may, but don't you have other cases apart from this?" Ruby replied teasingly.

"Yes I do, but the investigators are not as pretty," Jeffri bantered.

"I'll take that as a compliment. Good day, gentlemen."

✕

Leaving OJ's office, Jeffri called Shah to see if they could meet. Shah told him to come over to his kickboxing gymnasium in Pandan Indah. Jeffri took a taxi back to his apartment, changed into jeans and a T-shirt, stuffed RM5,000 into his pocket, and drove to Pandan Indah. Jeffri had been to the gymnasium several times, but not to work out. It was always for some business related to his street-pack cases.

Kick Ass Gymnasium (KAG) was in an old godown adjacent to Shamelin industrial area. Most of the surrounding buildings had been demolished and redeveloped into light industrial buildings or storage areas. Shah had told him he bought the property at a steal from an addicted gambler who owed him money and was waiting for the right offer to offload it. In the meantime, he turned it into a kickboxing gymnasium and used it as his office and recruitment center.

The gymnasium was dimly lit with yellow bulbs, except for the ring which was bright with fluorescent and stage lighting. The gymnasium interior was hot and reeked of sweat, cigarette smoke, alcohol and ointment. Two kids hardly older than 18 were beating each other in the ring, in what they claimed to be the latest sports craze of mixed martial arts. In Jeffri's opinion, it was purely street fighting with the barest of protective gears. You punch, kick, elbow, knee or wrestle your opponent to the mat and bash or choke him or her. That was what it was about: beating them to a bloody pulp or senseless.

Jeffri admired the ingenious individual who came up with the term 'mixed martial arts', got it sanctioned as a form of sport, and made tons of money. People all over the world — men, women and children — just love seeing other people beat each other up in a ring or cage, like animals all bloodied, and are now able to watch street brawls legally on live television in their living rooms.

There were about ten people in the gymnasium — including the two kids trying to kill each other in the ring, and another two on the wrestling mat getting some form of coaching. One kid was trying to kill a punching bag, but it looked like he was the one getting killed. The rest were around the ringside cheering the fighters on. Jeffri nodded to them, most of whom he did not know. The caretaker, a stout man in his mid or late sixties, whom Jeffri knew from his previous visits, was on a bench against the wall keeping an eye on everything. Out of politeness, he asked no one in particular if Shah was in and a few of them pointed to the rear.

Shah was on his handphone when Jeffri poked his head through the office door. He signaled Jeffri in and kept talking over the phone. Jeffri was grateful for the cold office, but it too reeked of sweat, smoke and alcohol. He took out the five thousand ringgit, placed it on the table and took a seat. Still talking on the phone, Shah took the money and put it in a drawer. After a few more 'okays', Shah terminated the call.

"That was my men, tailing your friend," Shah said, indicating the phone call.

"I thought he was at the office," Jeffri stated, surprised.

"He left soon after you did and went to Cheras crematorium. My men saw from a distance, your friend was confronted at the entrance and after some pushing and shoving, he left."

"Where's he headed to?"

"Still on the road headed for the city center."

Jeffri noted the concern in Shah's voice. "What is it?"

"He grew a tail, four men in an SUV. My men suspect they're a snatch team."

"Snatch? Why do they think so?"

"You don't need four men for a tail. You need two cars, one man in each, or at most two. But a four-man team in an SUV?"

"What do you think is going to happen?"

"They'll probably cut him off and drag him into their car. Then one of them will drive his car, but I doubt they'll do it that way in broad daylight, too many witnesses. I think they'll tail him until he parks somewhere, probably at his office, then take him. Unless, of course, they're reckless and don't give a shit."

Jeffri thought of the break-in at OJ's office and the desperation in the search and said, "Shit, this is not good. What do you suggest?"

"Call your friend and tell him to drive to AEON at AU2 Shopping Center. Tell him to park at the upstairs parking and go to Starbucks. It's open there, and we can watch if he's being tailed. And tell him to drive slowly, give me time to get my men in place."

"Why there? Why not somewhere near here?"

"Two reasons. One, I don't want to bring shit into my house, and two, AU is a Malay area, the Chinese will stand out like albinos and the shopping center is not crowded, easier for us to monitor the snatch team's movements."

Jeffri agreed with Shah's logic and made the call to OJ. OJ immediately started to narrate his encounter at the crematorium but Jeffri cut him off, told him to listen and closely follow his instructions. Shah poked his head outside the office and shouted for the caretaker, Tyson, nicknamed after the famous or infamous Mike Tyson. Jeffri heard Shah tell the man to get four men to AEON AU2 immediately and to stay loose and wait for his instructions.

Jeffri and Shah left in separate cars. He followed Shah onto Middle Ring Road 2 (MRR2) then took the slip road to AU Keramat. They made a left, passed Taman Hulu Kelang Police Station, and swung right at the junction before taking another right into AEON parking. Shah told Jeffri to go ahead to Starbucks and wait for his friend. Jeffri saw Shah give some instructions to his men and then walk away in the opposite direction.

Jeffri took a seat outside Starbucks and decided to wait for OJ before ordering his drink. He spotted two of Shah's men seated at the walkway flowerbed smoking. One of them was the kid trying to beat the hell out of his sparring partner earlier. Then he spotted Shah coming from the opposite direction and sitting at the Old Town White Coffee outlet facing him. Shah gave him a casual nod and turned his attention to the concourse next to a Subway outlet.

A few minutes later, Jeffri's handphone rang. It was from Shah: "Your friend's here. Don't move, just stay there and act normal."

Jeffri intuitively looked around.

His handphone beeped indicating a WhatsApp message — *I said act normal.*

Jeffri grinned.

He spotted OJ turning the corner next to the Subway outlet, and it took all his willpower to stay where he was. A few meters behind him were two Chinese men. OJ saw Jeffri and approached his table. He sat facing his friend and anxiously asked, "What's going on?" Jeffri casually observed the two Chinese men walking past them into Starbucks and standing at the order counter. One of the men turned to look at them, then quickly turned away.

"Nothing, I just wanted to meet you," Jeffri said. "See how you're doing."

His handphone beeped again — *Two, one in blue and one in black T-shirt just entered the ice cream shop across you. Don't look.*

OJ started to tell him what had happened at the crematorium, but Jeffri cut him short. "Didn't I tell you not to go?"

"My sister called last night and pleaded for me to come. And after what the inspector told us, I felt I needed to pay my last respects."

"Look OJ, I'm not going to lie to you, but seeing how things are developing, it's best if you lie low for a while. Like they say in the movies, let the storm blow over."

"Why? What storm?"

"Remember you told me about the files and the visit by the Chinese movie characters?"

"But I don't have the files."

"They don't know that. They think you do. I figured that was why your office was burglarized. Don't you see? Just your office and the conference room, not your ex-partner's office."

OJ took a deep breath. "Oh my god. What should I do?"

Jeffri's handphone rang. Shah said, "Tell your friend to pass his car keys to you. Then casually leave. Pass them to me as you walk to your car."

Jeffri stole a glance at the two men inside Starbucks. They were at the counter waiting for their orders. He told OJ to hand over his car keys and the parking ticket.

"Why?"

"Just do it. Where's your office season parking card?"

OJ did as told. "In the car at the door pocket."

"Now, let's casually leave and walk to the car park."

Jeffri turned to look at Shah, and he too stood and walked briskly behind them. As he passed them, his hand brushed against Jeffri's, and OJ's car keys and parking ticket changed hands. Shah went ahead of them, where two of his men were waiting at the car park. He passed them the keys and parking ticket with instructions. Jeffri sent him a WhatsApp message — *The office season parking card is in the driver's door pocket.*

When Jeffri paid his parking ticket at the machine, two of Shah's men were loitering by it. As soon as he pulled his ticket out, one of the men pulled the electrical plug, cutting the power supply to the machine.

They got into Jeffri's car and drove out of the parking lot. Through the corner of his eye, Jeffri saw the two Chinese men walking hurriedly to their SUV. One of them was pointing to OJ's car still in the parking lot.

Jeffri drove out and made an immediate turn into Jalan AU 2C1, then right onto Jalan AU 2A/23. He kept looking in the rear-view mirror to see if they were followed, a skill he picked up watching television on counter-surveillance techniques. OJ sat silently looking alarmed, but the Intense expression on Jeffri's face kept him quiet. Jeffri's handphone beeped. It was Shah — *Leave the area immediately.*

Unknown to Jeffri, when the Chinese men tried to pay for their parking ticket, the machine was not functioning. One of Shah's men who'd unplugged the machine told him he needed to go down to the car park office in the basement. Cussing under his breath, the man shouted something in Chinese to his team, who were waiting in the car ready to go.

Upon receiving the WhatsApp message, Jeffri drove out of the housing estate and turned back onto MRR2. OJ kept asking where they were headed. He had no idea. First he thought of driving to Shah's gymnasium, but then he remembered Shah's insistence of not wanting to lead the Chinese men there. Nothing else came to his mind, so he drove to his apartment.

2 7

✕

Safe in his apartment, Jeffri let out a heavy sigh and plonked on the sofa. He knew they'd just had a close call, and if it was not for Shah's criminal mind and quick thinking, OJ would be in the hands of the snatchers. He looked at his buddy slumped on the sofa, his face muddled and terrified. Jeffri believed he must have suspected what was going on, that he was in danger. How much danger, OJ might still not have figured out yet, and neither had he. *How important are the files to them, and how far are the triads willing to go to get them? Should I tell OJ I have the files? How would he react to the knowledge?* Too many thoughts in his head, he had to put them into perspective before making such a big decision.

*The first and most critical is OJ's safety. Where can I stash him until all this blows over? Should I ask him to leave the country? To Australia or New Zealand? On second thought, we're dealing with triads, and there are triads in both countries. The triads here could have links to the ones there. Perhaps Indonesia. The chances of the triads here having links there are probably lower. But then again, if he leaves the country, there's no way for me to keep an eye on him.*

*Second, the damn files. I need to keep the files in a safe place, and I need someone to know about them just in case something happens to me and I can't get to them. The question is, where and who?*

*Third, the hundred thousand, how and where can I get a hold of that amount to repay Shorty within thirty days? I can't cash in Kim Senior's check, not unless I want cute Ruby and her team to arrest me. Actually, it would be nice if Ruby put the cuffs on me, thinking more in the bedroom rather than taking me to the police station.*

*Fourth, how do I save OJ from the triads? What would the triads do to someone that broke their pledge or vow or whatever they termed it? I've seen Mafia or Yakuza movies, and these guys don't take broken pledges or vows lightly. They somehow loved blood and death, not theirs of course. They have this single-minded belief, killing solves everything.*

"Jeff, am I in danger?" OJ asked, looking straight at him.

Occupied with his predicaments, OJ's sudden question ended his mulling. He turned to face him. There was fear written all over his face, but there was also pain.

"I'm not sure, but it looks like you are."

"The triads?"

Jeffri nodded.

"Then I must leave."

"Why?"

"Because I cannot involve you and put you in danger, too. This has nothing to do with you. It was my grandfather's and father's doing."

Jeffri fell silent. He didn't know what to say. It was not OJ who involved him, but Kim Senior. There was guilt in OJ's voice as he stood to leave.

"I can take care of myself," Jeffri said as confidently as he could.

"I know you can, but this is not your fight."

"You have a plan?"

OJ looked at him, his face blank.

"Look OJ, why don't you stay here until we can figure things out?"

"How?"

"I don't know yet."

OJ asked if there was anything to drink, something strong. Jeffri told him no and made them a cup of strong black coffee each.

"Something happened today, and that was why you asked me to meet you at Starbucks?"

Jeffri felt OJ had the right to know, and hopefully the knowledge would keep him on his toes. He told OJ about getting help from his friends, help to keep an eye on him from the morning Kim Senior decided to fly without wings. He, however, left out the part about receiving the file and check from the deceased and the plea to save his son.

"And today my friend's men saw what happened at the crematorium. After you left, you grew a tail. My friends feared something bad was about to happen and needed to be certain, so we took precautionary measures. That was why I asked you to meet me at Starbucks."

"And?"

"They were right. You were being tailed."

"You serious?!" OJ was shocked.

"Yes." Hearing the fear in OJ's voice, Jeffri added, "It was probably nothing. They may have just wanted to keep you in their sight, you know, to make sure you don't leave town," he said smilingly.

"They followed me to Starbucks?"

"Yes, but when we left, my friends managed to stall them. For now, you're safe here."

"What about my family?"

"I figured they're safe. Your uncle must have made sure of that."

"You think that was why I was stopped by my uncle from attending the wake and cremation? To protect my family and me?"

"Most likely."

"What about my car?"

"Taken care of. It'll be parked at your office."

Jeffri's handphone rang, it was Shah informing him that OJ's car was parked at level B1 of Citibank Tower. He had sent his men around to Jeffri's apartment to hand over the keys and season parking card.

"Thanks."

"And they'll be taking your car and replacing it with one of my cars."

"Why?"

"I'm sure they would've taken your car number, and by now it's a marked car. I don't want you driving around in it."

"Thanks."

"By the way, I sent out some feelers to find out who they were."

"Thanks, really grateful for any info you can get on them. Shah, your guys are sitting on him, right?" Jeffri asked, not wanting to mention OJ by name.

"As long as you want and keep paying," Shah laughed.

2 8

✕

After giving strict instructions to OJ not to leave the apartment, not to tell anyone where he was, not to post anything on social media, and to deactivate his handphone GPS, Jeffri left. He drove the car loaned by Shah to Ampang Point and purchased a couple of T-shirts for OJ. Stopping at Giant Supermarket, he bought some frozen pizzas, sausages, bread, fruit and beers to stock at home for OJ. On his way out, he stopped at McDonald's for a takeout.

It was around 6:30 in the evening when he arrived back. OJ, with a vacant expression, was stretched out on the sofa in front of the blaring television. Jeffri doubted he was actually watching it. His heart felt the pain and turmoil his buddy was going through.

"Are you hungry?" Jeffri asked from the kitchen.

"Starving."

"Bought us McD," Jeffri said. "Got you a couple of T-shirts to change into and some beers. Thought of buying you a pair of briefs or boxers, but that's too personal."

"You're the best, always thinking of everything."

Seated at the dining table, OJ began talking about his situation. Jeffri felt there was no point in talking about it and getting all excited and dismayed when they hadn't gotten all the facts and information yet. He changed the subject to something he knew would take OJ's mind off his quandary.

"What's with you and Sarah?"

"Nothing," OJ replied rather too quickly.

"Where did you guys go after I left yesterday?"

"We hung around and had dinner."

"Then?"

"Then nothing. She left and I went home."

Jeffri made a face and laughed.

"Really, nothing happened."

"Okay, let me rephrase my question. What would you like to have happened between you and Sarah?"

OJ blushed.

"She's good-looking, stunning, smart, and she likes you."

"She does? How do you know that?"

"She told me so."

"When? What did she say?"

"I could see it in her eyes, her body language, how caring she was when you broke the news of your father to her. More importantly, how do *you* feel about her?"

"I think … no, I know I'm in love with her. I know, you're going to say it's a crush, but I can feel something different. Something I never felt before. Like, like … shit, I don't know how to explain it."

"Well, if you don't know how to explain it, it must be love," Jeffri laughed. "Have you told her your feelings?"

"Noo."

"You should. You know the saying: faint heart never won fair lady. And she's no ordinary fair lady," Jeffri said with a smile. "What do you know about her?"

"Not much. She went to college in the States. By the way, that's where her father is from and is currently residing. Her parents divorced when she was still in school. She works as a … a … I don't know what," OJ said, laughing. "She said she provides services for ADT."

"ADT?

"Any Damn Thing. That was what she termed it as. Someone wants something, she sources for that something. She gets a retainer, and when she manages to secure the something, she gets her commission."

"A trading agent?"

"I guess you can call her that."

"What's she sourcing for?"

"Didn't ask."

"You know she's Malay, right?"

"Don't we term them as Eurasian?"

"Yes, but she is Malay, therefore a Muslim."

OJ nodded but said nothing.

After dinner, Jeffri told OJ he needed to run some errands. He again reminded him to avoid answering calls unless it was from him, and also to refrain from going on social media and under no circumstances to divulge his whereabouts to anyone. He went to the bedroom and came back with a fresh towel.

"By the way, did your secretary Kimberly find out who was the last person that entered your office?"

"Yes, she did. According to the system provider, the last person who entered used my father's access code."

"You mean, your father gave his code to someone?"

"Looks like it, because he was ..." OJ stopped, not finishing his sentence.

"Who's the administrator for the codes in your firm?"

"I don't really know, but when I started working there, Kim arranged it for me. She got it from the Finance and Admin section."

"Okay, that's interesting. Has she told the inspector?"

"Yes."

"Let's leave it at that now. The spare keys are there in case there's an emergency and you have to leave the apartment," Jeffri said pointing to several sets of keys hanging next to the door. "You can sleep in my room. The spare room has no air-cond."

"I'll sleep outside on the couch," OJ said.

"Your choice. Don't wait up for me, and don't drink all the beers."

"Where're you going?"

"Meet up with some friends. See if I can find out anything about the guys following you."

"Why can't I come with you?"

"It's better if I go on my own. The friends I'm meeting are not exactly from your social circle," Jeffri joked. "You may spook them."

"You be careful, okay?"

"Always."

Leaving his apartment, Jeffri called Shah. As usual, Shah was at his gymnasium and invited him to come over. It was 8 eight p.m. and the area around the gymnasium was dark and tranquil. Most of the light industries and businesses were closed for the day. Jeffri turned into the gymnasium compound, which was poorly lit. He saw several cars and many motorbikes parked along the building. As he got out of the car, several more motorbikes came in and parked a few feet away from him. He was awed by how young they were. Most looked like they'd just left school, not older than 18.

He flashed them a polite smile and entered the gymnasium. It was stinkier than earlier. There were twenty to thirty of them, smoking, talking loudly, cheering and swearing. No one gave him a second look as he weaved his way through to the rear of the building.

The caretaker Tyson, was tending to a kid with a bloody nose and swollen eye, probably beaten by his sparring partner. *These kids have too much energy and aggression in them. Well, at least Shah's giving them a platform to let it all out without getting into real trouble.* He wondered if any of them did make it into the big-money ring. Tyson noticed him and Jeffri nodded to him.

Jeffri heard laughter from Shah's office. It sounded like there were women in there too. He knocked on the door and poked his head in. Shah immediately stood, pushing a woman off his lap, and beckoned him in. There were beer cans on the table and the office was clouded with cigarette smoke. There were three men in their forties and three beautiful women in their early twenties. They all gawked at him.

"Sorry for crashing your party," Jeffri apologized.

"No, no, just a few friends having a drink. Come, let me introduce you."

One of them was nicknamed Din Mayat. The other two were Abang Joko and Abang Bob. The three young women all had light brown hair. They looked Malay to him, but went by the names Nina, Coco and Pinky.

Jeffri had heard of Abang Joko and Abang Bob; Shah had mentioned them when seeking his legal advice. Abang Bob was a police detective dismissed for extorting money from foreign workers. Jeffri had advised him to cut a deal with the police: he put in his resignation and they might consider dropping the charges against him. After all, what the police wanted was to get rid of him, the bad apple. Instead, he was dismissed through disciplinary action without being charged in court. After his dismissal, he teamed up with Abang Joko and continued his life in crime, and he seemed to do well at it.

Abang Joko was a naturalized Malaysian born and raised in Aceh, Indonesia. It was said that he came to Malaysia in the eighties. If the USA is the Promised Land for the Mexicans and South Americans, Malaysia was likewise for the Indonesians back then. He started legally as a construction worker before he moved on to something bigger and better: crime. He married a Malay woman and for RM30,000 bought himself citizenship. Abang Joko was huge, a five-foot-nine-inch 260 pounder, mostly belly. It was rumored he was still wanted for several murders back in Aceh. There were also rumors he committed similar offenses here, getting arrested several times but never charged.

Jeffri had heard stories of how Din Mayat got his nickname. It was said that Din, short for Nordin, used to work as an attendant at the Kuala Lumpur Hospital mortuary. Probably due to his lack of academic qualifications, he was always put on the graveyard shift by his supervisor. To while away the quiet nights, he would drag a chair next to the refrigerated trays lining the wall, pull open a few body-boxes to expose the corpses' heads and chat with them. Sometimes, he would have dinner in their company. According to the story, the corpses never did talk back to him — until one night the corpse of a gunned-down hoodlum was brought in.

Out of curiosity, Din pulled out the refrigerated tray of the corpse to see what a gangster looked like. It was then that the corpse talked to him and gave him a brilliant idea.

*"What are you looking at?" the dead gangster asked.*

*"Nothing, nothing," Din answered, terrified. He was about to close the box when he heard the corpse cry.*

*"No, don't. It's dark in here."*

*Din was shaking. He thought of running out of the morgue screaming when the corpse said, "Don't be scared, I'm not going to hurt you. I'm dead."*

*"Yes you are, that's what scares me. Are you dead, I mean really dead?"*

*"Why don't you pull me out further and take a look at the hole in my chest? No man can survive a fucking hole in his chest."*

*Din calmed down, they kept talking, and it was then that the dead gangster planted an idea in his head.*

Jeffri never believed the bullshit about the corpse talking to him, but he guessed seeing the gangster did stir something wild in Din's brain. The morgue was scarily quiet especially at night, so no one in his or her right mind would want to loiter there. It was air-conditioned with a lot of storage space, and rent-free. Hospital staff going in and out of the morgue was a common everyday sight, no suspicion raised, no questions asked.

So Din started with smuggled cigarettes, knock-off women's accessories, cosmetics, generic and fake Viagra, sex toys, and whatever items the hospital staff needed. His business flourished and word spread. As he did not pay for police protection, the morgue was raided. He was charged with evading custom duty, conducting business without a license, and selling prohibited sex toys. He pleaded guilty and did time at Sungai Jelok prison. Din is a common Malay name, and there were many Dins in prison. To distinguish him from the rest of the Dins, the warden nicknamed him 'Din Mayat' because of his association with the morgue.

"If you're here for the fight, you're early," Abang Bob said.

"Fight? What fight?" Jeffri asked.

"Guys, can we have a moment? I need to sort out some business with Jeff," Shah said.

The men and women grumbled at their private party being interrupted and at being asked to step out.

"Leave the beer," Shah said, "this won't take long."

Nina, who was earlier on Shah's lap, gave him a peck on the cheek and said seductively, "It better not be long, or I'll let Abang Bob finish what you started."

Abang Bob grinned from ear to ear. "Always ready to assist a woman in need."

After the last of them left, Jeffri took one of the vacant chairs. Shah offered him a beer, but he declined.

"What fight was he talking about?"

"Just something we organized for the kids, you know, to identify potentials," Shah answered evasively.

"Are you running illegal fights, betting?"

"I can't stop them if they want to bet. Look, it's all in good sport and fun."

"If you say so. Did you find out anything about the guys today?"

"Not much yet. SUV registered to a Malay man who traded it in for the new Proton X70. My men are still working on where the SUV was ditched. I mean, to which used car dealer."

"Shouldn't it be Proton?"

"Proton doesn't do used cars. They normally offload it to a used car dealer. The dealer usually doesn't change the owner's registration until they sell it, cost-saving. Otherwise, they need to pay twice for the change of ownership."

"So if we know the used car dealer, we'll know who those guys were?"

Shah nodded. "Din Mayat recognized one of those guys when I showed the photos I took at AEON with my phone. He said the fat guy used to work as a bouncer at Noovo Club, Jalan Doraisamy. My men are checking on that. So far nothing yet."

"Are they related to any secret society or gang?"

Shah lit a cigarette. "You want to tell me what this is all about?"

"I'm not sure, I'm still figuring it out. Are those guys related to any secret society or gang?"

"They all are, one way or another. Why?"

"Can you find out which secret society or gang?"

"That's easy once we identify who they are."

"Shah, today's event scared me, and I need you to put on your best men to keep an eye on my friend."

"Why are you doing this, I mean, why is he important to you?"

"For one, he is a friend, and second, he gives my firm business."

"Okay, that's good enough for me. I'll put my nephew on him. He's a good boy, reliable and thinks on his feet."

"Thanks," Jeffri said and stood to leave.

"You don't want to stay awhile and join the party?"

"I'll take a rain check. Where did you get the girls from?"

"Abang Bob brought them. You want one? I can ask him to set it up for you."

"Thanks, maybe some other time."

Leaving the gymnasium, Jeffri's head was more muddled than before his chat with Shah. Using an SUV not registered to any of them was an indication the would-be snatchers took precautionary measures against being identified. Another indication was that they had connections and resources. The club bouncer was an indication they did have the muscle to do the job for them. Jeffri knew his wits alone would not be a match for whoever was going after OJ. He needed Shah or perhaps more than Shah on his side.

As he turned onto the main road heading toward MRR2, his handphone rang. It was Shah telling him OJ had just left the apartment.

"SHIT! What the fuck is he doing?"

"You tell me."

"Where's he headed?"

"Into town, my men are on him."

"Shit," Jeffri swore. "Tell your men to stay close. Do not let him out of their sight."

"No problem, but if he goes in for dinner or drinks, my men have to go in too."

"Okay."

"You're picking up the tab."

"Okay, just don't lose him."

Terminating the call, Jeffri took several deep breaths. He tried to figure out why OJ had acted that way. He'd specifically told him not to leave the apartment, yet something or someone made him disregard the advice. He knew OJ was scared shit, and unless something very serious happened, he would not have risked going out. Was his family in danger and they reached out to him for help? But Shah said OJ was headed for the city, and if he was not mistaken OJ once told him his family lived in Damansara.

It struck Jeffri: only one thing could make a man throw caution to the wind and put his wealth and life at risk — LOVE.

It had to be that woman, Sarah. *Stupid woman, but you can't blame her. She doesn't know of OJ's situation, she was probably thinking of cheering him up. It's OJ that's not thinking with his brain, but then people in love never do.*

After a while he calmed down and made a call. OJ answered after several rings, and there was a tinge of life in his voice. Jeffri knew what brought it about.

"Hey, buddy. What's up?"

"Nothing."

"You heading for somewhere?"

"Oh mmm, yes, meeting a friend."

"Who?" Jeffri paused. "She?"

"Yes she called, and we're just meeting to have a drink."

"Buddy, listen, I know you miss her and want her company, but please be careful. Under no circumstance should you go back to your apartment or the office."

"Why would I want to do that? I mean, go to the office."

"I don't know, but whatever you guys want to do, not these two places, okay? I've a strong feeling these places are being watched."

"Okay."

"You coming back later?"

"That's my plan."

"Okay. Unwind and have fun, but stay sober and alert. Call me if you feel something's not right."

"Sure, thanks."

2 9

✕

OJ's Grab ride headed for Healy Mac's Irish Bar at Jalan Changkat, a favorite nightspot for local hipsters, white tourists, expatriates and working Asian women especially from Vietnam and the Philippines. Pubs, grills and fancy Western and Middle Eastern restaurants lined both sides of the strip. One of the upmarket nightspots where you pay for overpriced food to be seen or to take a date to impress and hopefully score with.

It was a weekday, and OJ was surprised to see the large crowd. He thought Sarah would have picked a quieter place where they could talk and perhaps get a little romantic. Stepping out of the Grab car, he saw Sarah sitting by herself at one of the tables lining the walkway. He watched her from across the road for a moment and remembered what his friend told him; *faint heart never won fair lady*. He inhaled deeply, resolved he would tell her of his feelings, and crossed the road.

Just then Sarah turned to look outside, spotted him and smiled. OJ could see how beautiful she was. His heart cheered and all his worries evaporated. It was worth the risk of leaving the safety of Jeffri's apartment.

As he approached her table, Sarah stood and gave him a hug and a peck on the cheek. Her action was for the benefit of the group of men at the next table, who were ogling her from the instant she arrived. *That should stop those peering eyes*, she said to herself, but it did not.

The waiter, a foreign laborer, came to take their orders. Sarah ordered a Bloody Mary and OJ his usual beer.

"You look poorly," Sarah said. "Are you okay?"

"Yes," OJ said with a wan smile.

"Have you had dinner?"

"Yes, with Jeff."

"How is he, Jeff?"

"Okay, I guess. Why do you ask?"

"Just being polite," Sarah said laughing. "You two are not a couple, are you!"

"NO, of course not. We went to uni together, and my firm works with his firm. You can say we know each other well."

"Oh."

"I sensed you didn't quite like him."

"What makes you think that?"

"The other day when we met I thought I sensed a kind of, you know …"

Sarah laughed. "I thought it was the other way around. I sensed *he* didn't like *me*. Something about the way he looked at me, something in his eyes."

"Jeff's a good man. He talks straight, hard on the outside but soft on the inside."

Their drinks arrived and they changed the subject. Sarah did most of the asking and OJ the answering. Sarah discovered he was not attached, hated being a lawyer and wished he had pursued his dream of being an architect. They ordered finger food and refills. Sarah changed her drink to a sweet Martini, but OJ continued with beer. By the third mug, OJ was a bit woozy. He forgot he'd had two cans of beer at Jeffri's apartment before Sarah called. Four beers was his alcohol tolerance limit, but he was on his fifth.

Getting off his stool to let the blood in his legs circulate, he staggered and would have fallen if it weren't for Sarah's quick reflex to grab his arm.

"Ooops, sorry," OJ said, embarrassed.

"Steady there," Sarah said, still holding his arm. "You okay?"

"Yes, yes, just need to go to the gent's."

OJ stood holding the edge of the table until he felt confident he could walk to the toilet without tripping over the tables and chairs along the way.

"Okay, I'm okay now."

Sarah anxiously watched him as he made his way to the rear of the bar. Finally he disappeared from sight, and she smiled at the thought of him taking a leak in his state. She had seen worse situations during her college days. Men getting plastered and dropping to the floor out cold, or becoming boisterous and getting into brawls with other drunks. Luckily for her, OJ was not like that; he was always the gentleman.

After almost 15 minutes, OJ still had not reappeared. *Men don't take that long to pee. Women do, but not men. Could he be out cold in the toilet?* She was about to wave over a waiter to ask him to check on OJ when she spotted him by the bar. Someone was talking to him, it looked like they knew each other well. The man was holding his hand in a handshake and his other arm was on OJ's shoulder. OJ was nodding and nodding, and eventually the man let go of the handshake and patted him on the back as he walked away.

"Who was that?" Sarah asked.

"The accountant at my firm," OJ answered, his words slurred. "He was saying something about my father's passing."

"I think we should make a move. I've got an early day tomorrow, and you look like you need to get some rest."

OJ closed his eyes and inhaled deeply to clear his head. He felt woozy and leaned against the table for support. The table shifted under his weight and he went crashing to the floor, pulling the table with him. The crash took with it the chairs and almost downed Sarah too. The crashing sound of table, chairs and broken glasses attracted nearby customers and Shah's men who were watching them from outside.

Sarah, with the help of other customers, managed to lift OJ up and sat him in a chair. She called for the bill and paid. With OJ's arm wrapped over her shoulders, she walked him out. Once outside, she leaned him against a parked car and asked, "Where did you park?"

"I love you," OJ murmured.

"I know," Sarah said, grinning at the timing and situation he had chosen to express his feelings for her. "Where did you park your car?"

OJ shook his head. "Sarah, I love you. I truly do."

"You said that already."

"I did?"

"Yes, you did. Now tell me, where did you park your car?"

"No car, I came by Grab."

"Hmm, okay, stay here. I'll get you a cab."

Sarah managed to hail a taxi. Just then, she heard someone calling to her from inside the bar. It was the waiter with her change. She left OJ leaning against a car to take her change. OJ slithered down to the road.

Shah's nephew moved toward OJ and squatted next to him. "Hey, are you okay?"

OJ looked at him suspiciously.

"It's okay. I'm Jeffri's friend."

The mention of Jeffri's name brought a smile to OJ. He felt safe and mumbled, "My best friend."

"Who was the man you spoke to at the bar?"

"Man? What man? Oh, you mean Ng. Ng is my accountant."

Just then Sarah came back and with the help of Nik, they managed to get OJ into the taxi's backseat.

"Where do you stay?" Sarah asked, standing by the opened door.

"Jeff's place."

"Where's Jeff place?"

"Ampang somewhere. I don't know the address."

"What about your house?"

"Jeff told me not to go there."

"Why not?"

Before OJ could answer, the irritated taxi driver looked at Sarah and told her rudely he could not wait for them to sort things out the whole night. "The road is narrow. You tell me where to go or you get your boyfriend out!"

Sarah knew she could not leave OJ by himself in the taxi, not in his state. Not with all the stories she'd heard of the local taxi drivers' reputations. OJ could be robbed or, even worse, be injured or killed. Desperate, she got into the cab with OJ and gave the driver her address.

Nik instructed two of his team members to follow the taxi while he stayed back to monitor the situation for a bit.

A few minutes after the taxi left and made the turn onto Jalan Nagasari, an SUV suddenly appeared from the same road. It turned sharply into the one-way street of Jalan Changkat, almost colliding with an oncoming car. It screeched to a stop in front of Healy Mac's, facing the wrong direction. Two men jumped out of the SUV and dashed into the bar. There were horns blaring and a crowd of curious onlookers, eager for free entertainment, started to gather. Nik recognized the action, watching apprehensively. He suspected something was about to happen. If he was lucky, he would be entertained to a gang fight. The two men came out with the man he saw was talking to OJ earlier. They were talking in Chinese and pointing toward Jalan Nagasari. As abruptly as they arrived, the two jumped back into the SUV, made an illegal U-turn on the one-way street, and drove off in the direction where Sarah and OJ went.

Nik called his team members and warned them of a possible pursuit. He then called Shah to update him.

"If they're willing to attract attention to themselves, it means they're desperate. Tell your team to be extra-vigilant," Shah warned his nephew.

30

During the drive to Sarah's apartment, she wound down the taxi window to let in the fresh night air. She held OJ closer to the door with his head against the window. The rush of air helped clear his dizziness, and he asked, "Where're we going?"

"To my place," Sarah said, not too happy about it. "How are you feeling?"

"I'm fine, thanks. I'm sorry for behaving like a jerk back there, sorry I embarrassed you."

"Forget it," Sarah said with a weary smile and squeezed his hand. "Nothing I've not experienced before."

The taxi pulled up to Angkasa Impian Condominium guardhouse; Sarah produced her access card to lift the boom gate and directed the driver to the main lobby porch. OJ was feeling much steadier when he stepped out of the taxi. He paid the fare and thanked the driver. Sarah held on to his arm as she led him through the lobby.

"Are you sure it's okay for me to go to your apartment?" OJ asked as they waited for the elevator.

"If I said no, where would you go at this hour in your condition?" Sarah asked.

"I don't know, somewhere, anywhere."

"And get yourself mugged."

X

The elevator arrived and they got in. Sarah still held on to OJ's arm. She was afraid to let go, afraid he would fall again. OJ, on the other hand, thought she held on because it was how it should be for two people in love.

OJ had sobered up and was back to being good company again. Sarah, on the other hand, was a little hyped about her impending meeting with Philippe, her supervisor who would be arriving tomorrow morning. It was too early for her to call it a night just yet. She was hoping to chill out longer at the bar and drink a few more martinis before hitting the sack, but that was cut short by OJ's mishaps.

"Do you want to shower?" Sarah asked as she led OJ to the sofa.

"I'd love to, but I don't have anything to change into," OJ said, looking at her puppy-eyed.

"You can use the bathrobe, if you don't mind."

"I don't mind. I'm all sweaty and sticky."

Sarah went to the bedroom and came out with a fresh towel and bathrobe and passed them to OJ.

"You can use my bathroom. The other bathroom was never used, so there's nothing inside it. You can use my shampoo if you wish, but don't touch the other girly stuff. I don't want you to smell like me when you go back to Jeff's place," Sarah quipped.

OJ stood and just looked at her.

"Go on, I promise I won't peep. I'd like to have a glass of wine. Would you like one?"

OJ shook his head. "I've exceeded my alcohol limit. Can I have a cup of coffee?"

"Sure, with sugar and cream?"

"Black with a teaspoon of sugar, thanks."

When OJ came out of the bathroom, there was soft instrumental music playing. He recognized it immediately: Kenny G. Like what he loved listening to in the evening at his apartment, especially after a trying day at the office. Sarah had already changed into something more comfortable, he guessed it must be her sleeping attire: a loose T-shirt with a college logo and baggy silk shorts. She looked so casual and so beautiful. OJ noticed her glass was half empty, and she seemed relaxed and unassuming.

"Where do I put the towel?" OJ asked, holding it up.

"Sorry, let me get you the hanger," Sarah said, getting to her feet.

As she walked past him, OJ noticed she was not wearing a bra under the T-shirt. The bouncy sway of her breasts caused the T-shirt to move, outlining her nipples. An electrical surge shot through his body, pumping blood to his crotch. Sarah noticed the sudden movement of his bathrobe as she passed by and smiled inwardly.

She felt warm blood surge through her body too. She felt good about herself, about her body that could still excite a man. *It's been too long since I was with a man, since I've felt the warmth of a man's body.* In the one year plus since she came here, there were nights she desperately yearned for a man's touch.

Sarah came out with a hanger and took the towel and clothing from OJ to hang by the dining table chair. OJ was cross-legged on the sofa, afraid to move and expose his excitement in the form of an erection. Sarah sat next to him and took a sip of her wine. Her face too was slightly flush from the wine but more so from anticipation.

"Tell me why Jeff told you not to drive or go back to your apartment," Sarah asked.

"Eh, oh, I'd rather not talk about it."

"Why, don't you trust me?"

"No, no, I mean, yes, I trust you. It's just I don't want to worry you."

Sarah stared at him unblinkingly. That was all it took for OJ to tell her everything from the office break-in to him being tailed. Sarah noted the pained expression on his face and the fear in his voice. She moved closer and wrapped her arms around him. Having experienced what it felt like to live in fear from the unknown, she knew what OJ was going through. She too did not know who was after her or her child, and was still living in paranoia.

She pulled OJ's head to her shoulder, stroking it tenderly, whispering, "Everything will soon be okay." Her maternal instincts took over. She wanted to make him feel safe. At the same time, the years of not having an intimate relationship made her body crave more. She gently lifted his face and kissed him lightly on the lips. Not surprising to her, he kissed her back passionately. It felt good; he was a good kisser.

Disengaging his lips, OJ confessed repeatedly, "I love you." He started kissing her neck and nibbling her ears. Sarah moaned and responded. OJ held her neck and pulled her face up, kissing her. She dug her nails into his back. Like teenagers newly experiencing sex, they groped feverishly to undress each other, each filled with desire for different reasons. As he entered her, she gazed into his eyes. In his wild desire for her, she did not see lust, just love, and knew she could learn to love him. They moaned with pleasure and came together. It must have been the quickest climax they ever had. Exhausted and panting, they lay side by side on the sofa, listening to Kenny G playing 'Forever in Love'.

3 1

Sarah was up by 8 while OJ was still sleeping, exhausted from their second lovemaking and his emotional confession of love. She let him sleep as she tiptoed around to get dressed for her meeting with Philippe. She left a note for him on the bedside table:

*Didn't want to wake you. There's food in the fridge if you want to eat something. Don't know how long I'll be away. If you need to leave, just lock the door behind you.*

*Sarah*

✕

Walking into Vasco's @ Hilton, Sarah glanced over the dining area looking for her appointment. Not seeing anybody, she helped herself to a cup of coffee and took a seat by the glass wall facing the entrance. Then she spotted Philippe and another man walk in. Philippe was dressed in a polo shirt and shorts, while his companion was in a loud red Hawaiian shirt and shorts. He looked ridiculously out of place. They both had pale arms and legs. Sarah waved to them.

"Bonjour, Monsieur Philippe," Sarah greeted as they approached.

They pecked cheeks as Philippe replied to her greeting. "You know Roger?"

"Monsieur Roger," Sarah greeted and offered her hand.

"Ravi de vous rencontrer enfin, Mademoiselle Sarah." (*Nice to finally meet you, Miss Sarah.*)

"How was your flight?"

"Tiring, still adjusting to the time difference. We just need a little rest and we'll be ready to go," Philippe said. "I'm starving, let's get some breakfast before we talk?"

As they ate, Sarah refreshed them on what transpired between her and Dato' Tarmizi, which was not much except he had agreed to the meeting. She informed them of the arrangements she had made for them to have dinner this evening at Songket Restaurant.

"I don't want to take any risks, so I picked an authentic Malay cuisine restaurant. More like Malay-style fine dining," Sarah said, letting out a tiny laugh. "There's traditional music, and we can either dine indoors or al fresco."

"What risks?" Roger asked.

"Western restaurants. Dato' may be picky about halal and non-halal food."

"Good thinking," Philippe complimented. "Wouldn't have thought of that myself."

"The dinner is to break the ice and for you to feel him out."

"And him, me," Philippe responded.

Sarah nodded.

"Hopefully that will give you some indication of how to take it forward when we golf the next day. You'll ride with Dato', and Roger with me."

"Okay. I've been reading on the new government, their policies and directions," Philippe said. "Everything seems to focus on China. What are your thoughts on it?"

"China's influence has always been strong here. They've the money, technology, and clout in this region. It's easier for us to relate to them as part of us, because we are linked to them through ethnicity. As you may well know, the business community here is mostly Chinese, therefore it makes sense for the economic relationship and reliance with China to be strong."

Philippe and Roger nodded. "That makes it more difficult for us," Roger moaned.

"Not necessarily."

Roger raised his eyebrows.

"The government is controlled by the Malays. The Malays, well, on the surface are friendly with the Chinese, but deep inside they don't trust them. The Malays relate more to the Western communities in every sense: lifestyle, education, and so on. I mean, there are those religious segments that relate to the Arabs, but in terms of business and lifestyle, most are inclined toward the Western ways."

"Interesting. So you're saying the Malays are …"

"Hypocrites," Sarah finished Roger's sentence and smiled.

"I was about to say modern, but your definition is more accurate," Roger replied, laughing.

"Sarah, can you arrange for two sets of clubs?" Philippe asked. "I think it's better if we rent than bring along ours."

"I'm sure the pro-shop will have some, but I don't know if they will suit your needs. What about shoes?"

"We brought ours. It'll be fine. After all, we're supposed to lose, right?"

Sarah nodded and they laughed.

"Gracefully, like the real gentlemen the French are supposed to be."

OJ woke to the ring of his handphone. The time displayed on the screen was 10:12 a.m.

"Jeff?" OJ answered meekly.

"Where are you? You said you were coming back."

"Sorry, I was a bit tipsy and fell asleep."

"Where?"

"At Sarah's apartment."

"Are you coming back here?"

"Yes, yes. Can you WhatsApp me your address?"

Jeffri thought of telling him what had happened after they left the pub last night, but decided it could wait until he was back. He did not want to frighten him. After all, Shah's men were there to look after him. Instead he said, "Okay, I'll see you soon."

3 2

✕

OJ made the bed the best he knew how, then went into the bathroom to wash his face and get dressed. He wondered if he should stay and wait for Sarah. Last night's lovemaking lingered pleasantly on his mind, and he wanted more. He did not want it to be a one-night stand. He wanted to be with her and make it last forever. Then he realized he had nothing to wear except his soiled clothing and underwear. He'd also told Jeffri he was coming back. Perhaps he could go back, get some fresh clothing, and come back. *How?* If he locked the door on leaving, he would have no keys to come in again. Anyway, Sarah might not like the idea of him moving in uninvited. Dismayed, he called for a Grab.

He received a prompt on his handphone that the car was waiting for him downstairs. He let out a sigh of frustration and left the apartment. He got into the car and immediately after they passed the guardhouse, Shah's men on two motorbikes tailed them. One of the pillion riders informed Shah that their charge was again on the move.

As the Grab car slowed to take the long curvy road in front of Istana Pahang Kuala Lumpur, an SUV appeared from Jalan Ceylon and cut it off. The Grab driver swerved off the road and jammed the brakes by the curb, avoiding a head-on collision. Two men jumped out of the SUV; one of them yanked open the Grab car's rear door and the other crouched into the car to grab OJ by the arm, dragging him out.

Nik and his team members immediately reacted. They stopped behind the Grab car and Nik, who was riding pillion, jumped off the bike to assist OJ. The man from the SUV who was holding the door turned around as Nik rushed to assist OJ. Without warning, he stabbed Nik's belly with a knife.

Nik staggered back and fell to the ground, clutching his belly and groaning. His team members stood frozen, dumbfounded. They had never been in such a situation. It was always the other way around, them beating on a non-resisting loan defaulter. Without instructions from their leader, they were lost.

The two men from the SUV grabbed the moment to drag out OJ, who was paralyzed with fear. His legs jellied as he stared at the young man all bloodied on the ground. OJ caught a glimpse of an elbow, felt a sharp pain in his left temple, and warm blood ran down his cheek. His body went limp and the men shoved him into the back of the SUV. Before passersby realized what had happened, the SUV was gone.

One of Nik's team members called Shah to inform him. The other two just stood there lost and shaken.

"Fucking get him to the hospital!" Shah screamed over the phone.

"How? We're on bikes!"

"Fucking call 999 or stop a passing car!"

"Okay, okay."

"In the meanwhile, stop the bleeding. Take off your shirt and press it against the wound."

"My shirt?"

"Yes, your fucking shirt. Do it now."

"Okay, okay, okay, I'm doing it now."

"Call me back when you got him to the hospital."

Shah called Jeffri to inform him of what had just happened and that OJ was taken. Then he called Abang Bob, explained the situation, and asked if he could contact his old buddies from the police to immediately send a patrol car to the location where his nephew was and take him to the hospital.

"Nik, how bad is he?"

"I don't know. His boy said he was stabbed in the stomach. Bob, the boys are green kids. I don't think they can handle the situation. I really need him to get to the hospital. My sister would kill me if something bad happened."

"Okay, I'll call you back."

"Thanks."

Terminating the call to Abang Bob, Shah called Nik's boy and told him not to talk to the police, and to tell the other team members to return to the gymnasium.

"What police?"

"Abang Bob is trying to get a patrol car to help take Nik to the hospital."

"If they ask what happened, what do I tell them?"

"Tell them you saw some people fighting and when Nik tried to stop them, he got knifed. Tell them you do not remember their faces or the vehicle number."

"What about the Grab driver?"

"What about him?"

"He scooted off."

"Nothing you can do about that, can you? Just tell the police so."

"Okay."

"Call me when you're at the hospital."

And then Shah called Abang Joko for an urgent meeting.

Jeffri realized the situation had accelerated from dangerous to grave. The other party was desperate and willing to go to any extent to get what they wanted. *The question is, what do they want? Is it just OJ or is it OJ and the files? They probably think by having OJ they will have the files. They don't know OJ has no idea what happened to the files. Shit, if OJ is questioned — soon they'll know of me.*

Jeffri needed to act fast. Very soon the people who got OJ would be hunting for him. His apartment was not safe anymore, and he needed a new safe place to put the files. The file could be his and OJ's insurance. He grabbed the files from the kitchen cabinet and left the apartment. As he drove out, he racked his brain where to hide them. The first place that came to mind was his mother's house. *No, that'll be one of the places they'll look once they know of me and my involvement. Anyway, there's no reason to put my mother in danger. What about the man, Yusof? Give it to him for safe keeping. The problem is I don't know who Yusof really is or what he'll do with the files.*

He drove to the general post office headquarters at Dayabumi building on Jalan Sultan Hishamuddin. He knew post offices had P.O. boxes for rent. Perhaps he could rent one and keep the files there.

He drove into the basement parking and went a couple of rounds before he managed to get a parking bay. He put the plastic bag containing the files in the trunk of his car and went in search of the elevator to the lobby.

Dayabumi was a building that was the pride of the country, but was now rundown and in dire need of upgrading and maintenance. He could see faded paint on the walls and non-functioning neon signage. The lobby felt gloomy, absent of any feel-good ambience. Jeffri guessed that since the country had the Twin Towers, Dayabumi was forgotten, left to die a slow death.

He walked into the general post office and made inquiries on renting a P.O. Box. He rented it using his own name instead of his law firm Jeffri & Associates, a firm he suspected will soon be known to the people who took OJ.

He asked for the biggest box they had, saying he was a mature student with an overseas university who would be receiving lots of books and documents. The female clerk swallowed his bullshit. He paid the fee, and 15 minutes later he was given a key and shown to box number 85.

Jeffri retrieved the files from the trunk of his car and deposited them into the P.O Box. Satisfied they would be safe for now, he called Shah.

33

$\times$

When Jeffri arrived at the Emergency and Trauma Centre, Hospital Kuala Lumpur, Shah and Abang Bob were in a serious whispered discussion at the entrance. They saw him approaching and stopped talking. Shah's face was flushed red with anger and he signaled for Jeffri and Abang Bob to follow him away from the entrance and crowd. They followed him in silence to the motorbike shed where he leaned against a post with a NO SMOKING sign and lit a cigarette.

"How is your nephew?" Jeffri asked.

"All the nurses said was that he lost a lot of blood and is still in surgery," Shah replied, taking a deep drag on the cigarette.

"What did the doctor say?"

"What doctor? No bloody doctor came out to tell me anything."

"What actually happened?"

"Nik's boys said they saw the Grab car blocked by a black SUV. Nik tried to intervene and the bastard stuck a knife into his belly. Didn't even give him a warning to back off," Shah said, his voice filled with venom. "The bastard will pay for what he did to Nik."

Jeffri turned to look at Abang Bob, who just shrugged.

"Look Shah, I know you're mad, but I think we should try and work this out without resorting to violence."

Shah let out a cynical laugh. "You think this is a bloody courtroom where you can talk and talk and argue your case? You've been away from the streets too long, Jeff. This here is about respect, and if you don't retaliate, they'll think you're weak. The next thing you know they'll be running all over you, taking over your turf."

Jeffri inhaled deeply, letting out a tired sigh. What Shah said was true. But being a non-violent person, he still felt there must be an amicable way.

"Your friend was taken, and what do you think they'll do to him? Buy him coffee and talk?" Shah snorted. "He'll be lucky if he walks away from this with a broken arm or leg. I'm sure you understand what I mean."

"How did they know his whereabouts? Your men did not mention anything about OJ being tailed after the first incident."

"I know for a fact that they're sitting on your friend's car parked at his office, so they must have figured out he either used a taxi or Grab to move around. Nowadays everyone is using Grab. My guess, they must have someone in Grab or paid someone in there to monitor your friend's account. He also needs to turn on his GPS location to call for Grab."

"They can do that?"

"They can do anything so long as they pay. You're not thinking like us or them. You're thinking like a fucking lawyer. That's why I said you left the streets for too long. This is not like the child's stuff we used to play with. These are the real streets, grown-up games," Shah said mockingly and glanced at Abang Bob. "People get injured and killed."

Jeffri sighed.

"Look Jeff, my boys said the SUV came off Jalan Ceylon and blocked the Grab car. What does that tell you?" Before Jeffri could answer, Shah continued, "It means they knew your friend was in the car. How the hell did they know? The only explanation is they got a call from someone in Grab."

Jeffri digested what Shah said and admitted his deduction was right. All that was needed was for someone working with Grab to flag OJ's handphone number. The instant he called for Grab, they got him tagged.

"You hired me to protect your friend and I failed. In failing, my nephew is now undergoing surgery, fighting for his life. I'm not promising you anything, but I'll find your friend, alive or otherwise, and for my nephew, I'll make sure the bastard gets what he deserves."

"Please don't turn this into a gang war, or for that matter a racial clash," Jeffri pleaded.

"When you hired me, it was business, but when they hurt Nik, it became personal. You can stay out of it for all I care, but I've got to do what I got to do."

Shah and Abang Bob looked at each other. Jeffri could see they were on the same wavelength.

"I think you need to watch your back," Abang Bob said. "I'll assign a few men to watch over you."

Jeffri nodded. "Thanks. Shah, can you keep me updated? Likewise, I'll keep you updated too."

Shah nodded. "You have to pay Abang Bob for the protection."

Jeffri nodded. "How much?"

"Five thousand for a start, and we'll see how things develop," Abang Bob said.

"I'll get it for you by tonight. I'll call you later and set the meeting." He turned to face Shah. "Hey, Shah, I'll cover Nik's medical expenses too."

OJ regained consciousness, and felt a stinging pain around his left eye. He could feel blood caking on his cheek and knew the cut on his brow had opened up. He could not touch it as his hands were bound behind his back. He felt his left eye's vision get a little blurred and was certain it was inflamed.

He tried to recollect what happened. He remembered being grabbed, elbowed and shoved into the SUV. He remembered seeing a man stabbed. He remembered the fear and feeling of helplessness, and nothing else.

OJ blinked several times to adjust his vision and slowly turned his head to look around. The room was air-conditioned, furnished with a double bed, a box television, a small writing table, a mini fridge, two chairs and a coffee table. The windows were all covered with newspaper. Two men whom he recognized as those that grabbed him were seated on chairs around the coffee table. Both were busy playing with their handphones. He scrutinized them from the corner of his eye. They both looked normal, decent, no dragon or dagger tattoo or anything of that sort on the arms or neck.

There was a knock on the door, and the two men hurriedly pocketed their phones and pretended to be alert, watching over him. One of them nodded to the other, walked to the door and peeked through the peephole. He mouthed the word 'boss' to his partner before opening the door.

A Chinese man in his mid or late twenties, average height, clean-cut and in a white short-sleeve shirt and dark pants, like office clothing, stepped in. His eyes fixed on OJ. No sign of tattoos on the arms or a large gold chain around the neck either. To OJ, he could be any ordinary office-going person.

"Mr. Kim Junior," he said with a sarcastic tone, accompanied by a snigger. "We meet at last. You're not easy to locate, and sorry about the black eye. Johnny said you fell on his elbow. I see they managed to stop the bleeding."

The two men laughed heartily at their boss's joke. OJ glared at him. The man did not look anything like OJ had imagined a triad boss would look like. He was well-dressed and spoke with a non-threatening voice.

"Are you going to kill me like you killed my father?" OJ asked, surprised by his own question.

One of the men standing behind OJ struck him hard on the back of the head and said, "Watch your mouth."

The boss grabbed OJ's chin in a claw grip, bent down close to his face, and hissed, "Listen, you little piece of shit. Your father and grandfather were honorable men. You think I'd kill an honorable man like your father?"

"You kidnapped me. Your men stabbed an innocent man," OJ managed.

"Since you put it that way, I guess we have to kill you too, don't we?" The boss looked at his two men, released his grip and laughed. "But we've a lot of time for that. By the way, the police suspect you killed your old man. They said the office was a mess and you admitted to having a wrestling match with him. Perhaps it was you who threw your old man out the window. You know, to inherit his business and wealth. Otherwise, a weakling like you would never get anything from the old man."

"Fuck you," OJ cursed, his face flushed with anger. He was breathing hard and struggling to free himself from the chair. "Fuck you and your blood business. You think *I want* any of your business?"

The man laughed and dragged one of the chairs by the coffee table. He placed it a couple of feet in front of OJ and sat. His face turned serious.

"Let me introduce myself. I'm David Lau, the one you called to say your firm was terminating its service. Remember the call?"

OJ remembered calling a David Lau, whose name appeared on several documents in the old files. Then he remembered the visit by the two Chinese movie characters. It dawned on him that his life was in extreme danger. The terror he experienced when he woke up in Jeffri's bedroom a few days back returned. He bit his lips to stop them from quivering. He thought of Sarah, of their lovemaking, of not ever seeing her again. Tears welled in his eyes.

"Your grandfather made a vow to my granduncle that the Kim family pledges its loyalty as the keeper of our businesses. The pledge continues as long as there is a son that can inherit and continue the Kim legacy. This pledge was made in blood, in accordance with traditional rituals, and if broken, shall be paid in blood. Do you understand?"

OJ closed his eyes and tears rolled down his cheeks.

"The Kims were trusted keepers of our secrets. You think you can just break the pledge, made before you were even born? You think you can dishonor your grandfather and father?"

"I never wanted to be a lawyer, never did ..."

"You father knew of the pledge, and being an honorable man, he made sure you became a lawyer to honor your grandfather's vow," David said and lit a cigarette. "But what does a pig shit like you know about honor?" He stared, then abruptly stood, startling OJ and both his men. Standing menacingly, inches from OJ, he asked, "Where are the files?"

OJ looked up at him nervously and asked, "What files?"

"Don't play games with me. The files where you got my name and phone number. Where is it?"

"I don't know. I thought you took them the night you killed my father."

David slapped OJ hard on the face. OJ's head snapped to the right on impact. His left cheek instantly turned red and he winced, his eyes misty from the burning sting.

"For the last time, I did not kill your father. He was an honorable man, and I've no reason to kill him. You can tell me where you kept the files here and now or I'll let my men here have some fun with you. Either way, you're going to tell me where the files are."

"I don't know where they are. When I left the office on the night of my father's death, the files were on the table. When I came back that morning about 2 or 3 a.m., they were gone. That's why I thought you had them."

David looked at his men questioningly. They both shrugged.

"Who was the Malay man with you at AEON?"

"You mean Jeff? He's a friend from my university days, a lawyer that's doing criminal cases for us."

"Why was he protecting you?"

"Protecting?"

"My men said you left with him. Your car was left at AEON and was later found parked at your office building. You did not go back to the office or your condo."

"We went out for drinks," OJ lied. "I got a little tipsy and he took me back to his apartment."

"Where?"

"Ampang somewhere, I really don't know the address."

"His office?"

"Ampang Point, I think above the yong tau fu restaurant. I've never been there."

"How is he involved with you in this matter?"

"You mean the files? I don't think he knows anything," OJ lied. "It's just my father and me."

David gazed at OJ's face, searching for telltale signs he was lying.

"Well, Mr. Kim Junior, until I can get to the bottom of this, you'll be my guest here. My men'll see to it that you're well taken care of. But should I find out you lied to me, I'll not be as kind and civil as I am now." David paused and smiled. "You'll probably be fish food at the bottom of a disused mine."

David's handphone rang. He pulled it out, looked at the screen, turned on his heels and left. His two henchmen looked at each other, puzzled, but said nothing.

3 4

X

Jeffri went back to his office. The conversation with Shah weighed heavy on his mind. Shah's mission had changed, it was no more about protecting OJ. He could vividly see Shah's face, how furious and worked up he was. Shah wanted revenge, and that would make things difficult for him. Shah might not be upfront with him; he might withhold information to stop him from interfering with his quest for retribution. Jeffri needed an alternative person he could depend on to get information for him, but he couldn't think of anyone.

Jeffri thought of Yusof, the man his mother trusted. He remembered the old photo of Yusof in a police uniform he saw in his house. Yusof might be an ex-police officer, but Jeffri was confident he still had connections within the force. The problem of going to him was that he might want to know everything before agreeing to help. That was something Jeffri was not able to do without risking his buddy's life. Should Yusof pass on the information to the police, not only would OJ be in deep shit with the triads, he would also be in deep shit with the police. Anyway, telling the police of the existence of the files was like handing them over to the police and signing OJ's death warrant.

He thought of contacting Inspector Ruby, the cute policewoman investigating Kim Senior's death. How could he get her to help without telling her the truth, the whole truth? She was a smart woman; she would see through his lame excuses in asking for her help. She would demand to know it all and that was as good as giving OJ up for slaughter. Jeffri pushed the thought aside.

Arriving at the office, Jeffri told Juliana to take the day off and not to come in until he gave her the okay. Juliana gave him her usual inquisitor's glare.

"You went missing for almost two days without a call, then you come in, tell me to take the day off, and don't come back until you say so? What the hell is going on? Are you closing shop?"

"No, I'm not. I've just got a little situation and I need you to stay away for awhile."

"What situation? Am I not a part of this firm?"

"Better for you not to know."

"Right, because I'm not a lawyer, not smart enough to understand," Juliana said sarcastically. "I get it."

"No, it has nothing to do with legal matters. I just don't want you getting involved and putting yourself in danger."

"What danger? What shit have you gotten into this time? You fucked with someone and now they're coming for you, after the firm? Is that it?"

"No, nothing like that. At least not in the way you're thinking," Jeffri said and walked into his office.

Jeffri leaned back in his chair, closed his eyes and took deep breaths. He tried to put the current events into perspective, to resolve the issues.

*Kim Senior is dead; was it suicide or was he murdered by the triads? Most likely suicide, like the cute Inspector Ruby deduced.*

*Kim Senior removed the files, so he must have suspected the triads would come after them. Why didn't he use the files to negotiate for his and his son's lives? Was it because he believed the triads would not deal? Did he feel the files were not an equal and fair trade for their lives?*

*They broke into the office looking for the files. They must have thought OJ had the files. That he had stashed them somewhere, and because of that he was kidnapped. How do I get in touch with them?*

Now that Kim Senior sacrificed himself, would the files be enough to trade for one life, OJ's?

*Is OJ still alive? He has to be. They're probably beating the shit out of him to get to the files.*

*Would they know of me, of Jeffri & Associates? Sure they would, OJ would spill it all out. Ju's life would also be in danger.*

"Damn you, Kim Senior," Jeffri silently cursed.

With his eyes closed, he did not realize Juliana had come into his office with a cup of coffee. She placed the coffee on the desk and sat heavily on one of the visitors' chairs. The creaking made by the chair startled Jeffri and made him bolt upright.

"Shit," Jeffri exclaimed.

"Edgy aren't we," Juliana teased, grinning. "Sorry, didn't mean to scare you. Made you coffee."

"Thanks," Jeffri said and gave her a wan smile.

Juliana looked at her boss worriedly. She could see the exasperation all over his face.

"Jeff, boss, I don't know what's going on, but I'm here if you want to talk about it."

Jeffri smiled.

"I may not be legal-minded, but I'm a good listener."

Jeffri sighed.

"When I was in deep shit, you helped me. I'll never forget that, ever. Then you went beyond that and gave me a life, my baby a life. You never asked anything in return nor did you take advantage of me. I'm forever indebted to you, but I'm also not happy with it."

Jeffri arched his eyebrows at her. "Unhappy ... why?"

"Am I not attractive to you, not good enough for you?" Juliana asked, pretending to be disappointed. Before Jeffri could respond, she broke out laughing. "I'm kidding, okay. Look, you're really not yourself. So there's no way in hell you're going to resolve whatever it is that's eating you up."

To avoid Ju's piercing stare, Jeffri leaned across the desk for the coffee and sipped it.

"You need to let it out, talk to me. Tell me your thoughts and we can kick it about, see where it leads us."

"There is no *us* in this, just me."

"Okay, see where it leads *you*," Juliana said, grinning.

Juliana was not someone you could just shove aside. She was determined and relentless. After he made her promise not to breathe a word to anyone and to stay away from the office, he told her the summarized version of what had happened. He left out Shah's nephew being stabbed so as not to have her worry about his safety.

"I suspected it was the parcel you received, the one you're so secretive about," Juliana said. "So you and Shah have split ways?"

"I don't know for certain, but we have different objectives."

"This man, Yusof, your mother trusted him. When he helped you with the money, did he ask why you needed it?"

Jeffri shook his head.

"Didn't that tell you anything?"

"What?"

"That he was helping you because of your mother and you. Not because he wanted to interfere with whatever you're up to. To me, that's a good enough reason to trust him."

"But he's an ex-police officer."

"*Ex* is the key word. He has no glory to chase after, but more importantly, he has connections he can call on."

"What if he wants the police involved?"

"Tell him the reason you're going to him is because you don't want the police involved. He'll understand."

"And the files?"

"Say you've heard of them, but you don't know who has them."

"He won't buy it."

"No he won't, and he'll know you have them but you're not willing to hand them over to him or the police."

"You think it'll work?"

"Since you've got nothing better, it's worth a try."

35

One of Shah's men went to the Kim & Kim law firm pretending to be the building's car park staff, and asked to see Mr. Ng the accountant. When asked for the reason, he informed the receptionist that the security noticed Mr. Ng's car was not locked. He would like for Mr. Ng to follow him to lock the car for security reasons. The receptionist informed the accountant, and after a few minutes, Ng appeared. Together with Shah's men, they took the elevator to the car park.

As they exited the elevator, another one of Shah's men followed them. They walked along the parking bay, and a car approached and stopped next to them. The man who was following stepped up to Ng, grabbed his shoulder and jabbed a Cobra 9mm pistol to his back. The man pretending to be the car park staff pulled the rear car door open and shoved Ng in. When Ng protested, the man butt-whipped his head, then pressed the barrel onto his forehead and told him to shut up.

They pushed Ng to lie on the car floor and pinned him down with their legs, pressing hard on his head, chest, abdomen and thighs. The car drove off at a normal speed. At the boom gate, the driver paid using a Touch & Go card. There were two cameras monitoring vehicles leaving the car park, but there was no way the cameras could capture Ng on the floor.

The car eased into the flowing traffic headed north on the North-South Highway. Twenty minutes later, it exited the highway at the Sungai Buloh toll. After the Petron petrol station, they made a left onto Jalan Perusahaan 3 all the way till the end of the road and entered a workshop. Once the car was inside, the workshop shutter door was pulled down.

Accountant Ng was asked to get up and exit the car. Two men held him by the arms and forced him onto a plastic chair a few feet in front of the car. Shah came out of the office in the rear of the workshop smoking a cigarette, talking on his handphone.

"Okay, thanks, I'll see you back at the gym when I'm done here," he said and terminated the call.

Without saying a word, Shah struck Ng's head from the back. Ng bent forward and shouted angrily at him. He tried to stand to face Shah but was held down by the two men standing by his sides.

"What the hell do you think you're doing?" Ng demanded angrily. "This is kidnapping, a crime," he shouted. "You'll all go to jail."

Shah stood in front of him smiling. "That was just a taste of what's to come if you don't tell me what I want to know."

"What? What do you want to know? You don't have to kidnap me if you want me to tell you something. Do you know I work for a law firm and my firm will make sure you're prosecuted and sent to jail? Fools! You let me go now, and I'll forget all this."

"We've not even started and you already want to leave," Shah laughed.

He nodded to his men. The two men beside Ng grabbed his arms and strapped them to his back using a cable-tie. The driver went into the car, popped the hood, and started the engine. Another man popped the trunk and took out a battery jumper cable. He fastened the crocodile clips at one end to the car battery. Standing in front of Ng, he touched the two crocodile clips together, creating clicking sounds and sparks. Ng gawked at him, terrified, his eyes as wide as they possibly could open.

"What the hell are you doing?" Ng glowered at Shah. "You think you can get away with this? I have friends who'll come after you."

Shah ignored Ng's threats and gave the signal to continue. The man clipped the negative end of the jumper cable to Ng's left nipple and another man poured water all over him. Then they took a step back, waiting for Shah's instruction.

"Here's how this works. I ask you a question, and you give me an answer. If I believe your answer, my man here won't do anything. However, if I think you're lying, he'll clip the red clip to your other nipple. This'll go on until I get all the answers, or until your nipples are well done. After that we'll move on to your balls. You decide."

Shah took Ng's handphone and asked, "What's your passcode?"

"Four-three-two-one."

Shah punched in the passcode and the phone unlocked. "See how easy it is? What's your assistant's name?"

"May Ling."

Shah scrolled the contact list and found the name listed. He sent her a WhatsApp: *I'll be late, have to meet with a client.* He then put the handphone into Ng's pocket.

"Last night at Healy Mac's, you met with Mr. Kim?"

Ng nodded.

"After that who did you call?"

"No one."

Shah nodded to the man holding the jumper cable and he immediately clipped it to Ng's right nipple. Ng screamed in agony, tears running down his cheeks, and he struggled to break loose. Using insulated rubber work gloves, the two men beside him pressed his shoulders down hard. The man in the car revved up the engine to increase the electrical surge and drown out the scream.

"FUCK YOU, FUUUUUCK," Ng screamed, his body wiggling and twisting in agony.

Shah signaled to the man and he unclipped the positive crocodile clip. Ng groaned, taking big gulps of air. Saliva and tears dribbled from his mouth and face.

"Who did you call?"

"A friend," Ng mumbled as he gasped for air.

"What's his name?"

"David."

"What did you talk about?"

"Just the normal stuff."

Shah nodded to his man. The crocodile clip went on again. Ng screamed and shouted curses in Chinese. Tears of pain drenched his cheeks, thick saliva dripped from his mouth, and mucus oozed from his nose. Shah let it go on a little longer before he gave the signal to his man.

"What did you talk about?"

Ng seemed to faint, flopping his head to the side with his eyes closed. One of the men standing beside him grabbed his hair and yanked some off his scalp. Ng screamed and they laughed.

"What did you talk about?"

"Mr. Kim Junior, I told him I met Mr. Kim Junior."

"Why was this David interested to know where Mr. Kim was?"

"I don't know. He called the office several times looking for Mr. Kim Junior after Mr. Kim Senior's mishap."

"Who is David?"

"He's a client, a longtime client."

"What company?"

"Many companies: trading, property development, and many more. I always call his handphone."

Shah took Ng's phone from his pocket, scrolled the contact list and found David's number.

After they left the office, Jeffri told Juliana to go home or to the movies or shopping, just stay away from the office. He got into his car and drove to his apartment. He took a rolling luggage carrier from the bedroom, stashed the cash from the kitchen cabinet, and left. He drove to the general post office, took the files from the P.O. Box, and placed them into the luggage. Then he checked into Concorde Hotel along Jalan Sultan Ismail.

Jeffri expected his office and apartment would be the next targets of the triads. He needed a safe place until he could work things out. Checking into a hotel was the only thing he could think of for the moment. Concorde was perfect as the hotel was known for its Malay clientele.

He ordered room service and started going through the files. He needed to find out who these people were. Who was at the helm, and how to get in touch with them? He jotted down several names that appeared in the documents. Since 2012, the company Asian Merchants (M) Sdn. Bhd and the name David Lau Poh Seng seemed to appear in most documents.

He Googled Asian Merchants (M) Sdn Bhd and discovered it was into imports and exports, capital ventures, property development, art galleries, and entertainment. Diversified as it was, it was not a public listed company. Nothing much was known about the company except what they chose to publish online.

Jeffri carefully extracted the ledger and placed it in an envelope. He needed to make a copy and return the files back to the P.O. Box for safety. He took ten thousand from the stash and went downstairs to the business center to make a copy of the ledger. Then he drove to the general post office and placed the files in the P.O. Box.

As he was leaving the general post office, his handphone rang. It was Shah asking his whereabouts. Jeffri lied and said he was at his apartment.

"What time can you come over to the gym?"

"I can come now."

"Give me an hour. I need to get rid of this asshole."

"What asshole?" Jeffri asked anxiously.

"Nothing to do with you," Shah lied.

The crocodile clips did not move from the nipples to the balls; Ng sang like a karaoke champion. After Shah and his men were done interrogating Ng and got all the information, he told his men to get rid of him. The men started injecting small non-lethal doses of heroin into his arms. They watched as Ng got high, started mumbling, crying, laughing and slipping in and out of consciousness.

"Keep him here. Give him a small dose every two hours, at a different spot every time. Do a few on his ankles. Make it look like he's a hardcore junkie. Then at midnight, give him the last dose and dump him at a whorehouse," Shah instructed. "Leave a small pack in his pocket and let me know exactly where you dump him. I'll get Abang Bob to arrange for him to be picked up by the police. Make sure you don't leave any trace back to us."

The men nodded.

As he was leaving, Shah said, "Clean his wallet of cash and take his watch and jewelry, but leave his IC. Let the police figure things out."

36

When Jeffri arrived at Kick Ass Gymnasium, he did not see Shah's car at its usual spot. There were, however, a lot of motorbikes for this hour of the day. He decided to stay in the car until Shah arrived. After several minutes, two men emerged from the gymnasium, stood at the entrance and curiously stared at him. One of them went back inside and came back with more men. They all looked at him intimidatingly. Jeffri smiled at them to indicate he came in peace and meant them no harm, but it did not work.

Three of them broke away from the group and started walking toward him. These were men, not the kids who usually frequented the gym. Men Jeffri had not seen before. Two of them approached him on the driver's side, while one went around the car to the passenger's side.

"Can I help you?" asked the biggest of them.

"Thanks, I'm waiting for Shah."

"Shah's not here."

"I know he'll back soon. I'll just wait in the car until he arrives."

"What business do you have with Shah?"

"We're friends, and he asked me to come."

The three men looked at each other, and the second biggest of them said, "Why don't you wait inside?"

"Too stuffy, I'd rather wait here."

"Suit yourself."

The three of them walked back to the group. They went back into the gymnasium, leaving two kids behind to watch over him.

Ten minutes later Shah's car pulled in, followed by another car and six motorbikes. Jeffri's heart pounded with anxiety; he knew something was about to happen. In his heart of hearts, he knew Shah was preparing to go to war to avenge his nephew. This was something he was not looking forward to, something that could make things worse. This was not his style of resolving disputes, but he knew he was not in total control anymore.

Shah noticed Jeffri in the car, stopped at the entrance, and beckoned for him. Abang Bob waited with him as the other men moved into the gymnasium.

"What's going on?" Jeffri addressed the question to Shah.

"What do you mean?"

"Why so many men?" Jeffri tilted his head toward the gymnasium.

"We're organizing a search party," Shah said, walking into the gym with Abang Bob and him in tow.

"Search party?"

"Yes, a search party for your friend, Mr. Kim Junior."

As they entered the gymnasium, Jeffri estimated there were about thirty men and kids gathered around in pods, smoking and talking in a low murmur. The square-ring was empty and no one seemed to be training. Their eyes were fixed expectantly towards Shah, Abang Bob, and him as they walked toward the office.

Shah sat heavily at his desk, Abang Bob on the worn-out sofa, while Jeffri chose to stand. Shah and Abang Bob simultaneously lit cigarettes.

"You want a drink?" Shah asked.

"Yes, I could use one."

"Beer?"

"100 Plus, if you have."

"Just beer and Coke."

"Coke, thanks."

Shah opened the fridge beside him, took two cans of beer and a Coke. He tossed the Coke to Jeffri and a beer to Abang Bob.

"How's your nephew?" Jeffri asked, taking a sip of the Coke.

"Critical but stable, the doctor said. I don't know what the shit that means. He's in ICU, and the next twenty-four hours will determine if he survives or dies," Shah said disgustedly.

"He's young and strong, I'm sure he'll come through fine," Jeffri offered.

"I've arranged for four men to provide protection for you," Abang Bob said. "They'll stay invisible, but they're there 24/7."

"Thanks," Jeffri said and handed over the five thousand cash as agreed.

"This'll cover five days. Longer than that, I'll need more."

Jeffri nodded.

"Listen, when you're driving, make sure you don't go too fast. Give them the chance to stay close."

"Okay, I'll try and remember that." Turning to Shah: "What have we got so far on them?"

"The SUV at AEON, it was from Very Happy Used Cars in Cheras. It's a front for laundering money for politicians. The used car is owned by a guy called Ah Siew. He used to be with 036, but was kicked out for drugs. According to the caretaker, the SUV was rented out to Tian Mun Fatt or Ah Fatt, the ex-bouncer."

"We got this Ah Fatt's address from the rental record?" Jeffri was excited.

Shah and Abang Bob laughed.

"You think these people keep records? They're not AVIS," Shah mocked. "They rent out to people they know or were recommended by people they know, and it's all cash upfront."

"So, we're back to square one," Jeffri said disappointedly.

"Give me some credit, will you?" Shah said, annoyed. He took a sip of beer and said, "My men located Ah Fatt. He's now working as a driver-cum-bodyguard for a Dato' at Prosperity Property. According to the office, he's on leave for a week."

"What about the SUV that was used to snatch OJ?"

"False plate. Now here's the crazy part. The false plate was registered to a motorbike that belongs to none other than Tian Mun Fatt himself," Shah laughed. "Dumb asshole!"

"Taking the easy way to do things," Abang Bob interjected.

"So we got him?" Jeffri asked.

"Not yet, but my men are watching his house."

"What if he doesn't come back? I mean, before they're done with OJ?"

"I'll give it a day. If he doesn't come back, we'll put some pressure on the family. You know, to make sure he comes back to see his loving family," Shah smiled. "Oh, before I forget, I got this name for you, David. You know who he is?"

"Where did you get the name from?" Jeffri asked, surprised.

"Doesn't matter where and how I got it. Do you know him?" Shah demanded, staring at him intensely.

"No," Jeffri lied. He feared Shah's intentions.

"Your friend did not mention him to you?"

"No."

"Well, he's a long-time client of your friend's law firm, the man your friend's accountant called that night at Healy Mac's. That night the snatch team missed him by a few minutes, but got him the next day," Shah sneered. "I've got his contact number. I think I'll give him a call and set up a meeting."

Jeffri felt uneasy with what he suspected Shah had in mind and the path it would almost certainly lead to: a bloody confrontation and all-out gang war. He knew there would be no winner, just losers. He also knew Shah would not back off, not with his nephew lying in ICU. Perhaps if his nephew was out of danger, he might be a little more receptive to a non-violent solution.

"Shah, I know you're angry and you want revenge. I don't blame you. If it was my nephew, I might want the same," Jeffri started cautiously. "I'm not telling you to back off, but I am asking you to put on hold whatever you've planned for the time being. I'm asking you to give me time to find a solution where no blood needs to be spilled. If I fail, then you do what you feel needs to be done."

Shah looked at Abang Bob, then at Jeffri. His face contorted, his eyes narrowed; it looked like he was about to go ballistic. He stood and walked around the desk, stopping in front of Jeffri. Shah placed both hands on his shoulders and gripped tightly. Jeffri thought he had crossed the line, that Shah was going to bundle him out of the office. He noticed Abang Bob too had stood. Jeffri did not know if Abang Bob wanted to stop Shah or help bundle him out. Jeffri did not care; he desperately needed time to think and come up with a solution without matters being aggravated by Shah's actions.

"I'll give you twenty-four hours," Shah said in a low, controlled voice.

"Forty-eight," Jeffri pleaded.

"Twenty-four, take it or leave it."

Jefrri knew not to push his luck. "Thanks."

## 37

Leaving the gymnasium, Jeffri remembered something told to him by a seasoned trial lawyer: don't mistake action for progress. But Jeffri knew he just could not sit around doing nothing. He called Yusof, his mother's friend or lover that had helped him with the loan shark. He asked if they could meet, and Yusof told him to come over to the house. Jeffri headed for the MRR2 and Wazed his way there. Like his previous visit, Jeffri parked his car by the roadside and walked to the gate. He pressed the bell and waited. A few seconds later the gate swung open.

Yusof was waiting for him at the front door with a big warm smile. He hugged Jeffri, saying he was glad to see him again and ushered him in. Jeffri was beginning to feel a little weird with the hug-greeting, but said nothing.

"How have you been keeping? Did you manage to overcome your problem?" Yusof asked, not in a prying manner.

"I'm still working on it," Jeffri said, sitting on the edge of one of the single sofas.

"Have you had lunch?"

"Yes thanks," Jeffri replied, glancing at the clock on the wall, which showed 2:55 p.m.

"Can I get you a drink?"

"Cold water will do, thanks."

Yusof left for the kitchen, and Jeffri seized his absence to scrutinize the pictures on the display table and walls. Yusof had indeed been indeed a police officer, and a senior one at that. There were pictures of him and his family, wife and two daughters. There was one of his daughters in a graduation gown holding a scroll. Yusof came back with a glass of cold water, noticed Jeffri looking at the pictures, and smiled.

"My wife passed away several years back, cancer. My daughters are all grown, married and leading their own lives," Yusof said with a smile, and Jeffri saw loneliness in his eyes. "How's your dear mother?" he asked, taking a seat.

"She's fine, thank you. Sorry to hear about your wife."

"Thank you. It was a long time ago, and I've gotten used to being all by myself," Yusof said with a tiny smile. "Glad to hear your mother is doing fine. I've always known that your mother is a survivor." He paused as if lost in old memories. He suddenly switched back to the present and asked, "You said over the phone you needed my advice?"

"I'm sorry to bother you, but I really don't know where else to turn to."

"No need to apologize. This'll give me the chance to do right by you after all these years," Yusof said with a smile.

With his head jumbled up by pressing issues, Jeffri missed what Yusof just said. "Have you heard of Asian Merchants (M) Sdn. Bhd?"

Jeffri noted Yusof's eyebrows arch at the name, then immediately his face reverted to normal.

"Asian Merchants," Yusof repeated to himself. "It does sound familiar. Why are you interested to know about this company?"

"I'm not sure yet, but I think my friend is somehow tangled with them."

"That was why you needed the money, to bail out your friend?"

"Part of it," Jeffri lied.

"You're a good man," Yusof said, pleased. "Are they still after your friend?"

"In a way, yes."

"Are they after more money?"

"No," Jeffri said and took a deep breath.

"Okay, you don't have to tell me if you don't want to."

They remained silent. Yusof with a pleasant smile looked at Jeffri, as if saying, *It's all right.* Jeffri drank the water and took another deep breath.

"Asian Merchants is a company that was on the police radar for a long time. The police suspected it was founded and managed by the triads, but could not gather enough evidence to take them down. I heard they have powerful people backing them, you know, politicians, top civil servants, judges. The corrupted, there were and still are many of them," Yusof said with disgust. "If I remember it, the company went way back before independence. So you can imagine how entrenched they are."

Silence shrouded the living room again.

"I was in SB, Special Branch, and this was not my area, but still, I did hear background conversations about them. I also heard in the early days they were really nasty, you know, all the triads' things, but I guess those were the days. Now, they may just be a business entity like any other corporation."

Not knowing how to respond, Jeffri just nodded. In his mind, he pictured parangs and samurai sword-wielding opium-addled triad members attacking their adversaries.

"Do you know of a man named David Lau Poh Seng?"

"I'm sorry, no."

Jeffri remained quiet, lost as to how he should move on from there.

"Jeffri, there's this man they call the Ancient One. If anyone can provide you with any information, he would be the person."

Yusof stood up and disappeared upstairs. A minute later, he came down and handed a piece of paper to Jeffri.

"He can be found at this address. Tell him I sent you."

Jeffri thanked him, and again the hug before parting.

In the car, Jeffri took out the piece of paper. The address written was the seventh floor, Menara Promet, Jalan Sultan Ismail, which was close to the hotel he was staying in. He decided to park the car at the hotel and walk there. Driving back to the hotel, he wondered about the protection detail arranged by Abang Bob. What did he say — *they'll be invisible to you.* He checked his rear-view mirror. There were many motorbikes; the riders and pillions were all wearing helmets and looked the same to him. How would he know if Abang Bob's men were really monitoring him? Entering the hotel's basement car park, he pushed the thoughts aside.

Jeffri emerged from the lobby and walked along Jalan Sultan Ismail toward the junction with Jalan P. Ramlee. He turned to look along Jalan P. Ramlee that was lined with pubs, bars and restaurants all the way to the Twin Towers. One of the city's happening nightspots for tourists and locals.

He waited for the light to turn green, and his thoughts wandered to the Ancient One. *This guy must be really old to be called that.* He pictured a skinny man, probably a hundred years old, thinning long white hair, a permanently wrinkled forehead, a long thin mustache reaching down to his chest and a similar arrowhead-shaped beard. He would probably be dressed in an all-white Chinese long-coat. In movies, white is worn by the good guys and black the bad guys.

Waiting for the elevator in the lobby of Menara Promet, Jeffri asked himself, *Why was the Ancient One in a high-rise building? Don't all these kung fu masters or sifus live in temples or monasteries surrounded by their disciples?*

Coming out of the elevator on the seventh floor, Jeffri saw a directional signage pointing to the right: **Ancient Chinese Medicine**. *That made sense, the Ancient One practicing ancient medicine.*

Abang Bob, the dismissed detective, informed Shah that the handphone number he asked to check was registered to one Lau Poh Seng. A reverse check with the transport department using Lau's identity card number revealed he owned two vehicles: a black SUV of the same model used to snatch OJ, and a black BMW 5 Series. The address listed was a colonial bungalow converted into an art gallery on Jalan Kia Peng.

The art gallery was placed under surveillance, and within two hours Lau Poh Seng a.k.a. David Lau was identified and tailed by Shah's men. Shah gave strict instructions to his men not to confront or engage him under any circumstances. It pained him to give the instruction, but Shah was determined to keep the twenty-four hours promise made to his former leader, Jeffri.

David Lau was seen leaving the art gallery on three occasions: once to meet with several men for lunch at Lai Po Heen Restaurant at Mandarin Oriental Hotel; once to JKG Tower in Jalan Raja Laut, where the Asian Merchants office was located; and once to Wilayah Hotel at Jalan Tiong Nam.

There was nothing suspicious about his movements as reported by Shah's men, until Abang Joko asked why a businessman like David would go to Wilayah Hotel. The hotel was rundown and barely operational now. Abang Joko should know because the Tiong Nam area was for the last decade crowded with Indonesians, mainly from Aceh. Wilayah Hotel used to be one of Abang Joko's favorite haunts. It used to have a spa that was more than just a spa, providing women brought in from China and Taiwan.

Jeffri tentatively entered Ancient Chinese Medicine and was instantly flattened by a pong of ginseng, tree bark, leaves, dried animal parts, snakeskin and what not. The right wall was lined with shelves displaying animals, insects and reptiles in jars filled with liquid. Underneath it was a row of red plastic chairs occupied by a couple of elderly women. The left wall was lined to the ceiling with dark brown wooden drawers, like safe-deposit boxes in banks. In front of the boxes was a long counter from one end of the wall to the other. Two very tired-looking old men in black Chinese outfits were busy working behind it. They were taking dried chips of wood, leaves and roots from the boxes, weighing them, and then putting them on pieces of brown wrapping paper.

One of the workers looked up at Jeffri suspiciously. Jeffri thought probably because he was Malay; he guessed not many Malays came into Ancient Chinese Medicine. Jeffri approached the counter and asked if he could see the Ancient One. The man gawked at him.

"The Ancient One, your boss," Jeffri said.

"Yisheng?"

It was Jeffri's turn to gawk at him.

"Yisheng, doctor?

"Yes, doctor."

The man tilted his head toward the door on his right.

"Thank you."

He knocked on the door and heard a deep voice say, "Quin jin," which he presumed to mean 'come in', and pushed the door open. Seated at a round table was a heavyset man in his late fifties with thick graying hair, no mustache or beard. Nothing like what Jeffri had imagined. The man saw Jeffri staring at him, like he was shocked or seeing a ghost, and asked, "Yes, how may I help you?"

"Sorry," Jeffri said, realizing he was staring, "I'm looking for the Ancient One."

"Who may I ask is looking for him?"

"I'm Jeffri. Tuan Yusof asked me to speak to him."

"I'm him. How's the Trusted One?"

"Trusted One?" Jeffri asked, confused.

The man laughed heartily. "We were together in the force. After a few years, I left to answer my calling in Chinese medicine. There were four of us in the force that were tight, and we gave each other codenames. I was the Ancient One, and he was the Trusted One," the man explained.

Jeffri let out a tiny laugh, "Shall I address you as the Ancient One, or …?"

"I'm Tan Boon Kai, call me Tan. Why did Yusof ask you to see me?"

"I need to know about Asian Merchants."

At the mention of the name, Tan involuntarily pulled back from his forward sitting position.

"I'm sorry, did I ask something wrong?" Jeffri asked.

"No, no. Just that it's been a long time since I heard the name," Tan said with a tiny grin. "After I left the force, I heard many things about them, but I never had any direct dealings with them."

Jeffri nodded. Tan noticed the disappointment on Jeffri's face.

"You cannot learn ancient Chinese medicine without learning about ancient Chinese people," Tan said with a smile. "To understand Asian Merchants, you must know the early Chinese migrants here, because they go back all the way to the glorious opium days."

Tan stood, walked to the counter behind him and poured Chinese tea into small porcelain cups. Then he brought the clay teapot and porcelain cups on a brown circular tray to the table. He handed one of the tiny cups to Jeffri and held the other up. Giving a slight bow, he drained his cup. Jeffri did likewise out of not knowing how he should respond. *Why must they use tiny cups?* Tan refilled their cups.

"The founders of Asian Merchants were a group of opium traders. As opium traders, they were also the operators of opium dens. Those days, the trade was legal and encouraged by our British masters. The British were suspicious of the Chinese. They were deemed as anti-colonial, but the colonizers needed tin ore that the Chinese were mining. To cut the story short, the British legalized opium dens so that they could keep the Chinese stoned and not became organized as a force. How wrong the British were." Tan paused, then he smiled. "You must understand I'm giving you not the official version of history."

"You mean they're triads? But that was so long ago."

Tan laughs, "Triads have been in this country since the Chinese arrived in the nineteenth century. If you read history you will see their presence in the Larut wars in 1874, the dispute on tin mining."

"Wow."

Tan took his tiny cup and drained it. Jeffri refrained from following suit.

"Back to your question. Asian Merchants, the company, was legally established in 1960. Over the years, its members and associate members gained prominent positions in politics. A couple of ministers, one deputy minister and a few are still high-profile office bearers in political parties. They expanded from import and export into almost every sector, property development, financing at one time, manufacturing, you name it. The man at the helm during the pioneering days was Lau Yu Lek, but he is deceased. The company had brought in a Malay Dato' and a few other professionals to sit on its board."

"Is David Lau Poh Seng one of the board members?"

"Now, David Lau, that's someone you don't want to mess with."

"What do you mean?"

"From what I heard, he's in love with the old ways, the cleaver-brandishing and brass-knuckle ways … the colorful traditional triad ways. That's not their way anymore, I mean, the Asian Merchants. Now they run businesses. They already have solid footing in all the sectors, and there is no need for the knife-wielding and parang-slashing anymore. They leave all that to the gangs and thugs."

"But David Lau still does it?"

"Yes."

"Who's this David Lau?"

"Hmmm, that's difficult to answer," Tan the Ancient One said with a wide grin. "By that, I mean there are several stories about him. You see, Dato' Lau's family, his wife and two children, were killed in a road accident when he was just starting his political career. Yes he remarried, but they did not have any children. Some say his new wife is sterile, and some say the trauma of losing his family stopped him from starting a new one. Then one day, David appeared in his life. When asked, Dato' introduced him as his nephew, the son of his younger brother. That was the official version."

Tan took a slow sip of his tea, like he was deliberating whether he should continue. Jeffri looked at him, his forehead wrinkled.

"And the unofficial version?"

"This's where the stories get a little muddled. There were stories that David was his son from an affair with one of his campaign workers. To save his political career, which at that time was on a fast track, he managed to get his brother to raise David as his own. David's biological mother was paid and made to promise not to breathe a word of it to anyone. I was told even David did not know of it and never knew his real mother."

"The Lau family seems to have many skeletons and vows."

Tan the Ancient One chuckled. "Scandals and affairs are nothing new. If anything, there were more then than now. You just have to read the history of kings and queens to know it was a way of life in those days."

"Who has control over him?"

"I don't know, but if anyone does, it would be Dato' Lau Tze Lek."

"You mean the Deputy Finance Minister?"

"Ex-Deputy Finance Minister," Tan smiled. "Nothing was ever proven, but in tight circles of Chinese businessmen, you hear whispers he's the man behind Asian Merchants."

"Let me get this clear. If I'm in a situation with David Lau, I should see Dato' Lau Tze Lek?"

"I don't know what situation you're in with David Lau, but what I'm sure of is you do not want to deal directly with him."

38

✕

Back at his hotel room, Jeffri reflected on what the Ancient One told him about the triads. He did some research on the internet. He read about the Larut Wars and, as he expected, the Ancient One was right. He then read about the modern triads to understand what he will be facing. He discovered that after the 2014 massive operation to clean up secret societies and gangs undertaken by the police through their newly formed Special Task Force on Organized Crimes (STAFOC) and Special Task Force for Anti-Vice, Gaming and Gangsterism (STAGG), the gangland landscape, strategies and tactics changed. Big secret societies broke up into smaller units, relabeled themselves using numerical names rather than Chinese names, and set up legal business entities. Gang clashes and territorial disputes were settled through table-talks rather than bloodbaths. However, there were still the occasional clashes between gangs when amicable settlements failed.

Lately in Klang Valley, there seemed to be a revival of settling disputes using the old ways. Restaurants and entertainment outlets were attacked by bands of men with parangs and samurai swords. Fixtures, furniture and equipment were destroyed and workers injured. After talking to the Ancient One, Jeffri strongly believed David Lau might have his hands in a few of them.

Before he left, Tan the Ancient One had given him a name, a person that might be able to put him in touch with Dato' Lau Tze Lek, the Sifu or Godfather, whom Tan claimed to be the man behind Asian Merchants.

Shah knew the Tiong Nam area, once the hotbed for the triads, was infiltrated by the Indonesians, especially from Aceh. He sought the assistance of Abang Joko. He asked if Abang Joko's men could get the traders and food operators there to act as listening posts and lookouts for David Lau's BMW and the SUV used to snatch OJ.

Within an hour, he had a hundred pairs of ears listening to the beat of the streets and a hundred pairs of eyes watching vehicle registration numbers.

Jeffri lay in bed. He needed to come up with a purpose, what he wanted to achieve in meeting Dato' Lau. He could not approach Dato' Lau without an objective. He would be ridiculed if he was to ask Dato' Lau for help to forgive his buddy for breaking a traditional vow made by his grandfather.

*What was the vow made by OJ's grandfather? How could it be broken without any dire consequence? Did OJ know what it was? Was it written and documented in the files?*

Jeffri revisited the files. He found many documents in Chinese. *Could one of these be the vow?* He could find nothing that looked like it was written in blood or red ink. He needed someone he could trust to translate these documents, but who?

Jeffri knew time was running out for OJ. He needed to stop David Lau before it was too late. The saying "don't mistake action for progress" popped into his head. "Fuck the saying," he said, and made a call.

"Shah, I need some info," Jeffri said.

"What?"

"Do your guys know the address where OJ spent the night with the woman?"

"Why?"

"I need to talk to the woman, but I don't have her number."

"Let me check and call you back?"

Sarah was taking a nap, preparing herself for what she anticipated would be a long and draggy dinner with Dato' Tarmizi, Philippe and Roger. The doorbell woke her up. Since returning to Kuala Lumpur, she hadn't had any visitors except for the night she brought OJ home. No one knew of her existence in the condominium except for Lina, whose name she'd used to enter into the lease agreement. Her bad experience in the Big Apple with her son, Imran, made her take every precautionary measure not to reveal where she was staying.

Apprehensively, she got off the bed and walked barefoot to the front door. In her mind, it had to be OJ. Who else? She had never even ordered a delivery meal. The thought of last night brought a smile to her face. She guessed he wanted more, and so did she.

Looking through the peephole, she was shocked to see Jeffri's face. She tried to see if OJ was with him, but there was no sign of him

"What the fuck does he want?" she cursed under her breath.

The doorbell rang again, startling her, and she pulled away from the door.

"Who is it?" she asked, unwilling to open the door, stalling so she could come up with an excuse.

"Jeffri, OJ's friend. We met before."

"Where's OJ, and how did you find me?"

"Please, can I come in? It's about OJ. I need to ask you something, but I can't do it through the door. Please."

Jeffri heard the deadbolt click, followed by another click from the doorknob, and the door opened, revealing beautiful Sarah's apprehensive face.

"What about OJ? Is he okay? Where is he?"

"OJ's fine," Jeffri lied, not wishing to alarm her.

Sarah let Jeffri in and led him to the sofa. The sofa where she and OJ made passionate love for the first time.

"May I be blunt with you?" Jeffri asked, looking straight at Sarah.

"As blunt as you wish," Sarah replied, holding Jeffri's stare.

The black SUV used to snatch OJ was spotted by one of Abang Joko's Aceh traders parked in a back alley of Jalan Tiong Nam. Shah immediately deployed several men to monitor the SUV. He was anxiously waiting at his gymnasium for a report of a sighting, when Abang Joko walked in carrying a small black plastic bag. He placed the bag on Shah's desk and said, "Untraceable."

Shah opened the bag and took out a small package wrapped in newspaper. He slowly unwrapped the package and took out a .38 snub-nose Smith & Wesson. It looked like the standard model with a black steel body and wooden handle, something similar to those he had seen used by police detectives. He pushed the lock and flicked the cylinder out. All chambers were loaded. There were five bullets. He flicked the cylinder back into position. Shah had always preferred a revolver to a pistol. His reason was unlike a pistol, a revolver does not leave empty shell casings behind at the scene. That is one piece of evidence less, and therefore one chance less for the crime scene forensics to find a fingerprint.

"Only one?" he asked.

"Unless you want a 9mm Cobra," Abang Joko replied, lighting a cigarette.

"I need two at least. When can you get me one more?"

"I need a couple of days. Revolvers seem to be the flavor of the month. Found them yet?"

Shah shook his head. "Matter of time."

"What have you got planned?"

"Depends on how they want to play it."

"Let me know if you need my assistance."

"Thanks."

3 9

✕

It was close to 5:30 in the evening when Jeffri left Sarah's condominium. Sarah was upfront with him but non-committal. He did not expect her to agree right away, but things might work out according to his plan given time. *The question is, how long will it take?* Jeffri asked himself, having second thoughts. In his mind, only the wording of the vow made by UJ's grandfather could answer it.

Hitting Jalan Raja Chulan, he was caught in the after-office hour traffic crawl. Inching his way in the bumper to bumper traffic, he pulled out his handphone and called the number given by the Ancient One. Jeffri introduced himself and dropped the Ancient One's name. He detected calmness in the voice of the man on the other end at the mention of Tan Boon Kai the Ancient One. After agreeing to a fee of RM3,000 for the introduction, the man who wanted to be called Tony said he would call back.

"What shall I say is the purpose of this meeting?"

"Tell Dato' it's related to the Kim family. He'll know. Tony, if you can arrange for the meeting today, I'll double your fee," Jeffri said.

"When today?" Tony asked excitedly.

"Any time before midnight."

"Okay, I'll get back to you soonest."

Jeffri called Shah to inquire about his nephew.

"The doctor said there are signs of improvement, and they're confident he'll pull through," Shah said. "They said they'll be sure by tomorrow morning."

Jeffri let out a sigh of relief. He believed if the nephew made it, it would at least calm Shah down a little. His hunger for retribution may be satisfied with something less than blood.

"Great news. I'm sure he'll be fine," Jeffri said. "Any news on OJ?"

"We located the SUV used to snatch him, but nothing yet. I've put eyes on it just in case the bastards appear."

"Stay calm, okay, Shah? Remember, you gave me twenty-four hours."

"Yeah, yeah. Where're you? Why are you holed up in a hotel?"

"How did you know where I was staying?"

"Abang Bob told me. You want me to ask Abang Bob to put some guys on your office and house?"

Jeffri felt confident that Abang Bob's men were actually watching over him. "Could he?" On second thought, Jeffri said, "No, I don't want any confrontation. There's nothing for them to find anyway."

"Okay, your call. What's at Promet building?"

"Went to meet up with a man," Jeffri said without elaborating.

"Anything I should know about?"

"I'm working on something, but nothing's firm yet. I'll tell you once I have something solid."

One of Shah's men monitoring the black SUV spotted a Chinese man emerging from the back entrance of Wilayah Hotel, heading in the direction of the vehicle. As he neared the SUV, its indicator lights flickered, accompanied by a beep. The man reached the SUV, stood at the driver's door, and briefly scanned the surrounding area. Two of Shah's men on motorbikes rode into the alley, coming to the rear of the SUV. The man turned to look at them. Another two of Shah's men that were hiding behind a dumpster next to the SUV crept up behind the Chinese man and hit the back of his head with a blackjack.

The Chinese man dropped to the ground like a full garbage bag. The four of them loaded him into the SUV and drove off, escorted by three motorbikes. The driver called Shah and was told to blindfold the man and bring him to the gymnasium. The man regained consciousness and fought to break free, but a blow to his head with a helmet rendered him unconscious again. They bound his hands, blindfolded him, and sped towards Ampang Kuala Lumpur Elevated Highway (AKLEH), turning off to Kampong Pandan.

Reaching the gymnasium, they hid the SUV behind the gymnasium and dragged the unconscious man to Shah's office through the rear door. They sat him in a chair in the middle of the office. Shah asked his gym caretaker to bring the smelling salts and ran it under the man's nose.

After several passes, the man groggily regained consciousness. Shah took off the blindfold and gave him several wake-up slaps on the face. The stinging pain from the slaps did its job. The man opened his eyes. He struggled to break free. Four big strong hands held him down.

"What's your name?" Shah asked.

"Yat chew," the man cursed in Cantonese, which meant 'Go to hell.'

One of Shah's men standing by his side let loose a whooping smack on his head.

"Dew nay lo mo," the man cursed, meaning 'Go fuck your mother,' his head bowed in agony.

Not understanding what was cursed, Shah's men laughed. Shah told one of the men to call in one of his nephew's boys present during OJ's snatching. A moment later, a kid was escorted into the office.

"Is he the one that knifed Nik?" Shah asked.

The kid shook his head. He was told to leave the office. As soon as the kid stepped out, Shah gave the man a kick to his head. The man flew off the chair and landed heavily on the floor. Blood dripped from his mouth. He shrieked in agony and balled into a protective fetal position. Shah stepped over to him and landed another kick to his back. The man arched backward and screamed, spitting blood onto the floor.

"What's your name?" Shah asked, his voice low but threatening.

"Ah Fatt, Tian Mun Fatt," the man stuttered, spilling blood.

"That was easy, wasn't it?" Shah said with a tiny smile. "Who stabbed my nephew?"

"Johnny, Johnny stabbed the man."

Shah signaled to his men to lift Ah Fatt back onto the chair.

"Where's Johnny?"

Ah Fatt stared at Shah, defiance written all over his face. Shah grinned. He knew Ah Fatt was not going to sell out his friend so cheaply. He needed more persuasion. Shah pulled out the .38 Smith & Wesson from the back of his jeans and pressed the nozzle onto Ah Fatt's right kneecap. Ah Fatt gaped at him, wide-eyed. He slowly cocked the hammer. Ah Fatt shut his eyes tight, turned his head sideways, pleaded and begged.

"No, no, please, please no," Ah Fatt cried.

"Where's Johnny?"

"Wilayah Hotel."

"Which room?"

"Two-zero-one."

"What's he doing there?"

"Guarding ..." Ah Fatt stopped mid-sentence.

"Guarding Mr. Kim," Shah finished his sentence for him.

Ah Fatt nodded, and Shah uncocked the hammer and removed the revolver from his kneecap.

"How many of you in the room?"

"Just him and me. I was going out to buy dinner."

Shah gazed at Ah Fatt's face and brought back the .38 Smith & Wesson to his right kneecap. Before he could cock it, Ah Fatt cried, "True, just him and me, please, please."

"Who's David?"

"My boss."

"Which gang?"

"No gang. He hires people, pays them to do things. He tells us what to do, we do."

"He's a freelance boss, like the general with no army."

"Yes."

"Normally he hires people from which gang?"

"I don't know. This is the first job I'm doing for him."

"What about Johnny?"

"Johnny said he has done work for him before. He said David was from a powerful family, that he's got money and wants to start his own operation, his own outfit."

Sarah met Philippe and Roger at the Hilton Hotel, and they took the hotel limousine to Songket Restaurant, a Malay fine dining restaurant at Jalan Yap Kwan Seng. The restaurant was well-known for its cuisine and accompanying cultural performance. They were early and ordered their drinks while they waited for Dato' Tarmizi.

Roger asked for a beer and was politely told by Sarah that the restaurant did not serve alcoholic beverages. Roger raised his eyebrows disappointedly.

"Malay means Muslim here in this country. Restaurants are prohibited from serving alcohol. It's haram, and no pork either."

"You can survive a few hours without alcohol, can't you?" Philippe jested with Roger. "Do you want to order, or wait for Dato'?"

"Best we let him do the ordering," Sarah said.

Fifteen minutes later Dato' Tarmizi arrived, ushered by a hostess in a lovely light green kebaya. Sarah noticed Tarmizi seemed a little edgy. He kept looking behind him and around the restaurant. She remembered what happened during their first meeting, and casually scanned the restaurant. She did not spot anyone looking at them other than the casual glances of people coming and going. They stood to greet him, and Sarah made the introductions.

After Dato' ordered his drink, Sarah asked if he would like to choose their meal. He ordered beef rendang, fried chicken with thick soya sauce, yellow fish curry and vegetables.

"I think that should be enough," Tarmizi declared.

"We can always order more, should we want to," Sarah agreed.

"How was your flight? I'm sure you must still be tired," Tarmizi said, making small talk.

"The flight was good, thank you," Philippe answered. "So Dato', I heard you're an excellent golfer."

"Average," Tarmizi replied modestly.

Earlier, Sarah had suggested they avoid any subject related to the real reason for their presence in Kuala Lumpur, unless raised by Dato' Tarmizi. She also advised them to avoid any subject on the political situation in the country, the new coalition government infighting, and the drastic outflow of foreign investments. Philippe agreed there would be plenty of time to talk about the power plant deal while they golfed. The evening was spent talking about golf, the many beautiful and interesting places they visited, and football, mainly the Champions League which has a huge following in Malaysia.

Jeffri received the call from the introducer Tony, informing him the meeting with Dato' Lau was set for 9 p.m. Tony texted him the address for the meeting — in Taman Taynton View, Kuala Lumpur. Jeffri knew it to be somewhere in Cheras. He asked Tony to WhatsApp his bank account number and told him that he would bank in one thousand ringgit within the hour and the balance of five thousand after he had the meeting. After some protest, Tony reluctantly agreed.

Shah led a team of four men to Jalan Tiong Nam. He instructed two men to watch the entrance and alert him should David in his black BMW appear. He and two other men entered the hotel and approached the reception counter. An elderly Chinese man came out from the back room to attend to them. To avoid suspicion, Shah registered for a room using a fake name. He paid the fifty ringgit, took the key, and went up the stairs to level two to room 201.

Drawing his snub-nose Smith & Wesson, Shah kicked the lock set at the door. The plywood door flew open, and he and his two men barged in. Johnny, who was engrossed in playing games on his handphone, jumped off the chair. Before he could react, Shah's revolver was pointed directly at his chest. OJ, who was also caught by surprise, fell backward with his chair. Both OJ and Johnny gawked at Shah and his men, dumbstruck.

One of Shah's men lifted OJ up and untied him. The other man grabbed Johnny into a chicken wing arm lock. Shah stepped up to Johnny, pressed the revolver under his chin and snarled, "One word from you, and it'll be your last."

With an arm lock on him, Johnny barely managed to nod his acknowledgment. Shah called his men on standby outside the hotel to bring the car up front. The man, who was assisting OJ, grabbed hold of Johnny's hands and secured them with a cable-tie.

They took the stairs down, and as they passed the reception, Shah flashed a blue card to the elderly receptionist and said, "Police." He stepped up to the counter and demanded the elderly man return his fifty ringgit. The flare in Shah's eyes and the gun in his hand told the elderly man the point wasn't worth arguing.

Outside, Shah's men dumped Johnny into the trunk of their car. Shah told them to take him to his carwash in Pandan Indah. He walked OJ to his car. Driving away, he made a call to his gym caretaker. He told Tyson to send Ah Fatt to his carwash and lock him in the storeroom. Then he called Jeffri.

"I've got your friend," Shah said.

"OJ? How? Let me speak with him," Jeffri asked.

"Yes. Don't matter how, told you I'd get him and I got him. He's okay, just a little tired and dazed. Here."

Shah passed the phone to OJ.

"OJ, how are you?" Jeffri asked excitedly. "Are you okay? Did they hurt you?"

"I'm fine. Like your friend said, just a little tired and confused."

"That's okay. We'll talk when you're here. What's important is that you're safe. Can you pass me back to Shah?"

OJ passed the phone to Shah.

"Where do you want me to stash him?" Shah asked.

"Stash … oh, you mean to send him. Send him to me here."

"You're sure?"

"Yes, I am. This hotel is patronized mainly by Malays. The chance of him being recognized is slim. Anyway, Abang Bob's men are watching me, right?"

"Okay, will be there in fifteen. What's your room number?"

"Six-one-zero, see you. Shah, anyone got hurt?"

"Not yet," Shah said laughed and terminated the call.

Before leaving the car at the Concorde Hotel car park, Shah made OJ put on a baseball cap. He told OJ to walk with his head bowed to avoid the hotel CCTV cameras as a precautionary measure. They walked into the hotel through the back entrance and headed straight to the bank of elevators, avoiding the lobby and reception area.

Jeffri greeted OJ with a big smile and a hug. Shah told them he had urgent business to attend to.

"What urgent matter?" Jeffri asked, concerned.

"None of your business," Shah replied and left.

Turning to OJ, Jeffri asked, "What happened to your face? Are you okay?"

"It's nothing. I'm fine," OJ said, flashing a forced smile as he sat at the edge of the bed. He lightly touched his swollen eye and dried blood. "Who's he?" OJ asked, jerking his head toward the closed door.

"Shah, my childhood friend. We need to get you to a doctor, let him look at the cut again."

"I'm fine, we can do that later. I'll put some ice on it," OJ said, and took a can of Coca-Cola from the mini fridge and pressed it to his brow. "He has a gun. I thought he was going to shoot Johnny."

"Did he? Who's Johnny?"

"Noooo. One of the men who kidnapped me."

"Was he the one that stabbed the kid?"

OJ nodded. "Who was the kid?"

"Shah's nephew."

"Oh my god, I'm so sorry."

"Yeah, me too." Jeffri inhaled deeply, "Where's Johnny now?"

"Shah had him. His men threw him in the trunk of their car and left."

"Shit," Jeffri cussed, fearing the worst. "Do you know where they're taking him?"

"I heard something about a carwash."

"I think I know where it is. Have you eaten? Would you like to have something?"

"Can I get a burger or sandwich and beer?"

"Sure, we'll order room service."

Jeffri made the order for room service, and while waiting, he asked OJ to tell him everything from the time he was snatched. From what OJ told him, Jeffri made two conclusions:

The files were important to David for whatever reason. Perhaps there were incriminating documents in them which could be his bargaining chip, and

They did not kill Kim Senior, therefore they had nothing to fear with the police, at least for that death.

*How do I use all these facts to my advantage? David would be in a rage at losing OJ and was probably alerting all his men to look out for him. He might also be preparing to go to war against whoever took OJ from him. How do I stop it before more lives are lost?*

Jeffri told OJ he needed to go out. During his absence, OJ was not to answer any call or respond to any knock on the door. Their situation was grave and he needed to see someone to try and mitigate things. For the moment, Jeffri saw no reason to inform OJ of his visit to Sarah's condo and their little chat.

Shah headed toward AKLEH and turned off at Kampung Pandan Indah. He was anxious to confront the man who stabbed his nephew. Eager to inflict similar pain and suffering on him. A fitting retribution for Nik. His handphone rang; it was Jeffri.

"What?" Shah snapped, annoyed at his salivating thoughts being interrupted.

"Shah, where're you?" Jeffri asked, his voice filled with concern.

"On my way to attend to some business. Why?"

"Has it got something to do with the man, Johnny, you grabbed?"

"None of your business."

"Shah, please, I'm begging you. Don't do anything stupid. You gave me twenty-four hours and I still have until tomorrow. Please Shah."

The line went quiet. Jeffri could hear Shah's heavy breathing, like he was trying to control his anger.

"Shah," Jeffri said.

"Yeah, okay, you have until noon. After that, he's all mine."

The line went dead.

40

✕

Jeffri left the hotel at 8 p.m. and headed south toward the Kuala Lumpur-Seremban Highway. Traffic leaving the city was still heavy and it made him anxious. He used Waze and followed the verbal directions given by a very English-sounding female. Usually he would smile at the pronunciation of Malay words like 'jalan' as 'jelan', but tonight, it irritated him.

At 8:47 p.m., Waze announced; *you have arrived at your destination*. Jeffri decided to make a pass to observe the surrounding areas, and the Waze female announced, *in two hundred meters make a U-turn*. Jeffri said, "Oh, shut up," and turned the app off.

His destination was a huge double-story bungalow, more like a mansion with high brick walls and decorative stainless steel gate. The compound was brightly lit and so was the bungalow. Jeffri made the U-turn and parked on the opposite side of the road.

Jeffri tried to anticipate: would Dato' Lau be alone, would David be there, or would he even get to meet Dato' Lau? Would he walk out of this bungalow, or would he disappear like the journalist who walked into the Arab embassy in Turkey? After all, except for the introducer Tony, whom he only spoke to over the phone, no one knew of this meeting. Not even the Ancient One. *Shit, I should've made better preparations*. Instinctively, he looked front and back, trying to spot Abang Bob's men. None were seen.

✕

The saying 'Don't mistake action for progress', came back to haunt him. Pushing it aside, he told himself, *I have to, no, I need to do something, and this is doing something.* Jeffri stepped out of the car and walked across the road to the gate. He spotted a bell button and pressed it once. He could hear a faint chime of the electronic bell echoing from inside the bungalow.

Through the decorative gate, he saw two huge Dobermans running toward him. The beasts growled at him, showing fearsome teeth. "Fuck," Jeffri said, taking a few steps back.

"Duke, Prince, heel!" a woman's voice called from the front door.

The two beasts turned and ran to her, tails wagging, and sat with their tongues hanging out. One side of the gate opened, but Jeffri was too terrified to move. The woman noticed Jeffri rooted to the ground, said something to the two beasts, and they disappeared around the bungalow.

"It's okay, you can come in. They won't bother you," called the woman.

Jeffri let out a sigh of relief and forced his legs to move. As he passed the gate, he expected to see armed men guarding the compound. There were none — *they're probably inside with Dato' Lau.* His paranoia was running wild. The gate closed behind him, and as he approached the front door, the woman proffered her hand.

"I'm Isabelle, and you must be Encik Jeffri from Jeffri & Associates."

"Yes, and it's a pleasure to meet you," Jeffri replied, taking her long slender hand.

Isabelle was in her early thirties, tall and slender with long flowing jet black hair. Her eyes were not slit-shaped like most

Chinese. Jeffri figured she must have undergone cosmetic surgery. Her smile was pleasingly warm and sincere and her hand soft to the touch.

"Come in, Dato' is waiting for you in the study," Isabelle said, and led the way.

✕

The living hall was expensively furnished with beige leather sofas, a huge low-center table with matching side tables, a crystal chandelier, a showcase of exotic ornaments from all over the world, and lush, thick carpeting. *Luxuries of the rich and powerful.* Isabelle led him through a passage, Jeffri guessed, that went to an annex building. She knocked softly on the door, cracked it open, poked her head in and announced.

"Encik Jeffri is here."

She opened the door wide and gestured for Jeffri to follow her. Jeffri was surprised to see Dato' Lau was in a wheelchair. He looked old. To Jeffri, he looked more like the Ancient One than Tan the Ancient One of Ancient Chinese Medicine. Jeffri could not estimate how old Sifu was; his face was wrinkled, the skin under his chin flabby, his hands covered with liver spots and his white hair thinning.

Jeffri stepped closer to him and extended his hand. "Dato', thank you for seeing me."

Dato' Lau shook his hand, but said nothing in reply. Isabelle indicated Jeffri should take a seat, then she walked around the wheelchair and stood behind it. Jeffri sat, and Isabelle pushed the wheelchair closer to him.

"Tony said you wanted to talk about the Kim family," Dato' Lau went straight to the point.

Jeffri was surprised to hear the clarity and firmness of his voice. "Yes, and please forgive me if I'm in any way encroaching into areas deemed sensitive or private and confidential."

Dato' Lau nodded.

"Dato' knows of Kim & Kim, a law firm ..."

"Yes, of course. The late Kim Senior was a dear friend of mine and the family. What about the firm?"

"I didn't know the late Mr. Kim Senior personally, but I'm a friend of his son OJ, or Kim Junior. I came to know Kim & Kim had been the law firm which handled all matters for Asian Merchants." Jeffri paused for reaction.

Dato' Lau said nothing and gave nothing away through his facial expression at the mention of Asian Merchants.

"I was made to understand it all started with Grandpa Kim and continued through to Kim Senior." Jeffri took a deep breath, rearranging his thoughts. "When Kim Senior retired, the helm was to pass on to Kim Junior. Kim Junior was not aware of the vow or oath made by Grandpa Kim, and ... and upon discovering the undertakings, he ... he ..."

"Decided to break it," Dato' Lau finished the sentence for Jeffri.

"Yes, break the bond," Jeffri repeated, "but OJ meant no harm."

"As a Malay man, you may not know the implications of a vow or oath, I mean a traditional Chinese vow and oath. It cannot be broken without consequences, unless of course by mutual agreement. It can only be broken by the laws of nature or an act of god."

Jeffri nodded, "Dato', I apologize for my ignorance. May I know the nature of the vow made?"

"There was nothing written. In the old days, we did it through the time-honored traditional ceremony: by slaughtering a white chicken and prayers. Grandpa Kim made a vow that his family shall serve the Lau family until the last of the Kims. What it means is that so long as there is a male Kim in the family, he must make every effort to be a lawyer, and then serve the Lau family like his forefathers."

"I'm sorry; the terms were it had to be a male and that he should try to be a lawyer? What if he couldn't make it as a lawyer?"

"The females do not carry the surname once they're married, and their children won't have the surname of their grandfather. Then the law of nature ends the vow."

Jeffri pondered on what was said. "The vow is broken if OJ is dead, and there is no more male descendants of the Kim family."

Dato' Lau looked intensely at Jeffri. "In Kim Junior's case, yes, that's so."

"Dato' knows of David?"

"Of course, he's my nephew. I also know that he has Kim Junior."

Jeffri nodded. Interestingly, the news of OJ's rescue had not made it to the streets yet, or at least to Dato's ears. For whatever reason, David must have kept it under wraps.

"David's heart is in the right place, but his methods can be crude and reckless. He's young and hot-headed, unlike his sister Isabelle here. You see, he missed out on the old days and its ways. He heard too many stories from his uncles and granduncles about them. How issues and disputes were settled, I'm sure you know them too. I suppose when you're young and enthralled with too many glorified stories about the underworld ways, you would start to romanticize it," Dato' Lau said with a tiny smile. "David, well, he wanted to bring back the old ways. He felt muscle and brute force were mightier than the brain. Those days are gone, now we don't dirty our hands. Now, like all legitimate businesses, we get corrupt politicians and policy makers to do our dirty jobs," he genuinely laughed. "We don't need to go back to the old days."

Jeffri nodded understandingly. He supposed there were many who shared David's sentiment on resolving issues. He himself knew a few of them.

"Dato', what if I tell you I can get the files. Would that be sufficient to stop David from doing any harm to Kim Junior?"

"How, may I ask, are you going to get the files? I was made to understand the files were missing. David said Kim Junior must have hidden them."

Jeffri took the copy he made of the ledger and handed it to Dato' Lau. "Here's proof I can get my hands on the files."

Dato' Lau took a brief look at the photocopy, lifted his head, and asked, "Did Kim Junior give the files to you?"

"No he did not, in fact he doesn't even know where the files are."

"Interesting," Dato' Lau said, his eyes narrowed to look intensely at Jeffri, "and you can get them back for me?"

"Yes, I believe I know who has them, and I know how to get them back. I'll also promise Dato' there shall be no copy made of the files."

"It sounds to me like you already have them," Dato' Lau said, looking intimidatingly at Jeffri. "Returning the files may not be enough to break the vow. You see, the files rightly belong to me, to us."

"What if I give Dato' my word that OJ will be dead. Will that break the vow?"

Dato' Lau laughed and Isabelle smiled. "Are you going to kill Kim Junior, your friend? The man whose life you're here trying to save? No, I don't think so. I think you're going to fake his death, like in the movies, aren't you?" Dato' Lau let out a chuckle. "It has been tried by others before, and I assure you, it didn't work."

"No Dato', I'm not going to fake his death. OJ will be dead, but I need time."

"Time?" Dato's forehead contorted. "How much time?"

"Thirty days."

"Thirty days to kill one man?" Dato' Lau mused. "How are you killing him, with food? Are you feeding him to death?"

Jeffri noticed Isabelle stifle a smile, and he smiled openly at Dato's tease.

Wiping the smile off his face, Jeffri said, "I just need Dato' to trust me, and I'll make sure OJ is dead. Once the files are returned, Dato' must hold David back and allow me thirty days. It may be sooner, but let's stick to thirty days for the time being."

"Isabelle my dear, what do you think? Encik Jeffri is asking me to trust him. Should I?"

"I just need to understand one thing before answering," Isabelle said, addressing Jeffri. "Why are you doing this? You're a Malay and Kim Junior is Chinese. Why are you risking your life to save his?"

"In my eyes he's not Chinese, he's a friend, a friend who needs my help. I'm sure he'd do the same for me or his friends that need help."

"I admire your principles and belief in friendship. Such rare qualities in our country nowadays. We've become very racist. Yes, Uncle, I trust Encik Jeffri until otherwise proven."

"Thank you, Miss Isabelle." Jeffri noted she did not say anything about the title Miss.

"Isabelle has a level head, a business mind, unlike David. I value her views and judgement. As you requested, I shall hold David back and put a halt to whatever he's intending to do. When you return the files to Isabelle, you shall have your thirty days. Good night, Encik Jeffri."

Jeffri stood, extended his hand for a handshake, thanked Dato' and bade him good night. Isabelle walked him out and handed him her business card.

"It's been a pleasure knowing you," Isabelle said.

"Likewise, thank you. I'll be in touch soon. Good night."

## 41

While Jeffri was at Dato' Lau's house, Shah was at his carwash in Pandan Indah. The night was usually his carwash's peak business period, but he told the workers to close shop for the day and sent them off. Once the workers had left, Shah told his men to bring Johnny out of the trunk. Seated in the car waiting for his men to set things up, Shah took out his Smith & Wesson. It felt good in his hand; it fed his anger. He clicked the cylinder open and smiled.

The men sat Johnny on a plastic chair in the office at the rear of the carwash. Inside the car Shah lit a cigarette, taking several long drags, staring at Johnny who was quiet, looking defeated and terrified. His head was bowed, avoiding eye contact with Shah's men.

Shah barged out of the car, walked ominously toward Johnny and pulled out the Smith & Wesson. Without warning, he fired a shot to the wall behind Johnny. His unexpected action and the exploding sound made his men dive for cover, eyes fixed on him. The sound reverberated in the empty shop, the smell of gunpowder strong in the air. Face ashen, body shaking, mouth agape and eyes bulging with terror, Johnny looked up to see the revolver pointed directly at him. Three feet in front of him, Shah stopped and cocked the hammer.

Staring right into Johnny's eyes, he said, "That was for show. This is for you."

Johnny closed his eyes tightly and sobbed, which sounded like a prayer. Shah noticed the sudden wetness in Johnny's trousers and liquid dripping from the chair to the floor.

"Be a man, open your eyes," Shah barked.

Johnny nervously obeyed, but before he could say anything, Shah pulled the trigger. The revolver went 'tak', and Johnny screamed, falling backward to the floor. His body was stiff, unmoving in a fetal position, weeping.

Shah laughed until his eyes watered. Realizing what had just happened, his men joined in the laugh. They picked Johnny's limp body up and shoved him onto the chair.

"That was a good one, Boss," one of his men said.

"He peed in his pants," another one stated, followed by laughter.

"Scared the shit out of us too," said one.

Pleased with the stunt he pulled, Shah lit a cigarette and said, "Should have videoed it to sent to his boss."

"We can do it again," one of his men said.

"It won't work the second time. You won't get the same reaction. Did you see the expression on his face? Priceless. For that matter on your faces too," Shah said and laughed at his men.

He walked up to Johnny, who was still shaking and breathing hard. Again, without warning, he stubbed out his cigarette on Johnny's cheek. Johnny screamed, pulling his face away.

"Why did you stab my nephew?" Shah asked calmly.

"Sorry," Johnny repeatedly mumbled with his head as far away from Shah as he could manage.

"Why didn't you give him a chance, warn him to back off?"

"I panicked."

"Bullshit, he was not even armed."

Johnny did not answer.

"You want to show off to your boss that you're the *man*, the fearless one and no one fucks with you, right?"

Johnny tilted his head to look at Shah. His audacity to look up angered Shah. In his head, he pictured Johnny proudly telling his boss, David, how he had knifed this punk who tried to stop him, that they would not cause any more trouble. Shah snapped and let loose a vicious open-palm slap across Johnny's face. Johnny's head spun to the right on impact, almost throwing him from the chair. His cheek turned bright red from the sting. Shah spat on him and said, "Who's the *man* now?"

Shah pulled a flick knife out from his pocket. He twirled it around, releasing the blade. He grinned, enjoying the fear in Johnny's eyes. He brought the blade to Johnny's stomach at the same spot where his nephew was stabbed.

"It was here, right?" he asked Johnny.

Johnny sucked in his stomach and held his breath, waiting for the imminent thrust of the blade.

"You better pray hard to whichever god you pray to that my nephew makes it through tonight. If he doesn't, you'll suffer the same fate as him."

It took every grain of self-control not to continue bashing Johnny, to knife him in the gut like he did to Nik. Johnny's handphone rang. Shah's men looked at him for instruction. Shah told them to take the handphone from Johnny's pocket. The screen displayed 'Taiko'.

Shah pressed answer. "Wheeeeeey," he mocked in Chinese.

"Who is this?" David demanded. "Where's Johnny?"

"Johnny's indisposed right now. May I help you, Mr. David?" Shah chuckled, enjoying the moment.

"Jeffri, are you Jeffri? You're the lawyer my men told me about. Where're my men?"

"Safe for the time being," Shah said.

"You touch them, and you're a dead man."

Shah laughed into the phone, "For a man who's on the losing end, you talk big don't you? Asshole."

"Fuck you. I'll hunt you down like a diseased dog, that's a promise."

"Your man here, Johnny, knifed my nephew. He shall pay for what he did. That's the rule of the game. And you, you as his boss shall be held accountable too, and I'll deal with you when the time comes. In the meantime, watch your back."

Shah could hear heavy breathing from David's end, like he was blowing steam from his nostrils. He terminated the call and smiled. He knew he had the upper hand and had put David in a cautionary mode. He would have to surround himself with men, therefore reducing his street resources.

"Take him away," Shah instructed. "Handcuff him together with his buddy. I'll deal with him tomorrow."

"Do we feed them?" asked one of his men.

"Yeah, feed them if you wish. I want all of you to guard this place. Tell the workers to take tomorrow off, too."

On the way back to the hotel, Jeffri called Sarah. He asked if she would like to meet with OJ. Sarah said she would love to, but she had an early engagement tomorrow morning. Jeffri suggested she pack her clothing for tomorrow, check into Concorde Hotel, and go to her appointment from there. He would take care of the arrangements and expenses.

At the reception, he asked for a connecting room to his. He then WhatsApp-ed the booking confirmation to Sarah and told her to let him know when she had checked in. Sarah told him she would be finished soon and should be there in an hour.

Jeffri called Shah and asked if he could come to Concorde Hotel for a drink. Jeffri said he needed to talk and perhaps work out a strategy. Then he went to the Crossroads Lounge and waited for Shah. The lounge used to be a popular hangout for Malays and Filipinos. They used to have live bands from the Philippines featuring pretty young women as frontliners. They played contemporary pop songs with well-choreographed sexy dance moves. The place used to be packed. For whatever reason, the hotel management decided to convert it into a jazz lounge, and now the place looked dead. It suited him fine.

Jeffri spotted Shah at the entrance and waved him over. Shah joined him and ordered a beer. He looked tired, angry and impatient. Jeffri waited until the beer was served and Shah took a long swig at it, draining half the glass. He put down the tall glass and lit a cigarette.

"Everything all right with you?" Jeffri asked.

"Why shouldn't it be?" Shah answered with a question.

"You look unnerved. What happened today? How did you find OJ?"

Shah told him what had happened, leaving out the bloody smacking bits. Then it was Jeffri's turn to update him on his meeting with Dato' Lau. He left out the existence of the files and also the promise that OJ will be dead.

"You seriously got this Dato' to hold David back for thirty days?" Shah was perplexed.

"That was what I asked, and that was what he agreed to."

"Shit, I have to wait thirty days too."

"Wait for what?"

"Argh, forget it."

"To wait thirty days for what? What do you have planned?"

"Look, I can't hold the two assholes for thirty days. Where do I stash them? I'll require a hell of a lot of manpower to watch over them."

"Have you thought of letting them go?"

"No way, they're not walking just like that after what they did to Nik. No way in hell."

"Shah, let's wait and see how Nik comes out of this, okay? You said it's for Nik, so let his condition dictate the course of your action."

Shah drained his glass and signaled for another.

Jeffri eyed his friend, trying to read what was on his mind. "Shah, I know I'm asking a lot from you, but I'm trying to avoid further bloodshed. No one gains from it, not even Nik."

Shah lit another cigarette, saying nothing.

"I have Nik's interest at heart too. He was injured while protecting my friend. Let me think of something, something that'll benefit him and you."

"What do you have in mind?"

"I don't know yet, but I'll come up with something agreeable to both parties."

Jeffri's handphone beeped. It was a WhatsApp from Sarah: *Will be there in 10.* Jeffri told Shah that something just came up and he needed to leave. He called for the bill, paid it and pleaded with Shah to refrain from doing anything that could jeopardize his deal with Dato' Lau. Shah reluctantly agreed and said, "You better have something good for Nik."

"I promise. I'll keep you informed."

42

Jeffri went up to his room and found OJ curled up on the bed. His eyes were open but not seeing; he looked defeated and lost. Jeffri knew he was going through some sort of post-trauma syndrome. By now OJ would have realized he was the cause of the trouble he was in, and that he had involved his friend in it too. He would have realized that a man was lying in hospital fighting for dear life because of him.

Jeffri told himself, *Once this is all over, I need to get professional help for him. In the meanwhile, all I can do is be here for him.*

"Hey, buddy, there's someone coming to see you," Jeffri said.

"I really don't feel like seeing anyone right now," OJ replied without turning his head.

"Really?"

"Yes."

"Okay, I'll let her know," Jeffri said, pulling out his handphone.

"She?"

"Yes."

"My mother? Sisters?"

"Sarah."

OJ's face lit up like a lighthouse. "Sarah! When, where is she?"

"She'll be here soon. Now get up and shower. You don't want her to hug a smelly guy, do you?"

"But I don't have any change of clothing," OJ said, getting off the bed.

Jeffri took a T-shirt from his bag and threw it to OJ.

"Here, use this. We'll get some for you tomorrow."

Jeffri's handphone beeped. It was a WhatsApp from Sarah: *I'm checked in.* Jeffri WhatsApp-ed back: *Unlock the connecting door. We'll come over in a few minutes. Prince Charming is in the shower.*

He called to OJ, "She's here."

Jeffri heard the shower stop, and a moment later, OJ stepped out with a towel wrapped around his waist. Apart from the raw injury on his brow, Jeffri noted red bruising marks on his upper arms, neck and shoulders and figured they were made by his kidnappers when they grabbed him.

"Where is she? Downstairs?" OJ asked.

"Next door."

OJ was agape. "You're kidding me."

"No, I'm not. Put your pants on and I'll open the connecting door."

While OJ got dressed, Jeffri knocked on the connecting door and opened it. He stepped aside and invited Sarah to his room. As she entered, OJ came over and the two of them entwined into a single mass. OJ whispered into her ear sobbing, "I thought I'd never see you again."

Sarah broke away from the hug and held OJ at arm's length. Only then did she notice the raw cut on his brow. "What happened to you?" she asked, touching his face. "Did you get into a fight or bang into a door again?"

OJ looked to Jeffri, unsure if he should tell Sarah what happened. Jeffri moved away from the door and told them to sit. OJ and Sarah sat side by side on the edge of the bed holding hands. Sarah looked at Jeffri expectantly.

"I'm sorry I lied to you earlier about OJ. I did not want to unnecessarily alarm you," Jerri started, and was rewarded with an admonishing glare from Sarah. "What's important, OJ is safe for now, and I'd like to keep it that way. There will be people looking for him, wanting to hurt him for reasons that are better off unknown to you. I have a plan. I really don't know if it will work, but that's all I can come up with at this moment. I need OJ to have an acceptable and valid reason for doing what he did."

Turning to OJ, Sarah asked, "What did you do?"

OJ closed his eyes and inhaled deeply. "I'll tell you about it later. For now, let's listen to what Jeff has to say."

"The plan I have involves you," Jeffri said to Sarah.

"That was what you were hinting to me about earlier," Sarah said. "I thought you were just being you: nosy, crude and rude. When you pried into my personal affairs, I thought you saw me as a gold-digger."

"I'm sorry if I made you feel that way. I needed to know the truth."

"What did you say to her?" OJ scowled. "How dare you accuse Sarah of having such intentions."

"I'm sorry, it was the lawyer in me. I didn't mean to offend her in any way. I needed to be sure for my plan to have any chance."

"Apology accepted," Sarah said, putting her hands on OJ's arms to stop him from standing up to confront Jeffri.

"Thank you. Now, I'll let you both adjourn to your room, and OJ can tell you of his adventures. I need to attend to something urgent. I remind you again, please do not answer the door to anyone and do not tell anyone of your whereabouts. Should you need something to eat, order in through my room."

"Where are you going?" OJ asked, concerned.

"To make arrangements … to negotiate your freedom."

When OJ and Sarah went to their room, Jeffri took the wheeled luggage bag and left the hotel. He drove to the general post office at Dayabumi and emptied his P.O. Box of its contents into the bag. Putting the bag into the trunk of his car, he made a call. After several rings, Isabelle answered.

"Sorry to call at this hour. Did I wake you?"

"No, I was just reading. What can I do for you, Encik Jeffri?"

"Can we meet tomorrow? I have something to return."

"I'm sure Dato' will be happy to hear it. Why don't you come to the house at 10 a.m.?"

"Thanks, I'll see you at 10 tomorrow and sorry again for calling you at this hour."

"Don't worry about it. See you tomorrow."

## 43

✕

When Jeffri reached the hotel, it was almost 11 at night. Entering his room, he noticed the connecting door was slightly opened. Then he heard OJ call, "Jeff, you're back?"

"Yes. What're you guys doing up? I thought Sarah had an early appointment tomorrow."

"She does," OJ said, standing at the connecting door in a bathrobe, "but she's too hyped to sleep."

"People say sex is a great sleep inducer."

OJ blushed. Sarah appeared beside him and wrapped her arms around his waist.

"Not when the life of your loved one is in danger," Sarah said. "We need as much awake-time as possible."

"Well then, why are you guys in my room?" Jeffri jested.

"My man here needs re-energizing," Sarah laughed and gave OJ a peck on the cheek. "Can we order some drinks?"

"It's late. I don't know if room service is still open. Let me try and call."

Jeffri called room service and was surprised they were still open. He ordered two beers, a sweet martini and fried chicken wings. OJ and Sarah walked into the room and sat on the bed.

"OJ told me everything," Sarah said, looking intensely at Jeffri. "Everything he knows, but I suspect he does not know everything, does he?"

Jeffri smiled. "I don't understand what you mean."

Sarah flashed him a stern glare. "For one, he does not know where the files are, but I'm guessing you do."

Jeffri grinned. "Did you put OJ through the third degree?"

"I don't need to. Unlike you, OJ doesn't know how to lie," Sarah said. "You know why … because he loves me. You cannot have a healthy relationship based on lies. Don't you agree, darling?"

OJ nodded in earnest and was rewarded with a loving baby-pinch on his cheek.

"I did not lie. I withhold information until it's the right time to reveal it," Jeffri swaggered. "That's what trial lawyers do, the good ones."

"Yeah right. OJ's life is at stake, and I think this is the right time to reveal it all, don't you?"

"It's a long story," Jeffri lamented, "and you have an early date."

"Don't use me as an excuse," Sarah retorted.

"Okay, could I at least take a shower first?"

Shah received a call from his men informing him Ng, the accountant, was dropped off at Jalan Tong Shin close to Corona Inn. Shah made a call to Abang Bob, the ex-detective, and gave him the information. Within minutes, a mobile police vehicle picked up Ng and took him to the police station for possession and use of illegal drugs.

When Jeffri stepped out of the bathroom, the order from room service had arrived. OJ and Sarah were happily chatting and enjoying their drinks.

"You guys started without me," Jeffri jested.

"We're hungry after our workout," Sarah joked. "Come have your beer and tell us everything, and this time no holding back."

Jeffri told all, from the time he received the parcel from Kim Senior containing the letter and check. By the time he finished, OJ and Sarah were gawking at him.

"Why didn't you go to the police with the letter? It could've cleared me," OJ asked.

"I can't show them the letter. If I did, they would want the files. If the files were in the hands of the police, they would go after the triads, or in this case, Asian Merchants, and you would have been a dead man by now. The files kept you alive and the files will ensure David will not hunt you down, at least for thirty days," Jeffri explained. "The police are the least of my worries. According to that cute Inspector Ruby, they found no evidence of foul play. Anyway, what motive can they come up with for you to kill your father? You're already a partner and your partner, what's his name, can vouch to that. Eventually they'll close the case as suicide, which we know it was."

"Ex-partner, Tan," OJ stated.

"What do you mean OJ has thirty days? Aren't you giving the triads the files?" Sarah asked.

"Returning the files to them bought him thirty days. I've to figure out how OJ can break the vow made by Grandpa Kim without any dire consequences." Jeffri noted the sadness in his buddy's eyes. OJ knew what the consequences were. He knew why his father took his own life.

The room fell silent. Jeffri offered his beer to OJ who had drained his. Sarah got up, walked to the window and pushed the curtains apart. She stood looking outside, at the bright lights of the city. Without turning she asked, "How are you going to do that?" Her voice was cracked with emotion.

"Before I reveal my plans, I need to know where your relationship is heading."

"Meaning?" Sarah asked.

"Is your relationship based on wedding bell commitments?"

"I told you I love her," OJ replied sincerely. "I'll do anything for her."

"That I know. What I need to know is her side of the relationship."

"It's too early, but what I can say is I do have feelings for OJ. Where it leads to, no one can say for certain. You as a Malay should know, 'Kalau jodoh tak ke mana.' It's all in the hands of Allah."

"OJ, you said you'll do anything for Sarah."

OJ nodded earnestly.

"We've talked about this before, Sarah is Malay, therefore a Muslim. Are you willing to convert to Islam to be with her?"

"If that's what's required to be with her, yes."

"In this country, that's what's required if you want to marry her. Civil marriage is not recognized. The only way a non-Muslim can marry a Muslim is to convert to Islam."

"Then I shall convert," OJ replied resolutely.

"To convert to Islam is easy. All you need to do is recite with conviction the declaration of faith, the Shahadah. The challenge is to stay a Muslim."

"The Shahadah?"

"Yes, it's a declaration in Arabic. Which means, 'I bear witness that there is no God worthy to be worshipped but Allah, and I bear witness Muhammad is the Messenger of Allah.'"

"I shall declare my faith, and I shall stay a Muslim. I promise," OJ said with certitude, looking at Sarah's back.

"By marrying me, the triads will set him free of his grandfather's vow?" Sarah asked, turning to face Jeffri.

"No. Marrying you, the woman he loves, will be the reason he converts. What will set him free from Grandpa Kim's vow is his death. That was what I promised the triads. OJ will be dead."

"After he marries me, you're going to kill him!" Sarah glared at Jeffri.

"I won't be the one that kills him. The conversion to Islam will kill Kim On Juan."

"I don't think it works that way," OJ butted in. "The Chinese are not big on religion. To us, race comes first. I can be a Christian or a Hindu or a Buddhist, but it does not matter because I'll still be a Chinese. I will still be the descendant of the Kim family and bound by the vow made by my grandfather."

"Yes and no. It's going to be a hard sell, I'll have to put up a strong argument tomorrow. So, may I suggest we all get some sleep, or at least some rest? I know you guys have a lot to talk about, but I really need sleep. Good night, and try not to be too loud. Remember, I'm sleeping alone," Jeffri teased.

OJ stood and looked hard at his friend. His face expressed a maelstrom of emotions. "Jeff, you don't have to do this. You don't have to put your life on the line for me. It has nothing to do with you. It was my grandfather's stupidity, you don't owe me anything."

"Actually, I do. When you took over the firm, you could've called any lawyer to do your criminal cases, any firm, but you came to me ... a nobody in the trial circuit. You didn't know it but you saved me, my staff and my firm. Most of all, you kept my dreams alive. So say no more, go to your room, and make love with your beautiful future wife."

OJ, with tears in his eyes, lunged forward and hugged his friend. "Please be safe."

Sarah came over and hugged both of them. "Please save him."

# 4 4

As Jeffri drove out from the hotel car park, his handphone rang. He looked at the screen; it was Juliana. He decided not to answer it. He did not wish to break his train of thought. He was going over and over what would be the most important summation of his life. A summation in the chamber of the triads presided over by Dato' Lau and Isabelle. His success or failure would determine OJ's fate — whether he lived or died. His last play, whatever the outcome, would end today. The ringing stopped and was immediately followed by a voice message beep. *Call me urgent*, was the message.

Jeffri made the call and grumpily asked, "What's wrong?"

"The office was broken into, the place is a mess, everything was ransacked, everything," Juliana said in one breath.

"How did you know?"

"I was in the neighborhood and decided to check the office. When I went up, the front door was wide open and the office ransacked."

"What was stolen?"

"I don't know. Files were thrown on the floor. Do you want me to check the files?"

"No, leave it. I'll get Shah to send someone over to be with you. Call the police and make a report. Don't stay in the office, go downstairs and wait until Shah's men arrive."

Jeffri called Shah and asked him to send his men over to be with Juliana. To make sure she was safe, just in case the men who broke into his office decided to come back for a confrontation.

"You know who did it?"

"I suspect David's men."

"The bastard's really getting on my nerve," Shah snarled. "Okay, I'll get Abang Bob to look into it. He has police connections."

"Shah, don't get all worked up about it. Just make sure Juliana's safe. I'll deal with it later. Since you're sending your men, can you ask them to check my apartment too?"

"You think it's broken into also?"

"I wouldn't be surprised if it were. Just check it for me. Thanks."

By breaking into his office, David was grasping at straws. Jeffri theorized David had probably bragged he would get the files and assured — to whomever that needed assurance — the traitor would get what he deserved. Now OJ, the so-deemed traitor, was gone and the files still missing. To add salt to his wounded pride, two of his trusted men were held captive by people unknown to him. He was starting to lose face, and 'face' to the Chinese, especially the triads, is everything.

Jeffri knew he must tread carefully. David might have gotten a whiff of his earlier visit and might even be aware of his pending visit. After all, Isabelle was his sister. She might have told him to save his face. He, Jeffri could be walking right into a trap. *Shit. What the fuck have I gotten myself into?* He took several deep breaths. *Well, there's no backing out now. I just hope Abang Bob's men are there when I need them.*

He made the turn into Tanyton View and drove slowly. He kept an eye on the rearview mirror, hoping to detect Abang Bob's men. Two motorbikes passed him, but he could not identify the rider or pillion because of their helmets. He gave up and said, "Que sera sera, whatever will be, will be."

This time he parked on the side of Dato' Lau's bungalow. He sat in the car looking up and down the road, expecting to see a group of Chinese men suddenly emerging and rushing toward him. There were none.

He stepped out of the car, popped his trunk, and took out the wheeled luggage. He approached the gate, pressed the bell and waited for the vicious dogs to greet him. There were none. The gate swung open and he entered, walking to the open front door.

Isabelle was waiting for him. She was dressed in a gray office suit, and she looked as gorgeous as the last time they met. She smiled warmly, hand extended, and greeted him.

"Nice to see you again, Encik Jeffri."

"Likewise, and since this is our second meeting, please call me Jeff."

Isabelle smiled and said, "This way please."

Jeffri followed her through the same route he did last night. She walked with a mesmerizing sway that had Jeffri captivated.

"Are you staring at my bum?" Isabelle teased without looking back.

"Eh, yes, no, no, sorry," Jeffri stuttered.

"It's okay. I like a man who appreciates beauty when he sees it," Isabelle said with a chuckle.

"Yes, they're gorgeous."

"Thank you. I put in a lot of hard work to keep them the way they are," Isabelle laughed.

✕

Dato' Lau was seated on one of the single sofas. His wheelchair stood empty beside him. Isabelle beckoned Jeffri to one of the empty sofas and she pulled an upright chair beside Dato'.

"Isabelle said you have something of ours to return," Dato' Lau said without going into pleasantries.

"Yes, as promised," Jeffri replied and pushed the wheeled bag toward him. "Dato' will find it's all there."

"I'll take your word for it." Dato' Lau paused, as if thinking of what to say next.

Jeffri waited patiently, studying the old man's face.

"I heard Kim Junior is missing. Do you know of his whereabouts?"

Afraid the triads might put a tail on him to locate OJ, he replied, "At this very moment, no."

"Hmmm."

"Dato', forgive me for bringing this up, but do we have an agreement? Can you promise me that David will not, for the next thirty days, do anything to OJ?"

"You kept your part of the deal, so I shall keep my part of it. You have my word."

"Thank you, Dato'," Jeffri said, letting out a sigh of relief.

A moment of tense silence filled the study.

"Encik Jeffri, sorry, Jeff," Isabelle corrected herself, "last night you stated that Mr. Kim Junior will be dead."

Jeffri nodded.

"How will his death be proven to us?"

"Dato', Isabelle, I beg your indulgence as I present my case. As promised, Kim On Juan, or OJ, will be dead, and by our law he will be."

Dato' Lau and Isabelle looked at each other, then gave him a skeptical stare.

"OJ is madly in love with a Malay woman who goes by the name of Sarah. Dato' and Isabelle are aware in our country that being a Malay, Sarah is therefore by law a Muslim."

Dato' Lau and Isabelle nodded.

"It's silly, but yes it is so," Dato' Lau said, and indicated for Jeffri to continue.

"OJ's love for her is true and pure and he does not see religion as a barrier. In other words, OJ is willing to convert to Islam to tie the knot with Sarah. When OJ makes his Declaration of Faith, by our law he is no longer Kim On Juan. He'll be whoever he chooses his new name and beginning to be." Jeffri paused to read the expressions of their faces. "Let me assure both of you that OJ did not convert to escape his grandpa's vow. That never came up."

Isabelle seemed to have carved a tiny smile, while Dato' Lau displayed a blank unconvinced expression.

"I just love true love stories," Isabelle said. "Mr. Kim Junior has been through a horrifying and tragic event. I'm happy he found love and happiness."

Jeffri nodded.

"Kim Junior is a Chinese and will always be a Chinese no matter what religion he converts to," Dato' Lau said. "You cannot just convert to Christianity and be a mat salleh."

"You're perfectly correct, Dato'. However, we're here in Malaysia. Kim Junior, or OJ, had expressed his desire to remain here and not migrate to a foreign land. What Dato' says is true of other countries, but it's not true here. Our government and opposition parties are filled with Muslim fruitcakes. They somehow managed to confuse and mix secular and Shariah laws with the words of Allah. They put in place all sorts of secular laws, procedures and conventions that are not in accordance with Islamic teachings."

"How is that so?" Dato' Lau asked.

"For example, when a person converts to Islam, all his records with the National Registration will be changed. He shall be required to be under the care of the Religious Department for a specific period, so on and so on. By convention he will assume a new name, a Muslim name with a 'bin', and his father shall be listed as 'Abdullah', the servant of Allah. All these are man-made, which have no bearing in Islam." Jeffri paused, allowing them to digest what was said, and waited for questions or rebuttals. When there were none, he continued, "Legally, Kim Junior is dead and reborn as a new person, a Muslim. His children may be Malay, therefore a Muslim, not Chinese anymore. This is not noticeable as there are not many Chinese converts here, but I'm sure Dato' and Isabelle notice the Indian-looking Malays. They were once Indian, but now they're legally Malay."

Dato' Lau's eyes widened, and Jeffri knew he had managed to hold the old man's attention.

Jeffri pressed on, "As a Muslim, OJ shall forfeit all inheritance from his non-Muslim family, and likewise, his non-Muslim family shall not be able to inherit his wealth. This is a crucial point under the Syariah law. OJ the Muslim is prohibited from inheriting the Kim & Kim law firm as it was wealth from his father, a non-Muslim. Unlike converting to Christianity or Hinduism, a person who converts to Islam cannot, in Malaysia, reconvert easily to his or her original faith. It's like a full natural life sentence. His non-

Muslim family has no custody rights over his offspring. In other words, once OJ converts, the law of this country kills him as Kim On Juan."

"I didn't know it was that difficult and legalistic," Dato' Lau sighed. "In my opinion, he's better off dead, for it happens only once. By converting, he'll have to live it until his death."

"Yes, but OJ's in love and willing to make the sacrifice. As Dato' rightly pointed out, it's not easy and there's no turning back for him once he takes the leap of faith," Jeffri said with the most sincere expression and tone.

Dato' Lau closed his eyes, deep in thought. Jeffri waited in silent prayer. When Dato' opened his eyes, he continued.

"I beg of Dato' to please give him the chance to live his chosen life. The vow made by Grandpa Kim had derailed him, robbed him of the life he wanted as an architect. He was forced by his father to be a lawyer. Now he has a second chance at life to pursue his dream and a happy life. I'm sorry, but I was told Dato' too was given the same opportunity in life."

Dato' Lau allowed himself a tiny smile. Jeffri thought he must be recalling memories of how he escaped the tragic road accident where he lost his entire family, and how he was given the second chance to start a new one. The study fell silent once more. He could see Dato' Lau was still undecided, and he decided to play his last card.

"Dato' is aware of how our country is currently experiencing racial and religious tension like never before. What with this Indian Muslim extremist preacher propagating tension between Muslims and other faiths. A detrimental statement was made by Koon Yew Yin against our army, which is Malay-dominated."

Dato' Lau stared at Jeffri questioningly.

"Everything now, even a road rage incident between a Malay and Chinese, is being exploited and turned into a racial and religious matter. Once OJ converts as a Muslim, his untimely death might stir similar reactions from the media and public. It may fare poorly on Asian Merchants and David, and if I'm able to trace it all to Dato', I'm sure the police or any investigative journalist will be able to do so."

Jeffri paused and looked straight at Dato' Lau, making sure he was addressing him and him alone.

"But that is beside the point. The point is, the vow was made by Grandpa Kim and for two generations, they honored the vow. Kim Senior sacrificed his life, so that his son could be free. I do not see why more lives should be sacrificed. Please, I beg of Dato' to release OJ from the bond."

Jeffri noticed Isabelle's eyes well with tears. She probably knew what Jeffri was talking about, or she had a soft spot for romance, true love, and the happily-ever-after ending. She was a new breed of businesswomen in the triads. She leaned close to Dato' and whispered something to his ear.

"Isabelle suggests we hold a symbolic funeral rite for Kim Junior's death. Would he be agreeable to it?" Dato' Lau said.

"I'll ask OJ and revert soonest."

"Apart from you making sense of the racial and religious outburst, my dear niece Isabelle is a pushover for love," Dato' Lau said, turning to Isabelle with a fatherly smile. "She believes true love must be cherished, must be protected and given the chance to bloom."

Isabelle blushed. Jeffri waited patiently.

"Kim Junior is released of all his obligations to the vow made by his grandfather. He shall be free to choose his own life," Dato' Lau made the announcement.

"I thank you from the bottom of my heart, and I'm sure OJ and Sarah do too."

"You, Jeff, are an honorable man. You put your life on the line for a friend. I hope one day we could be friends," Isabelle said.

"I wish for that too."

"Is there anything else on your mind, Jeff?" Isabelle asked when she noticed Jeffri's reluctance to end the meeting.

"Actually, there is. When OJ was kidnapped, one of David's men stabbed a kid that was trying to help. OJ will not press police charges on the kidnapping, I can assure you. However, the injured kid's uncle is planning to retaliate. I seek Dato's permission to amicably resolve the stabbing with David so that we can avoid a gang war and more bloodshed."

"You have my blessing. While you're at it, I suggest you ask David to compensate you for the damage his men did to your office."

"Dato' knows about that?"

"Very little escapes Dato'," Isabelle said with a tiny smile. "Very little."

Isabelle walked Jeffri out. At the front door, she said, "One day, I'd like to have a drink with you. See if we can form some working relationship."

"I'd love that."

"You're honest, sharp and smart. Asian Merchants could always use someone like you."

"Thank you. I look forward to it."

# 45

It was almost noon when Jeffri drove out of Tanyton View, heading to the hotel. Not wanting to be disturbed during the meeting, he'd put his handphone on silent mode. Checking the phone, he had three missed calls and two WhatsApp messages. Two of the calls were from Shah and one from Juliana.

He read the WhatsApp from Shah — *Nik is moved to the general ward. Visiting him now.* From Juliana — *report made, nothing missing.*

He called Juliana, told her to put a temporary lock on the door and go home. He would take care of it on Monday. Then he called Shah and asked his whereabouts.

"Just leaving the hospital."

"How's Nik?"

"He'll live."

Jeffri thought Shah's voice sounded more relaxed. "I'm glad. Where are you headed?"

"Gym, why?"

"I'll come over. We need to talk. Want me to get anything?"

"No, thanks."

Jeffri called OJ and asked him if or when was Sarah coming back. OJ told him she had a golf game with some government people and should be back by 3. Jeffri told him he had something to attend to and should be back by then. He reminded OJ not to leave the room and to order lunch from room service.

Jeffri cut into AKLEH, took the slip road to Pandan Indah, and headed for Kick Ass Gymnasium. Shah's car was already parked at the gym when he arrived. Entering the office, Abang Bob and Abang Joko were there too.

"Heard the good news?" Abang Bob asked.

"Yeah, Shah told me,' Jeffri said.

"You want something to eat?" Shah asked. "We're having lunch."

"Yes, whatever you guys are having and iced tea."

Shah made a call and added Jeffri's order.

"Your office woman made the report. She said nothing was missing. By the way, your apartment was not broken into," Abang Bob said.

"Shah said you thought it was David's work," Abang Joko said.

"Who else? I got nothing of value in the office. He must have gotten my office address from OJ and suspected OJ must have hidden the files in my office."

"What files? You never mentioned any files to me," Shah interrupted.

"Nothing that matters anymore."

"What do you mean by that?"

"What I mean is that OJ's released of all his obligations, and David is on a very short leash. This's what I came to talk to you about."

The three men looked at Jeffri questioningly.

"The Godfather," Jeffri smiled, "gave me the blessing to settle all our disputes with David amicably."

"Meaning?"

"Meaning no gang war, no bloodshed," Jeffri said. "Now, what do you think would be a reasonable and acceptable compensation for Nik?"

"Fifty thousand," Abang Joko said.

"Two hundred thousand is more like it," Abang Bob asserted.

"I said reasonable. Two hundred thousand is too much," Jeffri said.

"How about one hundred thousand?" Shah suggested.

"I think anything between fifty to a hundred thousand plus medical expenses would be more than reasonable. Nik could never in his dreams lay his hands on such an amount."

Shah nodded. "What's the catch?"

"Withdraw the report. Nik gives a statement to the police that he could not recognize the assailant or remember the vehicle number. With a small donation, I'm sure Abang Bob can make the case disappear."

Abang Bob laughed.

The gym caretaker, assisted by a few kids, brought in the food, set it on the table and left.

"Where are Johnny and the other man? I hope you've not done anything to them," Jeffri asked.

"Nothing they don't deserve," Shah said casually. "How do you want to play this?"

"I'll set up the meeting tonight. Let you know the details once it's set."

"What if David doesn't want to play ball?"

"Don't worry, he will," Jeffri said with a grin. "Abang Bob, my friend OJ wants to convert to Islam. You think you could help arrange it for him?"

"Sure, let me know when, I'll handle it. That'll be my ticket to heaven, helping a new brother to convert," Abang Bob said, laughing. "Now that everything is okay, you want me to pull my men off?"

"Just to be safe, keep them on until we're done with David."

Jeffri bumped into Sarah at the hotel lobby. She looked exhausted, and her face was pinkish from sunburn.

"How was your golf?" Jeffri asked, waiting for the elevator.

"Golf was shit, but I think the pitch went well," Sarah said with a smile. "How was your day?"

"Unexpectedly well. I'll tell you all about it in the room."

They went up and entered through Jeffri's room. Sarah found OJ seated by the window in their room, staring out at the road below. Sarah gave him a peck on the back of his head and said she needed a shower.

"Why don't you go to Jeff's room? I'll join you guys after my shower," Sarah said as she peeled off her clothing.

"Jeff's back?"

"Yes."

OJ jumped out of his chair and rushed to Jeffri's room.

"How did it go?" OJ asked anxiously.

"Where's Sarah?"

"Taking a shower."

"Have you had your lunch?"

OJ shook his head. "I'm not hungry."

"Why don't you order something to eat and we'll wait for her? Then I won't have to repeat my story."

"Okay, you want anything?"

"Just iced tea."

Sarah walked in, wearing a bathrobe with nothing underneath. She was drying her hair with a small towel and she smelled sweet and fresh. When she sat on the edge of the bed, the split in the bathrobe dropped to the side, revealing her fair skin and firm thighs. She smiled when she noticed the two men's eyes. She pulled the robe flaps to cover the split.

"So what happened?" OJ asked.

"You, my friend, are a dead man walking," Jeffri said, looking seriously at him.

OJ closed his eyes and inhaled deeply.

"They didn't buy it?" Sarah asked, her hand reaching for OJ's.

Jeffri could not bear to see his buddy and his girlfriend's dejected faces and laughed.

"What's so funny?" Sarah retorted. "You think them killing him is funny?"

"Kim On Juan, OJ, is a dead man walking, but the new Muslim OJ, whatever his name will be, is a free man."

"You did it!" Sarah jumped off the bed and hugged him repeatedly, saying, "You fucking pulled it off."

OJ could not believe what he'd just heard. "What?"

"He did it, you're a free man," Sarah said and turned to hug him.

The momentum of Sarah's hug pushed OJ onto the bed and they lay hugging each other. OJ was crying happy tears, and Sarah was hushing him with, "Shhhh, it's all over, it's all over."

Jeffri's eyes welled with tears. Their tearful joy was contagious. OJ, or whatever his new Muslim name would be, was a free man, free of the stupid vow made by his grandfather.

There was a soft knock on the door and a voice called out, "Room service."

On OJ and Sarah's insistence, Jeffri told them about his meeting with Dato' Lau and Isabelle. He told them that since OJ will be a converted Muslim, Dato' Lau wisely recognized the racial and religious public outcry and the implication it would have on Asian Merchants if he was killed by them.

"I really don't believe Dato' wanted you dead. I believe all he wanted was the files, and killing you was David's idea. You see, David wanted to show them he could revive the old triad ways."

"You really think so?"

"That was my theory, we'll never know for certain. What I'm sure of, it was Isabelle's penchant for true love and a happy ending that saved OJ. Oh, by the way, Isabelle requested that we hold a symbolic funeral rite for your death."

"Symbolic ritual for my death?"

"They would probably cremate something of yours like a shirt or something. I was told they do such rituals for those lost at sea or eaten by wild animals."

"Really? There's such a ritual?" OJ asked, surprised.

"I don't know, I was just guessing. I've made arrangements for Abang Bob to assist you with the process of conversion. Help you memorize the declaration of faith and to recite it in front of an Imam or whoever the Religious Department appoints. By the way, I never knew your faith. Are you a Buddhist?" Jeffri asked.

"My parents are, so I guess I am too."

"Doesn't matter. You'll be a Muslim soon. Have you thought of a Muslim name?"

"I'll take care of that," Sarah said. "Got just the perfect name for him."

"I hope it's not your ex or someone you had a crush on," Jeffri joked.

Sarah made a face at him and they laughed.